I Was a Vacuum Cleaner Salesman

I WAS A VACUUM CLEANER SALESMAN

A novel by
Shelly Rivoli

iUniverse, Inc.
New York Lincoln Shanghai

I Was a Vacuum Cleaner Salesman

iUniverse, Inc.

For information address:
iUniverse, Inc.
2021 Pine Lake Road, Suite 100
Lincoln, NE 68512
www.iuniverse.com

BUYER BEWARE: This is a novel, the amalgamation of fictitious characters, corporations, events, and cleaning devices. Anyone who says otherwise shall meet with the steadfast gazes and firm handshakes of an endless stream of salesmen at his door.

ISBN: 0-595-27950-3 (pbk)
ISBN: 0-595-65722-2 (cloth)

Printed in the United States of America

For Mom, who let me copilot on Avon adventures once upon a summer; for Tim, who stood by me even in the presence of steak knives (and countless drafts of this novel); for Andy, who gave me the courage to dance in public and later in prose; and for all the men and women in this world who heard opportunity—and went knocking.

SALES

$12.84/hr. demo. small household
appliance. Flexible hours.
No exp. necessary.
Call 596-2444. EOE.

PART I

"Wouldn't you agree?"

"SHOOO."

I roll my shoulders back and try to implement that heel-toe action that comes so naturally to Mom's generation, but it's no use. The heels are too high and too narrow to put any kind of weight on. So I step on the front half of each foot, moving toward the glass door that reads "Chin's StormBurst." A green shamrock dots the *i*. On top of the words sits a painted leprechaun, pointing to a pot that overflows with green dollar bills. The rest of the door is painted with small, blue raindrops that make it impossible to see inside.

Step, step.

I pull open the door and feel the rush of conditioned air pouring over me. There's a high countertop to my left and I catch my balance against it a moment as my eyes adjust to the dark room. The countertop is high enough to have served as a bar in a past life, and a brass footrest along its base suggests that it has. It's topped with a paper sack from Big Burger and a name plaque inscribed with "Berta." I squinch my eyes and look around the dark room. It's lined with some kind of fuzzy wallpaper—and men.

Snots. It's all men, standing in a sloppy line along the back wall. But then: surely they aren't all here for—

"The end uh the line s'over there." Burp.

I turn on the front of my foot.

She must be ten inches taller than me. At least. Or maybe it's just that flame of hair rising up toward the ceiling. She points a freckled finger toward the beginning of a hallway, then rubs her chin with the back of her hand.

I open my mouth but nothing comes out.

She squeezes behind the bar, climbs up on a stool and reaches for the paper sack.

I take a deep breath and exhale: "Oh, but I have an appointment for an interview at eleven—I'm Diana Jensen."

She bares small teeth. "An' so does ever' body else here, lady."

She slides a clipboard down the bar toward me and goes deep for a handful of fries.

I take the clipboard and stand up as straight as I can as I step my way past men of all kinds: with neckties and loafers, with beards and briefcases, with ripped jeans and T-shirts, with cowboy boots—

"Hey there, little lady—if I get this job will I get to work with *you*?"

I chuckle along with the men and smile. "Not if I get the job first."

I step on, following the fuzzy red walls past the men's and women's rooms, on through a second room illuminated by a half-barrel hanging from the ceiling, on toward another hallway where I find the end of the line. Of men.

It must be a garbage disposal. Or maybe a garage door opener. Those are small household appliances too, aren't they?

Snots.

Why didn't I just ask what it is when I called about the ad? I should have asked more questions. I should have done some research. I should have—

"OUCH!"

The man smiles as he finishes adjusting his tie. "Sorry 'bout that, doll."

I should have just stayed home.

But then: rent is due in twenty-two days. And I can't live on spaghetti and oatmeal forever. Can I?

I take my place in line beneath the florescent Emergency Exit sign, behind the man wearing a Megadread concert T-shirt. He turns to face me, but no words come from under the blond mustache.

"Hello, I'm Diana."

Blink.

"Diana Jensen." I offer my hand for a shake.

Megadread studies the lapels of my blazer, then scrolls south to the high heels. He turns, offering only the ponytail straggling between his shoulders.

I turn on a narrow heel and contemplate the exit behind me. Of course, an alarm might sound, but what are the chances I'll ever be back here again?

But then: *somebody* in this line will get hired at $12.84 per hour—more than twice what the Dairy Barn paid. They wouldn't take just any slob off the street for that kind of money.

Megadread adjusts his belt and pulls the comb from his back pocket.

I begin checking off the boxes on the form: No, I've never committed a misdemeanor. Or a felony. No, I've never been *fired* from a job—not one I'd be foolish enough to mention at an interview. No, I don't have a medical condition that will prevent me from doing this job.

No, I'm not a veteran of a foreign war. Yes, I am a licensed driver. Yes, I am in possession of a functioning and insured automobile. No, I do not wear corrective lenses. No, I do not suffer from asthma or any other respiratory illness. Yes, I have answered these questions truthfully to the best of my knowledge.

I shift my weight back and forth from the front of one foot to the other and guess how many minutes have passed each time before I look at my watch. There's a dull ache in my back, but at last I can see a door and a large window at the front of the line. There's a big desk butted up against the glass, and a gray-haired man sits to one side of the desk. He wears a gray flannel suit and a tie and smiles kindly as he interviews someone—a woman.

How could I have possibly missed *her*?

A platinum beehive rests on her head like a swath of cotton candy, and a heap of golden chains glistens on her enormous, mostly-bare bosom. He continues nodding his head politely as the woman rambles on about something.

I can already tell he'll be wonderful to work for. Patient. Kind. Almost fatherly. The kind of a boss who would never fire you, no matter how many misshapen ice cream cones you'd tossed into the garbage.

And don't bother coming back—unless you're here to spend money!

The woman smiles and scribbles something on a sheet of paper for him; her breasts jiggle to punctuate. The man just listens politely, occasionally nodding his head. But then: he looks interested in something. Very interested in fact.

I push my shoulders back to reveal my new and improved bust line, made a full cup size larger now, thanks to my new aquati-bra.

They smile and stand and she reaches out to shake his—white-gloved hand?

She regards his glove, looks up at his face, then smiles. He exits the room with a handkerchief on the doorknob and a smile on his face.

Gulp.

The woman—the *woman*—invites the next man into her office.

I take a long, deep, soothing breath and visualize myself as the next Small Household Appliance Demonstrator. I am relaxed. I am calm. I am in control of my destiny.

My stomach gurgles.

I smooth my hands over my hair to make sure the bobby pins are still in place.

Megadread pulls the comb from his pocket again and rakes through the long, blond tuft.

I shift my weight from foot-front to foot-front and guess how many minutes have passed.

Three?

Nope, only two.

I watch Megadread strut into the office and give the woman a nod. He slouches into his seat, down, down, until his ponytail drapes up and over the back of the chair.

Thirty seconds?

Yes!

By the time the woman calls me into the office, my calves are cramping and my feet have swollen to the limits of my shoes. But I persevere.

Step, step.

After all, twelve dollars and eighty-four cents an hour is riding on this:

"Hi, I'm Diana Jensen." I lean across the wide desk and shake her hand firmly, just like Dad taught me. "Thanks for taking a moment out of your busy day to talk with me about this exciting opportunity!" I maintain eye contact.

So does she, without blinking.

"Diana, it's nice to meet you. I'm Brenda Sue Chin."

We continue shaking hands, firmly, staring without blinking. I try to remember the last time I saw a woman who is shorter than me. But maybe it's just the high heels. My eyes are beginning to twitch and tear when finally she gestures to the chair behind me.

"Please sit down."

We blink and take our seats.

"Let me just tell you the basics about the position we're hiring for, and then you can tell me if you think you're the right person for the job, okay?"

"Sure!" I smile and cross my legs.

She writes my name in the top left corner of clean sheet of paper.

"Now the advertisement you saw quoted the pay rate at $12.84 per hour, and did that sound acceptable to you, Diana?"

Gulp.

"Yes, I think so."

"Great. Now let me show you how we work out our pay scale around here, because you'll see that $12.84 is actually just the beginning rate. And it won't be difficult to make more than that—if you want to—once you've completed your training. Does that sound good to you, Diana?"

"Sure."

"Super. Now $12.84 is based on the average forty-hour workweek. Are you available to work forty hours a week…Diana?"

"Yes, I am." I nod and uncross my legs.

"Oh, wonderful." She smiles and writes down "40 hours" below my name. "Well, at forty hours a week, you should be able to complete…" and she writes down a few numbers, which beget fractions, which beget equations, which beget dollar figures, and before I know it I have all the statistical evidence in front of me that I can—without a doubt—make $12.84 per hour just by doing demonstrations. Better yet, I'll be working as an independent contractor, "which means that you can set your own hours and write off your auto mileage and lunches on next year's taxes. Does that sound good to you?"

"Yes."

Then she shows me how, by working just a few more than forty hours a week, I can make even more—but only if I want to. And I'm floating somewhere up near the fire sprinklers as Brenda Sue summarizes that I can make as little, or as *much* money as I want to. It's all up to me.

"Do you work well independently, Diana?"

"Oh, definitely."

"Great. All you'll need to do to get started is complete our FREE weeklong training session to become a certified dealer—but you seem pretty sharp, Diana."

"Oh, I am—and I'm a fast learner *and* a multi-tasker and I work well—"

"Terrific." She glances down at the lapels of my blazer. "Oh, and you can dress *casual* for training." She winks a green eye and reaches across the big desk. We seal the agreement with another long and blinkless handshake. Brenda Sue smiles and says, "You know, Diana, I've got a good feeling about you."

"You, too." I smile and feel a bobby pin slip down the back of my collar.

❧   ❧   ❧

"My OWN refrigerator."

I pat the side of the green appliance and smile. It's empty except for a six-pack of Green Hornet lagers, a carton of milk, and a half-empty jar of spaghetti sauce. I shut the door, then consider the letter at the top of the day's mail.

"My OWN utility bill." Until Christina gets back, anyway. I hurry through the mail, but there's still no letter from Christina. Not even a postcard.

I turn back to the refrigerator and take out a Green Hornet, twist off the cap and think of how I'll tell Mom and Dad about how I stumbled onto a better opportunity than working at the Dairy Barn.

Gulp. Ahh.

And how I don't need help making rent this summer, but thank you anyway.

Gulp. Gulp.

"Say, guess who you won't ever see wearing brown polyester again?"

Gulp. Ahh.

"Or a plastic visor?"

Gulp. Gulp.

Gulp.

"Guess who just got a 100% pay raise? WAHOOOO!"

Gulp. Gulp-gulp. Gulp. Ahh.

"Gee Dad, you know how you—"

"YEE-OWL! YEE-OWL!"

It's coming from the front porch. I step through the maze of moving boxes to the front door and balance on my toes to look through the peephole. I can't see a thing but the warped edge of the porch and the path to the alley.

"YEE-OWL!"

It's right on the other side of the door.

"YEE-OWL-OWL-OWL!"

I open the door a few inches and look through the screen door at a white cat. Or a mostly-white cat. I open the door all the way and see a gray stripe down the side of its body, starting at the shoulder. He paces back and forth, a few steps in each direction, and squints up at me.

"Well, now. A little fellow like you can make a big old racket like that?"

He's still squinting at me, looking a bit confused.

"Guess you were expecting somebody else, eh?" I open the screen door and squat down to introduce myself by way of letting him sniff my hand.

"Hi there, I'm Diana."

He sniffs both sides, and I scratch the top of his head.

"Diana Jensen."

"Vvvvrr. Vvvvrr."

"Nice to meet you, too."

He flops on his side and looks up at me and—oh my god—there are no eyes in his head! There's nothing there at all. Just holes where a couple of eyes should be.

"YEE-OWL!"

He's not-looking straight at me. I rub my finger under his chin and try not to look into those two dark holes going straight back to his brain. He shifts away from me and we both stand. He rubs his gray side along the bottom of the porch railing and slinks down the steps, then walks perfectly down the center of the path.

"See you later."

He rubs his gray side against the fence as he turns left onto the alley.

❧   ❧   ❧

I wear my khakis and a button-up shirt so that I'll look casual, but serious. Berta greets us at the door with a red slushee and red mouth, barking "You gotta go 'round back and up them stairs!" and we shuffle along the side of the building to where a concrete staircase begins. At the top we find a windowless room, lined with dark red wallpaper like the lobby downstairs. But the floor is covered in shag carpeting the color of oranges. The room is filled with nearly every man I'd seen on Friday—plus a woman in the back row and a girl in the front row who looks about my age. Our chairs face a whiteboard, where alternating red, orange, yellow, green, blue and purple letters spell "WELCOME!!!" A green box rests on the floor beneath the whiteboard—it's some sort of a square-shaped case with a handle on the top and golden buckles on the side. And what looks like a gold metallic sun lamp sits on the floor next to it. On the wall to our left, there's a bulletin board with a column of names down one side and some green paper shamrocks beside a few of the names at the top.

I search the room for someone friendly to greet, and maybe eat lunch with later. But everyone's sitting down and staring ahead at the whiteboard or down at their hands. So I take the last available seat, beside my old friend Megadread. He appears to have trimmed his mustache since Friday, but it still has handlebars.

"Well, hello again!" I smile weakly.

He doesn't.

"I love that T-shirt."

He looks down at the big red lips and tongue on his chest and flashes a tobacco-flecked grin. "It's a classic."

"Of course."

His grin widens, as do his eyes. "They're boss, man!" He punches the air with a fist, then settles back into his chair, spreading his knees just wide enough to gently touch mine. He gives me a nod.

"Yeah, the *bossiest*." I wiggle my eyebrows.

I can smell stale cigarettes as he laughs. I finally lean back in my seat and look toward the rainbow of letters on the whiteboard.

"Hey, you know what, man?"

I turn. "What, man?"

"I think you're all right." There's a black fleck on his front tooth. "*All right.*" He nods his head.

I sit up straight in my chair and cross my legs. "Well, that's what they tell me." I can see a large cardboard box under the bulletin board. "STORM-BURST" is printed across the side. It's big enough to hold a microwave oven. Or maybe a TV. There's another box behind it, flat and wide, leaning against the wall.

The floor vibrates as we hear footsteps thundering up the stairs outside. The door flies open and a hefty man in a green-striped shirt and blue tie lumbers up our aisle. He stops at the whiteboard, swivels on his heel, and throws his arms out to each side. "Welcome *everybody*!" His flesh is still swaying where it hangs over his belt.

He grins painfully wide as his chest heaves up and down. Everybody watches quietly as he continues smiling, heaving, and holding his arms out like a swollen Christ, dangling from a rainbow "WELCOME!!!" cross.

No one moves.

His right eye twitches a couple of times, and he rubs his nose with the back of his hand. Finally his hands settle onto his hips.

"Well, right about now you're probably all wondering 'Who the heck is this guy, and why is he smiling so *big*?' Is that right?"

His black eyes trace over us maniacally, until we each smile back at him.

"Well, just to tell you a little bit about myself, my name is Harold Chin, and my wife Brenda Sue—I think you all met the lovely lady earlier—we're the owners of Chin's StormBurst Center. We've been in the StormBurst business going on eleven years now, and with a track record like that, well, you know it's a solid business, right?" His dark eyes trace over us again as he waits for our response.

Megadread breaks the silence: "Yeah."

Harold's eyes shoot straight to him. He winks and nods his head. "That's right!" But then: no smile. Suddenly Harold looks very somber. "Now, I know that in this day and age there are plenty of people out there that'll try and tell you all kinds of things—wouldn't you agree?"

I nod, waiting to hear what Harold Chin is about to tell us.

A voice from the back of the room huffs, "They're everywhere!"

"That's right…" He nods with all manner of contempt for the human race. "Well, I can honestly tell you I've worked a lot of different jobs in my life; I've lived a lot of different places—and I've been handed a lot of lines, you know what I mean?" His black eyebrows rise, forming perfect triangles like a jack-o-lantern.

A few people nod their heads.

One man grunts, "You're tellin' me!"

I smile to be polite.

"And that's why nowadays I don't even *try* and tell somebody something if I can't back it up with some kind of—proof? Do you all know what I mean?" Harold looks around the room and waits. His eyes pause on each of us, until one by one we nod. Harold raises his eyebrows again and looks around the room. "Well, that's why I'm going to stop *telling* you things now, and start *showing* you what the StormBurst is all about. Does that sound good?"

"Yeah."

"Yep."

"Ah-haw."

"Right on, bro." Megadread nods.

Harold rests a foot on the corner of the green box, and a shiny penny glistens in his loafer. "Now has anyone here been to Ireland before?"

The room buzzes with no's.

"Well, if you don't have other plans for today, I'd like to take you to Ireland. Any objections?"

I hear some chuckles.

Megadread points a yellowed finger at Harold and asks, "But doesn't it take like a long time to get there, man?"

Harold giggles and tells him not to worry. He rubs his nose. "As a matter of fact, it will only take about as long as it does to go downstairs and walk back up here again. Could you do me a favor—I'm sorry, what's your name?"

"Ed, man."

"Well, Edmund…" Harold opens the top of the StormBurst box with the lid facing us so that no one else can see inside of it. He presents a clear plastic container, about the size of a punch bowl, with a green shamrock painted on the side. "Would you mind taking this downstairs to the restroom and filling it with cold water?"

Ed jumps up and takes the bowl. I uncross my legs and rotate my left foot to stop it from falling asleep.

Harold presses his left nostril with his index finger and says, "While he gets that for us, I'd just like to see a show of hands of how many of you have seen the *amazing* StormBurst before?"

Everyone looks around the room. Only one person, the woman in the back row who looks about Mom's age, raises her hand. She blushes as her hand slips down into her lap.

Ed returns with the bowl, now filled with water.

"Thank you…Edmund."

"It's just Ed."

"Okay everybody, this is what we call the *Pot O'Water*—and it's pretty obvious why, now isn't it?" Harold giggles and smiles at us. "But what isn't so obvious is how the StormBurst can clean all the air in your home, using just a simple Pot O'Water—without getting anything wet! Does that sound pretty amazing to you?"

I nod, along with everyone else.

"Say, have any of you ever noticed how when the sun shines in at a certain angle, you can see all kinds of dust and junk floating in the air?"

"Yes."

"Yeah."

"I guess so."

The voice in the back of the room bellows, "They're everywhere!"

"They sure are," Harold chuckles and picks up the sunlamp. "Well in case some of you haven't seen it, this little light of mine—" Harold pauses to giggle, then rubs his nose. "This light is going to show you the same thing. You see, we call it the *Ray O'Sun* because—"

Click.

"It's just like a ray of sun shining in your window, isn't it?"

And it is. Dust particles and fibers drift around in the golden beam beneath Harold's lamp.

A guy up in the front row snickers. "Now we know where boogers come from!"

The girl next to him punches his shoulder. "Shut up, Tyler. You're disgusting!"

"Do you see all that dust in the air?"

"Yeah."

"And do you know what *rides* around on those particles of dust?" Harold raises his eyebrows, then shouts: "Microscopic dust mites and bacteria!" He continues shining the light and lowers his eyebrows. "Did you know that forty *pounds* of dust accumulate in the average home *per year?*"

"No way!"

"Oh, man!"

"And did you know that, according to the EPA, indoor air can be as much as a hundred times *more* polluted than the air outside?"

"Oh, my god!"

"Whoah."

"Now, wouldn't it be nice if you could clean all that crud out of your air and have nice fresh air inside—as fresh as it is in the Irish countryside?"

"Yeah!"

"Definitely!"

"They're everywhere!"

Harold snickers and switches off the lamp.

"Well, that's exactly what I'm going to do with the StormBurst. Are you guys ready?"

We're ready.

"Those of you sitting in the back might want to come up closer to watch this part...yeah, just come right on around here..."

We form a semicircle around Harold as he reopens the lid of the StormBurst box and leans over it awkwardly. His shirt comes untucked at the sides, revealing pale bulges with sparse black hairs. He lifts out what looks like an Irish droid, or perhaps it's an electric Leprechaun. It stands about four feet tall with a bright green body and gold script letters spelling "StormBurst" down its front, like a shiny zipper. It stands on three green legs, each with a golden wheel for a foot. Harold sits the Leprechaun on top of the Pot O'Water so that all three legs straddle the bowl. He reaches between the Leprechaun's legs, lifts the bowl and clamps the two parts together with golden buckles. Harold tucks his shirt in casually as he takes a seat on top of the green box. "Could someone just plug this in over—ah, thank you." Harold turns the Leprechaun to give us a profile view, and holds the light above a three-inch opening that would surely be the Leprechaun's navel, if it were a Leprechaun. He switches on the Ray O'Sun. "Can you see that crud again?"

We can see the crud.

He presses a button on the StormBurst and with a growl, a grind, and a whoosh, the dust particles speed into the hungry machine so quickly that we almost can't see them. Harold shouts over the roaring motor, "Can everybody see that? You can take turns coming up closer if you need to. I just want to make sure everybody has a chance to see this..."

The noise is almost deafening.

"Ha-ha! Hasta la vista dust mites! So long, airborne disease germs!"

I can't help it, I have to scratch myself.

At last he shuts off the machine, and smiles. "Now, if you thought that it *looked* like the StormBurst was cleaning the air, I'd like to show you the proof? Do you want to see the proof?"

Of course we want to see the proof.

Harold unbuckles the Leprechaun and stands him on the carpet. He lifts the Pot O'Water in one hand, and shines the Ray O'Sun up beneath it, revealing a galaxy of dust and lint and pollen particles and "*skin cells—*which are the favorite meal of *dust mites—*and dust mites are the leading aggravators of *asthma—*and studies suggest they may even cause the development of asthma—especially in children and the elderly and those who suffer immuno-deficiency problems!" Harold sets down the lamp and points a finger toward the surface of the water. He takes a deep breath, "But when you see skin cells forming a filmy layer on the surface like that—can you see that? Do you see that scuzzy looking layer of film on the top? When you see that, then you *know darn well* that dust mites are drowning in there."

"They're everywhere!" Mr. Whiteglove stands bolt upright, waving frantic puppet-hands in the air.

"Yes they are. But the StormBurst will put an end to that!" Harold smiles and rubs his nose.

Whiteglove's eyes bulge and a vein rises, like mercury, up the center of his forehead. Slowly he sinks back into his seat.

Harold sets the lamp and water down on the carpet. "Did you guys like that?"

We liked that. And I finally know what I'll be demonstrating: an air-purifier. Loud, but powerful. Ugly, yet noble. Yes, asthmatics, allergy sufferers, even environmentalists perhaps will watch me with delight—will thank me for my small but significant contribution to their quality of life.

"Now wouldn't it be great if you could get all of that gunk out of your home for good?"

"Yeah."

"Definitely."

"Shut up, Tyler. You don't even have a home!" The girl stands to face the rest of us. Her chest heaves, her jaw pulses, and she shouts, "He still lives with his parents!"

We stare, in silence, until she sits down.

Harold's eye is twitching again. He takes a long, deep breath and pinches his nostrils for a second or two. "Damned allergies." He finally lets go and looks around the room at us. "Well, I'm not going to lie to you, but unfortunately it's not as simple as just cleaning the air in your home."

Ed sits up. "Dude, what do you mean?"

"Well, what I mean, *Ed*, is that if you want to get that dust and pollen and pet dander and whatever else is in your home's air *out* of your home's air, you're going to have to start from the ground up." Harold rakes his Ray O'Sun across the carpet and holds it knee-high, illuminating "a veritable sludge of domestic air pollution!" He looks around at our group and nods toward me, or maybe to someone behind me. "Tell me, where do most of the air pollutants in your home come from?" I try to look casually over my shoulder and, as I do, I see white.

"Dear God, they're everywhere! Everywhere!" Whiteglove races to the door, pausing only to produce a white handkerchief from his pocket with which he turns the doorknob.

We stare at the door as it closes, then at Harold.

Harold sits on the green case, pinching his nostrils, and staring at the ceiling. A moment later, he bursts into a fit of laughter.

So do we.

"Well, not everybody's cut out for this line of work, are they?"

Ed laughs and whispers "What a freaky dude, man!"

I can't tell if he means Mr. Whiteglove or Harold Chin. "Yeah, really."

Harold lets go of his nose and continues. "Okay, now, as I was saying, where do most of the air pollutants in your home come from?" I think he's looking at me. "More specifically?" He giggles.

I'd like to take a long, deep, cleansing breath, but I know what I'll be filling my lungs with if I do. "They're in—you're—uh—carpet?"

Harold grins. "Exactly! Okay everybody, so if you want to get rid of the dust and crud in the air—and on your TV screen, and everywhere else in your house, where should you start?" He's poised on the box and ready for action.

"The carpet!"

"Your rugs!"

"The floor, man!"

"Well, now I'm going to show you how the StormBurst can get that same dust and gunk out of your carpet—and everywhere else in your home. Does that sound good to you?"

"Yes!"

"Great. Now what's the tool we've traditionally used to clean the carpet with?"

Someone mumbles "Tool?"

Harold looks impatient. "A vacuum cleaner, right?"

"Right!"

"Well, let's just take a moment to see how the good old-fashioned vacuum cleaner can actually work against us." Harold excuses himself to the back of the room, where he opens a door and shouts, "This is what we call the *graveyard!*" He returns with a Windmaster 7000, just like Mom's. He plugs in the Windmaster and shines the Ray O'Sun above its exhaust vent. "I want you guys to come up here again, lean in…yeah, that's it…now watch really, really close…"

Click.

Poof!

Millions of dust particles blast out of the Windmaster. We back up immediately, stepping on each other's feet, scrambling for fresh air, but the Windmaster continues blasting dust and pollen and dust mite excrement and microscopic viruses and bacterium all over the room.

Click.

Harold grins in the abrupt silence. "*Cleaner*—I think NOT!"

We agree and slowly, cautiously, pull our hands away from our mouths and noses. Harold gestures to the other side of the StormBurst, and what looks to be the *anus leprechaunus*, but Harold calls it "the exhaust vent." He shines the Ray O'Sun above it and growl—grind—whoosh, not one spec of dust exits the StormBurst. "That's because *water* is Mother Nature's own household cleaning product, isn't it?"

Harold lifts his eyebrows and waits.

"Okay."

"Yeah."

"I guess so."

"But you're probably saying to yourselves, 'well, but that's not even cleaning the carpet, where the real filth is.' Am I right?"

"Yeah."

"Well, just hold on for a second and you'll see for yourselves…" Harold flips open the wide flat box and pulls out a glistening golden wand. He screws a green plastic handle onto one end of the wand, and what looks like a white plastic cloud—or maybe a giant puffy slipper—onto the other. No one utters a word as he inserts a long hose into the handle. Harold flashes a grin, "This is the specially patented Storm Chaser! It's what we use to clean the carpet—*really* clean the carpet!" He stretches the hose over to the navel of the StormBurst and plugs it in. His eye twitches. "Now, watch the Pot O'Water and you'll see for yourself just how well the StormBurst cleans carpet! Are you ready?"

"Yes!"

Growl—grind—whoosh, the Storm Chaser lurches forward, nearly escaping Harold's grasp. He works in a circle around the StormBurst box, and sure enough, between the leprechaun's legs, the Pot O'Water turns to brown.

"Ha-ha! But that's not all it can do!" and Harold proceeds to show us how the StormBurst is more than just an air purifier, a belt sander, a percussive massage tool, or a vacuum cleaner. It can even shrink-wrap sweaters for summer storage, freshen pillows and inflate a rubber raft in just minutes. "And even kids love the StormBurst!" He fills a cloud-shaped balloon, ties a knot, and tosses it into the air toward us. "Now, before I finish here, I don't want you to think I forgot about taking you all to Ireland. So are you guys ready for a trip?"

Of course we're ready.

"I'm trippin' already," Ed giggles.

Harold kneels on the floor and opens the green case. He removes a small plastic bottle with a green lid. "Now, I'm not at liberty to tell you what the special ingredient is in our Breath O'Ireland fragrance. In fact, no one's even told *me* what it is. Some people think it's shamrock extract; others think it's some kind of peppermint oil. Why a couple of my friends think it might even be Irish whiskey—you can bet I keep it away from them!"

We laugh with Harold.

Harold straightens his tie. "But whatever it is, I haven't met a person yet who doesn't love this stuff. So I want you all to close your eyes for just a moment while I turn on the StormBurst..." growl—grind—whoosh, "and take you on a trip to Ireland!"

The StormBurst slurps a few drops from the bottle and my head swims with the fragrance of carnations, or maybe freshly cut lawn. I try to watch Harold, but my eyes are closing, and I'm leaning back in my chair. I feel my knee touching Ed's, but it doesn't bother me. I'm in Ireland...and in Ireland everyone is...beautiful.

Click.

We open our eyes to see Harold sitting perfectly upright on his green case. He's beaming. "Now you haven't just *seen* the proof—you've *smelled* it too! Ha-ha!"

We giggle.

"So now that you've all seen the StormBurst, wouldn't you agree it's a pretty amazing machine?"

"Yes."

"Definitely."

Harold removes the Leprechaun from the Pot O'Water, which has now accumulated filth and crud and junk from the air, the carpet, even Ed's combat boots. He shines the Ray O'Sun up through it and grins with delight as the lamp barely illuminates the murky water. "And wouldn't you agree you'd rather have all of this filth *outside* your home, instead of inside it?"

"Yes!"

"Of course."

"Because if you don't, you know, I'd be happy to come over and dump this *in* your home!"

We laugh, heartily.

"But seriously," Harold's eyebrows pull up into black triangles again, "you can see how the StormBurst can make your life easier all the way around, can't you?"

"Yes."

"It not only keeps your house cleaner, it keeps you and your family healthier. And isn't good health the greatest gift of all?"

"Yes!"

"So, if I could make it *possible* for you to own a StormBurst today, you'd be interested, wouldn't you?"

"Yeah—no—wait, I mean—"

We look at each other awkwardly, then back at Harold, and the room buzzes with explanations of how, since none of us has a job—except for this—

"And that's the demonstration!"

❄   ❄   ❄

We watch a slideshow that explains the history and evolution of the Storm-Burst. It begins with a tattered black and white photograph of Brendan P. Callahan, the son of Irish immigrants who were overwhelmed by the dusty conditions of California's gold country. We see a slide of Brendan P. Callahan's diary where he wrote about his mother's nightly prayers to the saints, begging for a good Irish rain. The gruff voice on the tape recording chuckles, "Well, Brendan's parents never struck gold themselves, but he surely did years later when he created the world's first motorized dust-free cleaning device—what we now call the StormBurst."

We spend the first couple days in small groups memorizing each segment of the same demonstration Harold showed us, and we take turns "shrink-freshening" an assortment of old sofa cushions and assembling the Storm Chaser. Wednesday morning, Harold explains to us how to use the shampoo attachment, too, though he assures us we'll probably never have to use it; it's not even *officially* part of the demo.

"Just ask your customer if she might be interested in getting the StormBurst's exclusive shampoo wand—FREE. That's easy enough, isn't it?"

"Yes!"

And by Thursday morning, we're working on what Harold calls our "closing techniques." He explains that the close of the sale is simply when we get our customer to "put his money where his mouth is—or *her* mouth, because at StormBurst we don't discriminate! Right?"

"Right!"

"And it's easy enough to do since the customer already agrees with you that the StormBurst is pretty *amazing*. Who wouldn't?"

We shrug our shoulders.

"But," he emphasizes, "Your number one job is to make sure they *realize* they're agreeing with you. That's why you need your customers to say yes—or at least nod their heads—every time you make an important point. Can you all do that?"

"Yes!"

Harold flashes a smile. "That way, when you reach the final question—what's the final question? Ed?"

"Uh, so if I could like make it *possible* for you to own a StormBurst today, man, you'd be interested wouldn't you?"

"That's right! Then that person either has to say yes or contradict everything else he's told you in the past thirty minutes! And no one wants to be a liar, right?"

"Right!"

A somber look passes over Harold's face. "I'll be honest with you, though. You know, for each of you, there might come a time when someone won't say yes…" He passes out a Xeroxed list of possible scenarios where someone might hesitate to say yes at the close of the demo. And for each scenario, there's a catchy phrase to help us remember how to turn "worst-case situations into StormBurst revelations! Does that sound good to you?"

"Yes!"

And after just a few days of training, Harold is willing to entrust us with the most important secret of good salesmanship.

We lean forward in our seats.

"Don't sell—*solve!*" Harold throws his arms out to each side. "Making a sale," he continues, "is just a matter of solving a customer's problems. Like helping them find the right solution to get rid of all of the pollen, dust and filth from their homes—and finding a way to *easily* fit a StormBurst into their budgets."

And to imagine, I'll make $12.84 per hour just for helping people.

That afternoon, Brenda Sue joins us to announce a special kick-off weekend extravaganza that she and Harold have organized just for us. "I want you all to go home and call up every friend, neighbor, relative—heck, even the Avon lady!" She snorts. "And you're gonna ask them for their help!" She bulges her eyes at us, then grins. "All you need them to do is give you about thirty minutes of their time to watch you practice your demonstration, and tell you what they think of the StormBurst! Could you use some more practice?"

"Yeah!" We chuckle.

Harold shouts, "Then practice in front of as many people as you can!"

Harold and Brenda Sue smile at each other, then back at us.

Harold throws his hands out to each side. "And we're gonna have some prizes!"

Brenda Sue continues, "That's right! Starting tonight, for whichever one of you goes home and schedules the most practice demonstrations for this weekend!"

Ed sits up in his chair, "What's the prize, man?"

Brenda Sue grins with delight, "*Welllllll,*" she fondles one of the thicker chains on her chest, "for that you'll get a genuine 10-karat GOLD-plated key chain. But THAT'S just the beginning!"

Harold rubs the tip of his nose. "Yeah. We're going to have prizes *all weekend long*—for the dealer who completes the most practice demonstrations, for the dealer who gets the most referrals over the weekend—don't forget to ask for referrals! And let's see, and for the dealer who drives the most miles over the weekend!"

Brenda Sue wags a jewel-studded finger at us, "Don't forget to keep track of those miles now!"

"But the top prize will go to the dealer who *sells* the most StormBursts over the weekend!"

The room is silent.

Brenda Sue adds, "Now, you remember how impressed you all were the first time you saw the StormBurst—don't be surprised when all your friends are too!"

"What's *that* prize?"

"Well, Ed…" Harold's eyebrows rise up into triangles, "Your own Storm-Burst!"

Holy snots.

Harold and Brenda Sue wait for us to settle down. She retrieves the longest chain from deep within her cleavage. "Now the best part is, if you win that machine, well, you can keep it for yourself…"

"Wow!"

"Oh my gosh!"

"No way!"

There's a flash of green behind her eyes. "Or you can sell it and keep *all* the cash."

❈   ❈   ❈

"I need to practice a presentation for my new job in front of as many people as I can, by Monday—in their homes. And they don't have to buy *anything*."

"How long is this presentation?"

"About half an hour."

Mom calls every teacher in her school district, and every professor she's met from Dad's college. She sets appointments for me from nine in the morning to nine at night, with one starting on each new hour, except midday when she's scheduled an hour's lunch break for me. The only catch: They all live in Cornston, 45 minutes away.

"Mom, how on earth did you get so many people to agree?"

"Honey, do you have any idea how many Girl Scout Cookies, candy bars, Christmas ornaments and rolls of wrapping paper we've bought from *their* children over the years?"

I do. And I thank her.

My first appointment is, of course, with Mom and Dad, on Friday evening at 7 p.m. When I arrive, the table is set with Mom's china and the cloth napkins. They're ready to feed me dinner and celebrate my new "career" as Dad calls it, with his tongue planted firmly in his cheek and a bottle of sparkling cider in his hand.

I tell them thank you but that I stand a good chance of "winning a big bonus," so I'll have to eat later, on the road.

They carry their plates to the sofa and watch as I lug in the equipment from my car: The green demo case, the StormBurst Box and the Storm Chaser/ Accessory box. I look at the shampoo wand, wedged behind the passenger's and driver's seats, spanning the floor of the backseat, and decide to leave it there.

It's not even officially part of the demonstration.

Mom watches Dad, nervously, as he cuts the roast beef on his lap.

"By the way, I love the new sofa! What do you call that color?"

"Ecru." Mom smiles.

Dad points to the boxes, "That all fit inside your Rabbit?"

"Yep." I stretch the extension cord across the floor.

Mom giggles. "So, no room for your laundry?"

I take my seat on the green demo case, with just the coffee table between us. "Okay, Mr. and Mrs. Jensen. Thanks for having me over today—this evening. I really appreciate your time." I take a deep breath.

Dad clears his throat gently and points his index finger at a newly formed smile on his face.

I take his cue and smile back. "I know that nowadays, it seems that everywhere you look, someone's trying to tell you—indeed, to *sell* you something, and well, it's hard to know what to believe, now isn't it?" But I'm already staring down at the coffee table trying to remember what comes next. I look up at Mom and Dad again. Mom is concentrating on chewing her roast beef and Dad will probably be asleep in no time if I don't find a way to pick up the pace. But there's still a list of things they have to agree with before I can get to the good stuff. "So, um, don't you think it's better when somebody *shows* you something—instead of just telling you about it?"

They stare blankly.

"Would you agree with that, Mr. Jensen?"

Dad sits up and clears his throat, "Well of course, honey," and waits to see if he's answered correctly.

"Great." I nod.

He smiles.

"And would you agree with that too, Mrs. Jensen?"

Mom nods her head and pats the corners of her mouth with her napkin.

"Great. I'm glad you both agree. That's actually why I'm here today—tonight, because, let's face it, Mr. and Mrs. Jensen, I could call you up on the phone, or even show up on your TV set in one of those crazy infomercials, but let's face it, you wouldn't *really* believe any of it, unless you saw it for yourselves. Isn't that right, Mr. Jensen?"

"That's right." Dad winks at me.

"I can tell you're a wise shopper, Mr. Jensen, and I'll bet you are too, Mrs. Jensen."

Mom smiles back, cautiously, and sets her plate on the coffee table.

"Well, without any further to-do, I'd like to show you the StormBurst."

"Oh, good!" Mom smiles at Dad and pats Dad's lips with her napkin.

"But before I do…" I'm staring at the coffee table again, searching for what comes next. "Have you ever been to Ireland?"

"Oh, why yes!" Mom clasps her hands together.

No one ever said yes in training, but I improvise. "Well, that's great! Then you must remember how fresh the air was?"

Dad wrinkles his brow. "Well, not in Dublin, sweetie."

"Oh, yes, there was terrible air pollution—*smog*, right honey?"

"Yes, and did you know that they still used coal for heating there up until 1990? It's just terrible for the environment. You know, I had my class do an experiment once—"

I clear my throat until he stops. "I meant in the *countryside*. The air was very fresh in the Irish countryside, now *wasn't* it, Mr. and Mrs. Jensen?"

"Oh, of course it was." Dad begins to button up his blue cardigan.

"Yes dear," Mom smiles and nods, "the air was *very* fresh in the countryside."

"Well, good. As long as you liked the fresh air in the *countryside*, I think you're going to love the StormBurst!" I smile at them both and open the box to reveal the Pot O'Water.

"Ah-ha! So this is it?" Dad finishes the last button.

"Oh! Well—wait…" I consult the coffee table. "Did you know that 40 *pounds* of dust accumulate in the average home *per year?*"

"Not in this house, it doesn't!" Mom nearly drops the plate off her lap.

Dad smothers his grin with the palm of his hand.

I reach for the Ray O'Sun. When I look up again, Dad's whole face has turned red from not-laughing.

Click.

"And did you know that, according to the EPA, indoor air can be as much as a hundred times *more* polluted than the air outside?"

"Good heavens! Look at that dust." The crease is beginning to show between Mom's eyebrows.

Dad raises his eyebrows as he takes a long, deep breath. But it's no use. He can't stop giggling.

"Professor Jensen, what's the microscopic organism found throughout the home that feeds on human skin cells?"

Mom wrinkles her nose.

Dad drops his smile and rubs his chin, thoughtfully. "On the body or off the body?"

I grin, "Mostly off."

"Dust mites!" He grins back at me, excited to hear more.

Mom sighs, "Good heavens. I think I've lost my appetite for the next week." She pats her mouth with the napkin. "Do you mind if we move on, sweetie?" She forces a polite smile for me.

"Fine." I consult the coffee table for what comes next. "Now, wouldn't it be nice, Mr. and Mrs. Jensen, if you could clean all that crud out of your air and have nice fresh air inside—as fresh as it is in the Irish countryside?"

Mom glances down at her watch. "Oh, sweetie it's almost time for your next appointment—with the DeYoungs! I'd better call and let them know we're running behind." She excuses herself to make the call.

Dad rubs his chin, thoughtfully. "Did I ever tell you about that car we rented in Ireland? It was so small your Mother's suitcase barely fit in the trunk!"

"Really, Dad?" I click the Ray O'Sun on, then off.

"That was some vacation all right. You know, over there they don't think anything of drinking beer with *lunch*!" He chuckles and shakes his head.

"Hard to imagine."

"Yes, indeed. I'll never forget that trip, that's for sure. The vacation of a lifetime."

Mom returns. "All right, they said to just give a call when you're on your way." She sits down on the sofa with a smile. "Where were we now?"

For some reason, the demonstration takes nearly three hours to complete. Dad helps me move the coffee table to clear enough space to unfold the shrink-fresh bag while Mom calls the DeYoungs to apologize—and cancel.

"It's okay, Mom! Tell them thanks anyway."

Dad winks at me and sets down his end of the plastic bag. "I think you've got your work cut out for you tomorrow—she's called everyone we know in Cornston!"

My stomach gurgles. "Yeah, I know."

"Oh, sweetie, it sounds like they were really looking forward to seeing you! They said if you still need more practice, you're welcome to stop by any time."

"Thanks, Mom." I stuff the Ecru sofa cushion into the plastic bag and stifle a yawn, but Mom and Dad can't hold back.

Dad rubs his eye with his fist. "Okay, honey, are we almost through?"

"Yeah, almost." I tap into my final reserve of enthusiasm. "This is my favorite part, watch!"

Growl—grind—whoosh—

The cushion flattens into a pancake between the layers of plastic.

Dad bolts upright on the ecru sofa.

Mom squeals, "That's about the most amazing thing I've ever seen!"

And suddenly we're all awake again.

When I inflate the balloons, Dad jokes, "Say does that have an adapter for tires, too?" He and Mom cackle like a pair of drunken hyenas.

"As a matter of fact, Mr. Jensen, it does."

But when I show them the Pot O'Water at the end of the demonstration, Mom pales. And suddenly, this is my favorite part of the demonstration:

"So, Mr. and Mrs. Jensen, don't you agree that the StormBurst is a pretty amazing machine?"

"Oh, yes!" Mom exclaims, her gaze fixed on the Pot O'Water.

"Absolutely, without a doubt," Dad says, good-humoredly. "Say, can I take a sample of that—I'd love to get a look at it with a microscope!" He winks at me and I begin to smile back.

But then: this is no time for jokes.

"So wouldn't you agree, Mr. And Mrs. Jensen, that you'd rather have all of this *dust* and *dirt* and *filth* outside of your home, instead of in your carpet?" I look directly at Mom.

"Oh, yes!" She shrieks, and clutches Dad's sleeve.

Dad looks nervously at Mom. Mom looks only at the Pot O'Shame.

"And can you see how the StormBurst will keep your home cleaner all the way around?"

Mom nods to the pot, "Oh, yes!"

"And isn't health—and since the StormBurst will keep you healthier—isn't your health the greatest gift of all?"

"Yes!"

Dad shifts on the sofa and clears his throat. "Well, I suppose so—"

"So, if I could make it *possible* for you to own a StormBurst *today*, you'd be interested, wouldn't you—Mr. and Mrs. Jensen?"

"Yes!" Mom shrieks again.

Dad tries to say something, but I'm faster.

"I thought so! That's *wonderful*. We accept many forms of payment: cash of course, Visa, MasterCard or Discover, and we also have a number of payment plans available—which method would work best for you, Mr. and Mrs. Jensen?" Then I do exactly what Harold taught me to do: I shut up and wait.

Dad's pulse quickens at the side of his neck. He unbuttons his cardigan.

"Visa!" Only then does Mom look at Dad. She pats him on the knee as she adds, "I can't wait to try it on the lampshade in the den!" She's glowing.

So is Dad.

I have to bite the sides of my tongue to keep from speaking too soon. As Harold said, it's the surest way to kill a sale.

Mom smiles at me, then looks at Dad.

Dad looks at the StormBurst, then at me.

Mom says in her softest voice, "Honey?"

Honey says nothing.

I resist the urge to move the coffee table back to its place as I wait for Dad's response. I listen to the second hand of my watch ticking, ticking, ticking—

Dad takes a long, deep breath and says, "Well, that all sounds well and good, you two, but Diana still hasn't told us how much this machine costs. Diana?"

"You're absolutely right, Mr. Jensen." I pull out the clipboard and pen and begin writing as I say, "For the marvelous StormBurst, the patented Storm Chaser, and all of the attachments you've seen here, it's just fourteen thirty-seven!" I smile confidently, then shut up and wait.

Dad's nostrils flare. "Did you say *fourteen thirty-seven*?"

"Oh, Hal, just think of the frequent flyer miles we can rack up on that new card!"

Dad's Adam's apple rises and falls. "*Fourteen? Thirty-seven?*"

Gulp. "Now, Mr. Jensen, I know you might be thinking that's a bit high for a vacuum cleaner, but of course, as you saw, Mr. And Mrs. Jensen, the Storm-Burst is a far cry from *just a vacuum cleaner*, isn't that right?"

"Oh, yes!" Mom smiles.

Dad doesn't. He starts to button up his cardigan again, but stops mid-way and stares at the coffee table.

I force a smile.

"Hal, *you said yourself* that it's an amazing machine!"

It's a tone I've only heard once before. And as I recall, it led to their first trip to Ireland.

Dad finishes buttoning up his cardigan and looks over at the Pot O'Water-loo. "Well, I just think that for a purchase of *that size* we ought to think this over first." He crosses his arms. "And *discuss* it." He clears his throat.

"Oh, Hal, we just saw the thing in action—on our *own* carpet. What more is there to discuss?" Mom smiles and pats him on the knee. "Get your card, honey."

Honey doesn't budge.

I take out my calculator. "Now, my boss will allow me to give you a $100 credit for your old vacuum cleaner…if you go ahead and invest in the amazing StormBurst *today*."

But the room is silent. As they both stare at the coffee table in its new location beside the bookcase, I realize they're waiting for *me* to fix things.

Dad clears his throat again and leans against the arm of the sofa, away from Mom. He examines his hands, the cuticles, and bites at a hangnail.

Don't sell—solve!

But how?

Mom's eyes are beginning to water. She folds her hands on her lap and blinks rapidly toward the ceiling.

I search my memory for a StormBurst Revelation.

Turn their fight into a double delight.

Mom would be delighted with the StormBurst. But Dad? I try to casually pull my accessories brochure out of the green demo case. My pulse thumps against my temples as I flip through its pages. The tire pump adapter is $45. It would still leave me with a $155 commission, including a credit card bonus—of $50.

Holy snots. Two hundred and five dollars? For three hours of work?

"Well, you know, Mr. and Mrs. Jensen, I can see how much you both like this amazing machine. But I can also see that Mr. Jensen still has some reservations about whether or not your household will be able to get the *full value* of this amazing machine. Is that right, Mr. Jensen?"

Dad takes a deep breath, then clears his throat. "Uh, yes. That's right, Diana."

I smile and nod my head. "Well I can certainly understand that, Mr. Jensen. That's why, if you purchase the StormBurst today, I'll not only give you the $100 credit for your old vacuum, I'll also throw in the tire pump adapter at no extra charge to you—would that set your mind at ease, Mr. Jensen?"

Mom takes a long, deep breath and continues staring at the murky water.

Dad looks at Mom, the water, then me. Slowly, slowly he surrenders a smile.

I take a long, deep, cleansing breath through my teeth as I maintain my smile.

Dad's eyebrows lift. "Please tell me that at least *some* of this will be going toward your tuition?" He reaches for his back pocket.

"Well, of course it will…Mr. Jensen."

Mom giggles.

Dad looks at Mom and pats her on the knee. "All right." He winks at me.

"Fantastic," I reach out and give him a firm handshake.

❀   ❀   ❀

Just thinking of Mrs. Gruber ties my stomach in a knot. I can still picture her standing in front of the blackboard, waving the long wooden pointer at us and shouting, "Settle down! *Goddamnit* I said settle down!"

She answers the door in a quilted pink housecoat with a shower cap on her head. "Well, Diana Jensen! For Christ's sake! Let me get a look at you!" She is hefty and stout and generally mean-looking, like a bulldog in fuzzy slippers. "Is it really you?"

I try my best not to look at her harelip. "It sure is, Mrs. Gruber."

"By GOD, it's been a long time." She looks me up and down and I wonder if she knows she's wearing a shower cap. "Well get in here! You're letting the *goddamned* flies in!"

I follow her through the kitchen that smells of pancakes, maple syrup and eggs, and into the living room where her breakfast plate sits on the TV tray, empty except for a puddle of syrup.

"So how old are you now?"

"Uh, I just turned twenty-two last month." My stomach gurgles.

"No kidding? *Jesus Christ,* I must be getting old!" She snorts and yanks the shower cap off her head, revealing a thin frizz of white hairs and the pink scalp beneath. "How old would you guess I am, Diana?"

"Oh, well, I don't know…*seventy*?" Gulp.

She bulges her eyes and cackles, "Ha-ha! I'll be *eighty-three* come September! Not doing too bad for an old lady, eh?"

"Uh, no. Not at all, Mrs. Gruber." I try to smile.

"They keep telling me I ought to retire, but what the hell else would I do?"

"Oh, well, I don't know."

"Huh-hum!" She nods more to herself than to me. Her hand rises into the air with a crooked finger pointing at me. "I'll tell you what my secret is, Diana."

I press my hand against my abdomen to try and muffle the noise. "Okay."

Her harelip spreads wide enough to reveal a couple of teeth. "A glass of wine, *every day*." She nods her head at me. "One glass. No more, no less. Every single day."

"Like a vitamin?"

"Huh-hum, that's right!" She sets the shower cap on the end table and I feel my stomach begin to relax. For a moment. "Well, then! What in *god's name* is this all about?"

It takes me a couple of trips to carry my equipment in, but as soon as she sees the StormBurst boxes, she asks, "Well, don't I get steak knives or something?" It looks like she's sneering at me, but I tell myself it's just the harelip.

"Oh, I don't have any steak knives yet." I untangle the cord on my Ray O'Sun.

"What do you mean, *not yet*?" she demands.

"Well, uh, they don't give us steak knives until after we've sold a few, 'cause, um, they take them out of our…commissions."

"Well that's just stupid!" She plops onto the orange loveseat and sighs, "Huhrump!" with the last syllable sounding something like a small fart. Again, I tell myself it's just the harelip.

I watch her from the corner of my eye as I close the demo case. I decide to let the dust mites and bacteria go just this once, in the interest of time. After all, I've still got a full day of appointments ahead of me. Tomorrow, too. "Have you ever been to Ireland, Mrs. Gruber?"

Mrs. Gruber snorts and slaps the arm of the love seat, "Is that how this presentation begins? Ireland? What are you selling here, Irish Coffee? *Christ almighty!*" She cackles and runs her fingers through the thin frizz.

"You just have to answer 'yes' or 'no.'" I try to smile.

"Well of course not! *Jesus Christ*, do you think I'm made of money?"

She watches me with a critical eye and never once says "yes." But I can get her to at least nod her head and even make an occasional "Huh-hump!" I assume that means yes.

"As you will see when I shrink this cushion from your sofa—"

"Is that your natural color of hair?"

"Pardon?"

"You're not using *peroxide*, are you?"

The adrenaline rush helps me cut the demonstration time in half. It's only an hour and twenty minutes later when I take her to Ireland, for the first time ever.

"Just close your eyes a moment and take a deep breath and—you'll feel like a million dollars!"

Growl—grind—whoosh—

I shout, "Just close your eyes, and take a long, deep, soothing breath!"

"Huh-hump-huh-hump-huh-hump!" She nods. "That's good!" I think she might be smiling.

At last, I hold up the Pot O'Water, surprising myself, I think, more than Mrs. Gruber. There's a thick layer of sludge about half an inch deep at the bottom.

"And Mrs. Gruber, wouldn't you rather—"

"Well *son-of-a-bitch!*"

"Yeah, I know. So wouldn't you rather—"

"How much is this thing, Diana?"

My mind reels. I should have eaten some breakfast. "So you like the Storm-Burst then?"

"Yep. How much is it?"

"Well," I take a quick breath and reach for my clipboard. With my pen firmly between my fingers, I say "The StormBurst-with-all-the-attachments-you've-seen-here is just fourteen thirty-seven."

Her bottom lip pops out and I hear my morning coffee gurgle in the silence. "You don't mean fourteen dollars, do you?"

I try to smile politely, "No, I don't mean fourteen dollars, Mrs. Gruber."

"Well *son-of-a-goddamned-bitch!*" She massages the arm of the loveseat.

A sudden pain stabs through the wall of my stomach. I flinch, but I try to cover by looking at my watch and confirming I've still got two full days of this.

She releases a dramatic sigh, followed by a big "Huh-hump" with the small-fart suffix. "*Son-of-a-goddamned-bitch!*"

I do my best to stay put, to hold on to the pen, to keep my mouth shut—until it suddenly dawns on me that Harold Chin has never met Mrs. Gruber. I drop my clipboard on the carpet, stand up, and begin winding up the extension cord.

Mrs. Gruber clears her throat. "Well, you know, that's more than I just sold my old car for." She looks at me sadly.

But I don't budge. Maybe I'm just tired. Maybe I've got low blood sugar. Or maybe I'm just tired of being afraid of a mean old lady in a pink housecoat.

Whatever it is, I can feel something peculiar deep inside of me. It quivers. It twangs. Then, finally, it snaps. "Well, I'll bet this thing runs a hell of a lot better than your *old car*, doesn't it?"

Mrs. Gruber's eyes bulge. Her lip pops out and my stomach growls. I ready myself for a grand parade of four-lettered nouns and verbs, followed by multi-syllabic salutes to the main players from the Christmas pageant. But she just sits there on the corduroy loveseat, staring like she has no idea who I am or why I'm in her house.

But then: her mouth pulls up at the corners, and her harelip spreads wide across her front teeth and gum.

I smile back at her.

"You're right about that! Whew! What a clunker! Good riddance!" she chuckles.

And I jump in on the high note, just like Harold taught me. "Well, the *good* news is, we'll take cash or credit, and we have lots of different payment plans available." She's nodding her head. "So what can I arrange for you, Mrs. Gruber?"

I convince her to go with the payment plan of $200 down, and $65per month—it's the only plan I remember talking about in training. We fill out papers on her kitchen table, surrounded on three sides by a wallpaper border that's nothing but goose, goose, goose.

"*Goddamnit already!*" She throws her pen down on the papers and huffs.

Gulp. "WHAT?"

"Stupid pen's out of ink."

I laugh out loud. "Is that all? You almost gave me a heart attack!"

Mrs. Gruber cackles a bit.

"Here, use mine."

"Thanks, Diana."

Mrs. Gruber mumbles "Huh-hump, huh-hump," as she works her way down the terms and conditions page, initialing each line.

I'm so relieved to have the whole thing over with, I give her my extra bottle of Breath O'Ireland "In lieu of steak knives," I say. I make a quick, local call to Mom and ask if she could cancel my next two appointments while I drive back to Harveston for a new machine.

"Oh, sweetie, congratulations! Of course I'll call and cancel—or should I reschedule?"

"Well," I look over at Mrs. Gruber as she attaches the upholstery tool to the StormBurst. Holy snots. I just made a hundred and fifty-five dollars. "Tell them I'll give a call to reschedule."

Mom's Windmaster had barely fit across the back seat, but Mrs. Gruber's Karmair is even bigger. She brings out her spool of twine and watches as I stand on a kitchen chair and hoist it up on top of the Rabbit. I tie it sideways, then lengthwise, then crossways to be safe. We stand back and survey the tangled heap on top of the luggage rack.

She grunts, "Looks like huntin' season!"

We chuckle and, before I know it, she's pulling me toward her for a hug—and a kiss! She puts her fuzzy harelip right on my mouth.

"Diana, I can already tell you'll make one *hell* of a salesman!"

❀   ❀   ❀

The lobby is abuzz with dealers laughing and sipping coffee, and x-dealers griping and returning their equipment to Berta, who is both laughing and griping while masticating a chili cheese dog.

For breakfast?

Nine o'clock sharp feels a lot like a knife between the ribs. But maybe it's just a slipped vertebra from hoisting those vacuum cleaners in and out of the car.

I find my way to the coffeepot, pick up the remaining half of a glazed old-fashioned, then trudge around back and up the stairs—where Brenda Sue and Harold greet me with hugs.

"There she is!"

"That's our girl!"

I stagger to my chair.

Honorable mentions are given to two dealers who also made sales during the kick-off weekend: Ed, who sold one to his Mother's in-home care provider, and the woman who'd said she'd seen a StormBurst before and apparently sold one to herself—with a substantial discount.

Harold and Brenda Sue ask me to come to the front of the room. I try to remember if I washed my face this morning as they swaddle me in a green satin jacket, which has an embroidered rainbow running up one sleeve. I must look like a drunken racecar driver, Green Hornet Speed Racer perhaps.

"The most demonstrations!" Brenda Sue smoothes the jacket over my shoulders, then claps her hands and smiles at me.

Harold opens his wallet and pulls out a crisp bill. "And here's some gas money for our dealer with the most miles driven!"

Twenty? But I must have filled up five times.

I spot some new faces in the room, but then they blur behind Styrofoam coffee cups and bismark donuts. My eyes rest on the empty seats at the back of the room.

Harold puts his hand on my shoulder, "And the most referrals!" He hands me a bumper sticker that reads: "Kiss me! I work for StormBurst!" A green shamrock dots the *i*. I stuff the twenty and the bumper sticker into the pocket of the green jacket.

Brenda Sue walks to the back of the room, then bends at the waist, erasing herself above a perfectly round hind end. Her gold-fringed boots step gingerly through the shag as she slides a StormBurst box across the carpet. She doesn't stop until she's directly in front of me. "And for the most StormBurst *sales* during the kick-off weekend…here it is, Diana, your very own StormBurst!"

There is more clapping. I hear Ed's voice shouting, "Right on, man!" and somewhere above the heads and faces and vinyl chairs, a fist punches the air.

Brenda Sue takes both of my hands in hers. I stare at a giant green stone on her index finger, in a setting that's wide and bulky like a man's. "So, Diana. Are you going to keep it for yourself…?"

Harold, Brenda Sue and a couple of the dealers shout together "Or SELL it!!!"

I pull my hands back and put them into the pockets of the jacket. "Well, you know, I need the money for school next year, so I'll probably—"

Brenda Sue squeals, "Ah-ha! She's gonna SELL it!"

The dealers cheer and applaud in a blurry smear between one fuzzy wall and another. Someone whistles as I rub my eyes.

Brenda Sue presses her hands on my shoulders, and the dealers quiet down. "Diana, why don't you tell us a little bit about your *favorite* sale this weekend?"

I rub the twenty between my index finger and thumb inside my pocket. "Well, I suppose…" I feel her press my shoulders again, "I guess it was when my parents bought it, 'cause, um, they just really liked it a lot, and I didn't think they would." She releases her grip and claps.

"Isn't that wonderful?"

Everyone claps.

Harold shouts above the commotion, "Let's all congratulate Diana on her *seven* sales this weekend!"

There is even more applause. I hear "Shit!" and "Jesus Christ!" and then "That's fucking insane." And I suppose it is.

I start to make way toward my chair, but Brenda Sue catches my sleeve.

"Now before you sit down, Diana, there's something else we have to mention. Something else you did this weekend that we never *guessed* was going to happen—"

Harold chimes in, "That's right! Listen to this…"

Brenda Sue rubs her hands together as if they are cold, but I still feel the hot sticky prints on my shoulders. "Every once in a while, someone breaks the Chin's StormBurst Kick-Off Weekend record. And Diana, you did it!"

"You broke the Chin's StormBurst Kick-Off Weekend record! Isn't that great?" Harold's eyebrows rise with delight.

"Let's hear it for Diana!"

"One hell of a salesman!"

Everyone claps as Harold walks across the room and returns with a small golden trophy—shaped like an electric Leprechaun.

"Congratulations!"

I take the trophy, my first ever, and read the small brass plaque on the base of it: "Chin's Kick-off Champion."

That's when the giggling starts.

"Thank you."

I clamp my teeth together to keep from giggling out loud, but then my knees start to shake.

"You can sit back down now, Diana," Brenda Sue whispers.

"Thank you," I say through my teeth. Some of the dealers congratulate me as I make my way back to my seat, next to Ed.

Harold begins passing out small booklets—songbooks. He looks quite serious as he tells us to open to page twenty-two. The dealers I don't recognize stand up. Then, one by one, the new dealers stand. We look around at each other, nervously. Harold holds his songbook before him like a church choirboy and asks, "Who would like to lead today?"

A white-haired man in the front row, wearing a blue plaid sports jacket, raises his hand. "Thank you, Bruce." Harold gives a nod and the room fills with song:

> This Ray O'Sun of mine,
> I'm gonna let it shine.
> This Ray O'Sun of mine,

I'm gonna let it shine.

Let it shine, let it shine, let it shine.

We repeat the song over and over until all of the new dealers are singing to Harold's satisfaction. Brenda Sue claps and stomps as her cotton candy hive bobs in syncopated rhythm. She tilts her head back and sings toward the ceiling in a key all her own:

Let it shi-hi-hine!

Let it shi-hi-hine!

I'm gonna-gonna-gonna let it shi-hi-hine!

Harold's eyebrows rise into triangles, and he splits the room into halves, directing us to sing in a round, and then faster and faster, until no one can keep up anymore and we all sit down, laughing.

"Excellent! Sounds like we have some strong new voices among us!"

We pass our songbooks forward and Harold tells us it's time for A.D.T., which he quickly explains to us new dealers means "Advanced Dealer Training! We have it every Monday to help you stay at the *top* of your game! Today's subject is closing techniques." Harold calls up two of the dealers I don't recognize, then whispers a hypothetical scenario to them and lets them go to work. The rest of us watch and learn.

The dealer, James, is trying to close his customer, Mike, who wants to buy a StormBurst, but "just not today." James does a pretty good job of getting to the bottom of why Mike says "just not today."

Mike, it turns out, is the kind of customer who prefers to save up his money first, and then pay with cash. James compliments Mike on his responsible spending habits and proceeds to solve the problem with a 90 days same-as-cash option. A group discussion follows.

"Did you all see what James did there?" Harold lifts his eyebrows.

"Yeah."

"So don't forget now, if you meet a customer like Mike, we have a 90 days same-as-cash option that can solve their problem. Okay?"

"Okay."

"And don't forget, whenever you can't solve a customer's problem yourself, just give us a call! Right?"

"Right!"

Harold smiles and takes his seat.

Next, Brenda Sue calls up each dealer who has made a sale in the past week and hands them shamrocks to add to the bulletin board, each representing a sale. Brenda Sue explains that at the end of each month the dealer with the most sales is awarded "Dealer of the Month" and gets the best parking space outside. Bruce is the current dealer of the month.

"And he has been for five months running!" Harold shouts.

Brenda Sue points to my seven shamrocks and shouts, "But it looks like you've got some competition now, Bruce! Better watch out for Diana there!"

Bruce smiles and adjusts his tie.

Then Brenda Sue presents the dealers with their weekly paychecks, one at a time, as she reads off their grand totals.

"Juan, two hundred and fifty-five dollars!"

"Mike, one hundred seventy-five dollars!"

"Bruce, four hundred eighty dollars!"

"James? No you didn't have any sales last week, remember? Yeah, nice try, wise guy!" She snorts.

The new dealers, she explains, will get their checks at the next Monday morning meeting. "It takes a week to process your paychecks," she nods.

After the meeting, Harold leads us new dealers back down the stairs and to another wallpapered room, with its own entrance by the dumpster.

"This is the phone room—where you'll do some of your most important work!"

I count eight desks, ten telephones, and countless stacks of phone books, but zero windows. We are each handed Xerox copies of three different phone scripts. Harold explains that one is specially written for our non-buyer referrals, while a second script is for our buyer referrals. Then there's a third script for the speedboat drawing he says we'll learn more about later on. We're always supposed to call our buyer referrals first if we have them, then the non-buyer referrals. Bruce is already seated at a desk, arranging his referral files.

Harold smiles at the wide-eyed new dealers. "Just follow the scripts, and you'll be fine."

But I have to get going back to Cornston. I owe several people machines and Mom is anxious to get her FREE shampoo wand. Plus, I still have demonstrations to do for all of Mom and Dad's friends I missed over the weekend. Harold helps me load up the Rabbit, which only fits three StormBursts at a time. I can fit two StormBursts on the backseat, and I seatbelt the third Storm-Burst in the passenger seat. My demo case is already in the trunk. We double-check the rope securing the Storm Chaser/Accessory boxes on the luggage rack.

"Maybe you should rent a moving truck to deliver all of those machines—Ha! Ha-ha!"

I smile, but I'm too tired to laugh.

PART II

❀

"SEEING IS BELIEVING."

It's a long, hot drive to Cornston. The first appointment of the day is with Nancy Rickreal, who Mom calls "the first lady of Cornston University." She's hosted the annual Ladies' League charity tea for children with Leukemia for ten years running.

"What do you mean a cute little thing like you doesn't have a boyfriend?" She calls to her husband on the other side of the bathroom door, "Howard! Can you believe this cute little college girl doesn't have herself a *boyfriend*?"

I stare at the enormous mahogany door, relieved I can't hear the man on the other side.

"Well, let's go into the living room." She smiles and waves for me to follow her lead. The living room is large with a ceiling that must be two stories above us. It's decorated with what look to be real oil paintings and an enormous red rug with golden fringe. Centered before the bay windows is a black grand piano.

"So what's the matter—don't you *like* boys?" She chuckles and turns to squeeze my arm. "Oh, I'm just teasing you, Diana! Better to wait for Mr. Right than settle for Mr. Right Now! Right?"

"Right."

"Although, there's nothing wrong with a Mr. Right Now once in a while! Ha!" She winks at me. "Care for a martini?"

I swallow hard. "Please."

I sit on the green demo case in the middle of the big red rug. She digs something out of a candy dish and pops it into her mouth. She grins. "You're just going to love this, Diana! Watch…" She turns a key in the side of the rosewood credenza and shrieks with delight as the top rises, as if by magic, lifting the crystal candy dishes and decanter skyward to reveal a modest arsenal of pure, distilled sin.

"What do you think?" She grins and blinks her pale blue eyes at me.

"I think it's…I've never seen anything like it!" I scan across the labels: Beefeater, Johnny Walker, Absolut, Goldschlager—

"Now, what's your *favorite* martini?" She rubs her hands together and beams with enthusiasm.

"Oh, my *favorite*? Martini, you mean?"

"Let me guess…" She paces back and forth in front of the rosewood credenza. "You're a—oh, good heavens, I forgot to ask! Have you had lunch yet Diana?"

I look at my watch. It's 11:32 a.m. "Oh, yes, yes I have." I smile.

"Terrific! We had a late breakfast, ourselves." She cocks her head to the side. "Have you ever had a jellybeantini?" Her eyes and smile are wider than any human being's should be.

"Hit me."

"That's my girl!" She throws her arms in the air for a moment of brief, ecstatic joy, then whispers, "I'll be right back with the ice!" She skitters across the room in her navy blue pumps.

"Okay, I'll just go and get the rest of my things," I announce to the empty room.

I make two trips to get the rest of my equipment, but I'm still alone in the living room. I look around at the room, the brocade drapes and the metal sculpture of something I can't quite identify hanging over the fireplace. One of the paintings must be a portrait of Nancy when she was young—about my age. She's wearing a royal blue formal gown with one bare shoulder and a small tiara on her head. I stretch the extension cord across the room and plug it in behind the piano.

She returns with a silver ice bucket and tongs. "Now we're in business!" She goes to work at the bar, then shouts over her shoulder, loud enough for the neighbors to hear, "Howard! Get out here! We've got company, Howard! Don't be rude!" She grins over her shoulder at me. "Men!"

I click the Ray O'Sun on, then off.

She pours the liquid into two jumbo-size martini glasses and reaches up into the candy dish.

Plop. Plop.

She skitters toward me and hands me the martini glass with a pink jellybean resting at the bottom. "You know, Diana, my nephew Lewis is back in Cornston for the summer. He goes to Dartmouth—and he's *single*!" Her eyes flash, "Cheers!"

"Cheers."

She taps my glass almost hard enough to break it.

"He's pre-law—HOWARD!!!"

I swallow hard to keep the firewater from escaping upward and through my nose.

"What do you think?" She sets her glass on a coaster and rubs her hands together in anticipation.

The heat seeps down through my esophagus, melting the muscles in my neck along the way. "It's incredible." I smile.

A gray-haired man in a sports jacket wanders into the living room, then pauses as if just realizing he's forgotten something in another room.

"Howard! This is Diana Jensen—Hal and Betty Jensen's girl!"

He forces a small smile as he steps toward the green demo case. And me.

I reach out my hand for a shake.

"Howard Rickreal—the Third." He nods and shakes my hand.

"Diana Jensen—the one and only." I smile and nod back.

"Howie, baby, what's your poison today?" Nancy pets his shoulder.

Howard Rickreal the Third considers the cardboard boxes in his living room. "Better make it a Tullamore Dew." He adjusts his tie and settles onto the sofa.

Nancy pours him a glass and settles beside him on the sofa. "So, Diana, you're selling something?"

I take another sip of the jellybeantini and swallow it as fast as I can. "Oh, well, actually I demonstrate it first. I mean, I'm more of a demonstrator." I set my glass on the edge of the marble slab that appears to be intended for use as a coffee table.

Howard sips from his glass, then stares at the amber liquid in his hands.

"But if we want to buy it, we'd buy it from you, right? That's why you're here, isn't it?" She smiles and blinks her pale-water eyes.

"Well, yeah." I smile and reach out for my glass. "Of course you can buy it from me." I take a double sip and smile.

"Well, do you want to show us what it is?"

Gulp. "You bet." I wink at her and she wiggles with enthusiasm.

Howard takes a sip.

"So..." my tongue feels a little thicker than usual. "Have you ever been to...Ireland?"

Nancy slaps Howard on the shoulder. "Howard! Have we been to Ireland? Good lord, almighty!"

Howard gives a half smile and nods at me.

"Well, terrific..." I grin and take another sip, swallowing as fast as I can to keep from tasting it. "Then you're going to LOVE the StormBurst!"

Nancy's smile widens. "Oh, it's something *Irish*! So can we see it now?"

I take another sip and set my glass on the rock. "You bet!" My cheeks are happily warm. "Oh—but first you have to get me your vacuum cleaner!"

They explode with laughter.

I do too.

Nancy shakes and quivers with an occasional snort and wipes a tear from her eye.

Howard heaves and releases high-pitched sighs between bouts of chuckling.

I take another sip. And another. "No, seriously…" I try to take a deep breath, but the giggles keep pouring out of me, "I really do need to see your vacuum cleaner!"

The laughter erupts all over again.

I lift my glass and, this time, I taste a hint of watermelon.

Nancy wipes a tear from the other eye, "Well, oh, dear…Diana we don't actually have a vacuum cleaner here." She kicks off her navy pumps and sits on her panty-hosed feet. "You see, our cleaning woman brings her own equipment." She's still grinning as she reaches for her glass.

Howard's shoulders still bounce visibly as his chuckling slows to light giggling. "Oh, boy…" He shakes his head.

I set my glass back on the big rock. "Well, then I guess I'll just have to fill this darn thing with water and show you what it does!" I stand and wrestle the Pot O'Water out of the top of the StormBurst box.

Nancy stands, "Diana! Can I freshen your glass?"

I look over my shoulder and see my glass, surprisingly void of liquor. "Well, sure!" I look around the room, reorienting myself. "I'm just going to go fill this thing with water and…I'll be right back!"

Howard shouts, "We'll be here!"

They chuckle together.

I drift down the hall to the mahogany-paneled bathroom and fill the Pot O'Water. When I return, there is a full glass waiting for me, this time with a green jellybean at the bottom.

"So, the main thing you have to understand about this is…" They smile at me from the couch. "Water is Mother Nature's little beauty product!" I try to clamp my lips together to keep from laughing, but it's no use. I just spray a plume of saliva across the red rug and laugh right along with Howard and Nancy. "Well, anyway, you know, the water's really amazing because it traps all the dust and crap—oh, pardon me!" I take another sip as they giggle. "And you know, regular vacuum cleaners just spew half of it back out again—cause they're dry. You follow?" I reach for my glass.

Nancy sighs and fondles a lock of hair. "Well, is that why vacuums always smell so *bad*?"

"YES!" I jump to my feet. "But smell this!" The room sways gently and we're all still laughing but I hit the switch anyway.

Growl—grind—whoosh—

I shout, "Now wait a second!" and I scramble over the Storm Chaser box and pull out the pieces. Howard and Nancy are laughing and nodding at the machine but I can't hear what they're saying. I'm having trouble attaching the handle, so I run back over to the demo case and get the Breath O'Ireland. I put my hand next to my mouth to amplify the sound, "CHECK THIS OUT!" I squirt a few drops, maybe five or six, into the StormBurst and run back to the Storm Chaser.

Nancy screeches, "LORD ALMIGHTY! HAVE YOU EVER?"

Howard bellows, "WHAT IS THAT STUFF?"

They both grin and sip and I roll the Storm Chaser over to the Leprechaun. "NOW CHECK THIS OUT!" I shove the Storm Chaser hose into the Storm-Burst and it lurches ahead across the giant red rug without me. "SNOTS!" I run to catch up with it. With the green plastic handle in my hand, I turn with a smile to show Howard and Nancy how easy it is to use, "IT JUST GLIDES RIGHT ALONG! SEE?"

They smile and nod.

I wave at Nancy to come over to where I stand. I put the Storm Chaser handle in her hand and she squeals, "LOOK HOWARD! I'M A CLEANING WOMAN!!!"

We all laugh as she waltzes with the wand, getting tangled up in the hose. I help to unwind it from around her pantyhosed legs and finally shut off the machine.

I look between the legs of the leprechaun and can't help but grin. "Now, if you thought that it *looked* like the StormBurst was cleaning the rug…" I take a sip and set my glass back on the rock. "Would you like to see the proof?"

Nancy grins.

Howard raises his glass toward me, "What the hell!" He smiles and takes a sip.

"All right, then!" I have to sit on the rug as I unbuckle the StormBurst. "Is it just me or does this thing look like a Leprechaun?" We pause to consider the machine.

Nancy snorts, "More like a troll!"

We giggle and I lift the Pot O'Water. "Here's the proof!"

"Good lord! That came out of *this* rug? Louisa just cleaned yesterday!" She shakes her head with frustration.

"Well…it is a pretty amazing machine, isn't it?"

Howard raises his eyebrows "I guess so!"

We all sip from our glasses and I sit back down on the demo case, or at least one corner of it.

"So how much is it, Diana?"

"Oh, the StormBurst? Uh…fourteen thirty-seven." I look around me for the clipboard. I slide off the demo case, onto the thick red rug, and search through the case.

"Well, Howard, we could always just have Louisa use this thing when she cleans our house."

"I suppose so."

"Oh, we take cash or credit or…" I brace myself against the giant rock as I rise. "We also have these payment plans."

"Howard, get your card out."

❉   ❉   ❉

I can't believe it's been over a week since I drove Christina to the airport. And the whole cottage is still in boxes. But then: I've got the whole summer to unpack before she gets back. I open a Green Hornet and plop on the beanbag chair in the middle of what I like to call Cardboard Central.

She could have called by now to let me know she got there okay. I'm sure she called her mom at least. I suppose I could call her mom to see, but I don't want to talk to her mom. I want to talk to Christina.

"YEE-OWL."

The grungy white face sniffs at the screen door then raises a paw as if to wave at me.

"Hey there, White Kitty. Let me get the door for you."

He steps inside the doorway and sniffs my bare shin.

"So what have you been up to?"

He sits on his haunches and lifts his head up toward mine, then turns it slowly from side to side as if taking in the scenery with his dark eye-holes.

"Well, I've mostly been working, myself. But it's paying off—that's for sure! I'll get the paycheck for my first weekend on Monday." I scratch the top of his head. "But the best part is I don't smell a thing like French fries!"

He flops on his side right there in the entryway and gives a big sigh.

❧   ❧   ❧

There are no donuts today, just coffee. When I ask the dealer, James, where they are he snickers, "That's just for when we've got new dealers." He dumps the powdered creamer into his Styrofoam cup and slurps without stirring. He makes a pouty face and bumps my shoulder with his fist, "Ahhhhh, don't sweat it sweetheart! We'll have 'em again next week." He winks.

It's just six of us upstairs this week, plus Harold and Brenda Sue. The whiteboard reads in all green letters: "MAKE NEW FRIENDS, MAKE NEW MONEY!!!"

Brenda Sue spreads some paper shamrocks in her hands. "Let's do the board! Bruce! Get up here, three of these are yours!"

Bruce smiles and takes his shamrocks from her, then staples them to the bulletin board.

"James! One of these is yours—and it's about time!" She winks and hands him a shamrock.

"Ted…two of these have your name on them. Good job!"

The man grins and shouts, "YES!" and jogs up the aisle to Brenda Sue.

"Diana! Hot-diggity-*damn* girl! Seven more shamrocks for you!"

I take the stack of paper shamrocks from her and she lifts her hand to give me a high five.

As I staple my shamrocks, one by one, Harold shouts, "Oh, no, Bruce! Looks like she's passed you up—*already*!"

I look over my shoulder as everyone chuckles, except for Bruce.

"Now today…" Brenda Sue picks up a stack of white envelopes from the tray of the whiteboard, "I'm gonna save the best for last, 'cause when you all here *these* numbers, you won't be able to *wait* to go on out and sell yourselves some more machines! Especially Diana! Ha!" She stomps a brown leather boot on the carpet. "Harold? What can you teach us all for Advanced Dealer Training today?"

Brenda Sue takes a seat in the front row and Harold centers himself before the whiteboard. His eyebrows rise into triangles as he presses the tips of his fingers together. "Have you ever started a conversation with a complete stranger?"

I cast a quick glance at the other dealers and catch James rolling his eyes. Bruce raises his hand and says softly, "I have."

Harold grins and folds his arms. "What would you say if I told you that for every fifth stranger you said hello to, you could make an extra *five thousand dollars*—per year?"

Ed ventures, "Uh, hello?"

Harold beams, "That's right! You'd say hi to a lot more strangers, wouldn't you?"

❈   ❈   ❈

I pause a moment to kiss the envelope before it disappears into the ATM. Eighteen hundred seventy-four dollars and fifty-two cents.

My half of the rent for five months.

Tuition for a semester.

Three hundred and seventy-four hours of work at the Dairy Barn.

❈   ❈   ❈

"Hello?"

"Hi, Mrs. Ramirez?"

"Who's this?"

"Oh, this is Diana Jensen—"

"Is this a sales call?"

"No—um, your friend, Cathy Weimer, asked me to give you a call. She needs your help to earn a FREE carpet shampooer, and all you have to do is give me about thirty minutes of your time."

"What do you mean?"

"Well, you see, I'm demonstrating a new product and I just want to get your opinion of it. That sounds pretty easy, doesn't it?"

"We're not interested."

"But your *friend*—"

"Cathy's not my friend, we just work together."

"Oh."

I've run out of leads that know me as "Hal and Betty's girl," and it doesn't take long to see that Harold's phone scripts are a death sentence. If I'm going to keep up my sales average, I'll have to be more creative. Resourceful. I'll have to figure out what the other guys are doing—and do it better.

"Hi, is this Lois?…Hi, Lois. This is Bruce calling you with some good news—do you remember when I stopped by last week and entered your name in our speedboat drawing?…Well, I'm afraid you didn't win the *grand prize* for the, uh, boat, but as one of our finalists, you're entitled to another great prize!…Yes, ma'am, a set of stainless steel steak knives, backed with a lifetime warranty!…Oh, no, ma'am. You won't have to wait for them to come in the mail. In fact, I'm going to deliver them to you *in person*."

Yes, the steak knives. Sure I'll get docked six bucks for each set I give away, but so long as these commissions keep rolling in, who cares?

"Hi, Joyce?"

"Yes?"

"Oh, hi there. This is Diana Jensen calling on behalf of your friend…Louise Platt. Well, she thought you might be interested in getting yourself a new set of steak knives—FREE. All you have to do is watch the same demonstration *she* did, for about thirty minutes."

"Oh? What's the catch?"

"Oh, there's no catch! You don't have to buy a thing. My company just wants to know what you think of it." And it's true. Because as soon as I show people the StormBurst, they think they need it.

※   ※   ※

It's a small, shingled cottage plunked between towering cedars right at the intersection of 18th and McKinley. I pull into the graveled driveway and notice a sign near the front door, "Pottery and Natural Gifts," just as a rush of children greets me, each with a crop of the reddest hair I've seen.

"Are you the StormBurst lady?" her little face looks up from between flat sheets of red.

I take in the four additional freckled faces tilted up toward me. "Yep, I guess I *am* the StormBurst lady! Who are you?"

I catch a couple of names—Brian and Gregory. The smaller brother pokes at a praying mantis on the driveway. The girl-child pulls on my wrist and smiles up at me with robin's egg eyes. She whispers, "I'm Jenna Jean."

"Hi, Jenna Jean. Are your parents home?"

Gregory adjusts his glasses and points to the front door.

"Thanks. I'll let them know I'm here."

I'm escorted the door, hoping Polly and Leroy Fletcher will have half of their children's enthusiasm. Polly meets me at the door, wearing a long tie-dyed sundress. She has red braids as thick as my wrists that hang down to her waist, where I can't help but notice the youngest of the Fletcher clan prepares for his earthly debut.

"Oh! You must be the StormBurst lady!"

"Well, yes. I'm Diana."

Polly ushers me into the living room, which is so much darker than outside that I can scarcely see anything except for a fish aquarium just over Polly's shoulder. "Now which church are you affiliated with?"

I think I see an angelfish in the tank as my brain fumbles over her words. "Oh—church? Well, to be honest, I don't usually go, really. I mean, it's not that I don't—"

"Well, that's cool that you help them out anyway—St. Mary's right?"

"Oh, you mean StormBurst?"

"Of course!"

"Oh, goodness, we're not a part of any church—not that I know of anyway. We're just a business—"

"No kidding? Well, that's cool. I just figured you guys were part of that Noah's Ark clothing drive they do every summer—you know, *StormBurst* and everything."

"Oh, right."

"They always stop by. Whatever the kids *haven't* worn out, they get!" She snorts, which is enough in itself to make me giggle. "So do you go to church at all?"

"Me? Oh, well, it's been a while." I try to glance at my watch, casually.

"Yeah, we didn't really go for years, you know, all the rules and everything." She rolls her eyes. "I mean, if God really wanted all *those* rules, why would he bring us into the world naked? You know?"

"Well…yeah."

She rubs her belly. "But then they started up that First Church of Jesus for Original Thinkers, over on Howard Street, you know? Have you seen it?"

"Is that the one with the exclamation point on top—instead of a cross?"

She snorts, "Yeah, kind of hard to miss, huh? It's pretty relaxed. The kids even like it."

"Really?"

"Yeah. Hey, can I get you a glass of iced tea or anything?"

"Oh, that sounds great. Thanks."

She disappears through swinging doors and—

"SCRAAAAAAW!"

I drop my demo case on my foot and look over my shoulder. I have to squinch my eyes to make out what must be the shape of a giant birdcage, housing a…large…red…macaw. He jigs his head up and down, up and down, and whacks his beak against the bars.

The whole room reeks of animal, but I can't put my finger on which kind. I start untangling the cord of my Ray O'Sun and search the room for an outlet. I stumble upon a glass terrarium sitting on the floor, filled with sawdust. No lid. I walk around it, carefully, as I head outside for the rest of my gear.

When I come back, the kids are leading what looks to be a German Shepherd-Beagle-Wiener dog puppy by its collar into the living room. Gregory adjusts his glasses and proclaims, "This is Toby. We got him from the pound."

Jenna Jean shrieks, "They were going to *kill* him!"

I pat him on the head. "Hello Toby, it's very nice to meet you."

The children wander in and out of the room as I continue setting up. "I wonder if there might be an electrical outlet hiding in this room somewhere…"

Brian volunteers, "You could plug it in over there, except for the fish tank's plugged in there and they'll all *die* if you turn off the heater!" He studies me carefully, making sure I understand the seriousness of this matter.

"Well, I certainly wouldn't want to…" Bright flashes of orange, yellow and red bob up and down in the light. "Wow, those are beautiful!"

"They're Dad's. We don't get to feed them 'til we're older." Jenna Jean rubs a wet finger across the glass.

"I see."

Toby settles onto the floor, just to my left. The kids accumulate on the sofa, watching me curiously.

"What'cha gonna do?"

"Well, what I'm gonna do is show you a machine that does all kinds of cool stuff. Unless you guys want to play outside instead."

Not one of them moves.

"What kind of cool stuff?" asks Gregory.

"Oh, you'll just have to wait and see."

"When can we see it?" asks Jenna Jean.

"As soon as your parents are ready to watch."

"Mom's on the phone with Aunt Kelley," explains Jenna Jean.

"Oh, really?" I look around the room again. "Okay, well, we can just wait."

Brian screws his finger into his ear. "Are you our new babysitter?"

"No, I'm not a babysitter."

"She's the StormBurst lady, dummy," reminds Gregory with a brotherly whack on the arm.

"SCRAAAAW!"

There's a flutter in the corner and I see the macaw climbing onto the roof of his cage. "Say, is that door supposed to be open?"

Gregory rushes to the cage, "Yeah, this is Jerry-Bird! He likes the door open so he can sit on the top and stuff."

"Aren't you afraid he'll fly away—or *bite* somebody?"

Gregory stands on a dining chair and takes Jerry bird on his wrist. "Nope. He's got his wings clipped so he can't fly—not at all. If he tries, he falls on the floor. Wanna see?"

"Oh, that's all right. Say, is your dad here today?"

"Yeah, but he's outside," Jenna starts a braid in her little sister's hair.

I sit there on the demo case, smiling for a while, wondering if I might actually be the new babysitter. The children stare at me. Toby flinches, then digs for a flea on his belly.

"Tell us a story!"

"Oh, well, I don't really know any good ones."

"Make one up!"

I smile.

"Hey, you wanna watch TV with us?"

"No, thanks. I'm going to start showing this cool machine to your parents any minute." I wiggle my eyebrows at the kids.

Jenna Jean stands on the sofa and shouts, "I know a story!"

"Wonderful."

"Um, once, upon a time," she wipes her nose with her hand, "there were *three* bears." Her eyes bulge at me.

"There were? Really?"

She nods her head.

"Where did these three bears live, Jenna Jean?"

"They lived in the *woods*." She nods.

"Well, what on earth did these three bears do for work?"

"Work?"

"Yes, how did they pay their rent?"

Jenna Jean looks over at Gregory.

Gregory grins.

Brian volunteers, "I know! I know! The, um, Daddy Bear made gorganic vechtables for everybody. He had a *farm*."

Jenna Jean looks back at me and nods.

"But what about Snow White? Where was she during all of this?"

Jenna Jean's eyes bulge, "She met the prince and he gived to her a apple."

There's no sign of life coming from the doorway Polly disappeared through earlier.

"SCRAAAW!"

"Well thank you Jenna Jean, that's a wonderful story."

Brian walks up to me and puts his hand to one side of his mouth to tell me a secret. Then, loud enough for all of the kids to hear, he says: "Toby doesn't have any balls. Know why?"

I check my watch. I've been sitting on the demo case for twenty-three minutes.

"The veteran cut them off. Know why?"

Brian drops his hand from his mouth and starts bouncing on his toes. I scratch my ankle and look over at Toby, scratching his ear with his hind leg. "So he can't hump other dogs and make puppies!"

The group is consumed with laughter. I smile and scratch my ankle again. "So how old are you guys?"

Polly returns with a glass of iced tea for me, as promised. "Sorry that took so long. I almost forgot I had to call my sister-in-law this afternoon—she's having a partial mastectomy in the morning. Do you get regular mammograms?"

I take a long, deep, soothing sip of iced tea. "Oh, this tastes great, thanks. What kind of tea is this?"

Polly flips a long braid over her shoulder and settles onto the sofa next to Jenna Jean. "Oh, well it's kind of a home-brew: Chamomile, Ginseng and Lemon Spice. It's supposed to give you energy but mellow you out at the same time, you know? Leroy calls it 'Yin-Yang-Zing'. Isn't that cute?"

"Yeah, that's pretty clever." I take another sip. "Say, I'm going to need just a couple of outlets for this demonstration—"

"Oh, here. We'll just unplug the TV and the VCR." I squeeze my forearm behind the giant TV. "Do you need more?"

"Nah, this should be great, thanks. So, is your husband going to join us?"

"Oh, did you want him to?"

"Sure! The more the merrier, right?" I force a smile.

"Okay, he's um, in the studio—he does pottery, you know? It might take a couple minutes though. Do you mind waiting?" She sits bolt upright with her hand on her belly, and blushes. "I can't sit still for more than a minute before this one starts a jig!"

I smile. "No, I don't mind waiting."

"Brian, go get your Dad—tell him the StormBurst lady's here."

The littlest girl is drifting off to sleep against the arm of the sofa. Jenna Jean starts a new braid in her sister's hair. "So, Jenna Jean, is it fun to have a little sister to play with?"

Polly smiles at her as she screws her face up into a serious scowl, thinks it over, then releases a long, dramatic sigh. "Well, sometimes it's fun. And sometimes she breaks stuff, you know? Cause she's just *too little!*"

"Yeah, I hear you."

A smile washes across her face. "Do you have a little girl?"

"Oh, god no!" They look surprised. "I mean, not yet. I'm not even married."

Gregory chimes in, "Aunt Kelley's got *two* kids and she's not married."

"Oh, well there's that too." I try to smile politely. Polly winks a blue eye. I look around the room again and gesture to the open terrarium. "So what's in there?"

Jenna Jean asserts, "That's Piggly. He's a *hedge-hawg.*"

Gregory continues, "He's boring 'cause he only wakes up at night when we're sleeping. So we don't even see him hardly."

Jenna Jean summarizes, "He's a *stupid* pet."

All agree, including me.

"SCRAAAW!"

Brian leads a denim-overalled Leroy into the living room. His black, wiry beard is exactly the same length as his black, wiry hair, all of which appears to be spattered with clay. We shake hands, and at last the demonstration's under-way.

"Have you ever been to Ireland?"

The kids all jump to their feet and shout out,

"No!"

"I want to go!"

"Mom and Dad have!"

"What's Ireland?"

Polly and Leroy crack up and nod their heads to say yes they have.

"According to the EPA, dust mites—"

"What's that?"

"Well, they're like little tiny microscopic animals—like germs! And they live in your bed and pillows and the carpet—"

"Yuck!"

"Can somebody get your vacuum cleaner for me?"

"I will!"

"No, I will!"

I had no idea the demonstration would be so entertaining for kids—enough to actually hold their attention, in spite of the living zoo around us.

"SCRAAAW!"

Every time I ask a question, I don't just get one or two answers, but seven! Of course, shrinking the sofa cushion is such a big hit that we shrink just about every cushion in the house before I can move on to the balloon inflation.

"Do *my* pillow!"

"Okay, who wants a balloon?"

"Me!"

"I do!"

I notice Polly and Leroy are having just as much fun as the kids, and Toby doesn't even seem to mind the noise from the StormBurst. Soon I realize I'm smiling an honest-to-god real smile.

When we finally board the 747 for Ireland, and everyone is seatbelted in, all seven close their eyes and wait for the mystical land to appear before them out of the fog. I drop in the Breath O'Ireland…one, two, three…and do my best to roll the *r* as I sing out: "Brrrrrrrrrrriiiiiiiiiiiiiiiig-a-doooo—DEAR GOD WHAT IS THAT?!"

The Fletchers quickly deplane and find me standing on top of my demo case, watching the small ball of fur finish rolling across the floor and stop bolt upright, on hind legs, right in front of the StormBurst.

The Fletchers are in hysterics. Brian falls off the arm of the sofa and onto the floor laughing uncontrollably. Polly clutches her belly with both hands, laughing as tears roll down her cheeks. Leroy rubs a hand over his beard as he chuckles.

I do my best to maintain my balance on top of the demo case.

The littlest girl stands on the arm of the sofa, squealing with delight. The younger brothers dog pile on top of Gregory. And meanwhile the rat-fuzzed-super hero stands stone still, his nose gently testing the Irish breeze.

Gregory shouts out above the roar of the StormBurst, "THAT'S MR. WHISKERS!"

Brian screams, "HE'S A *REAL* PRARIE DOG!"

Toby barks and spins in a circle, then digs for a flea, then barks. The kids are still laughing, and so are Polly and Leroy. Polly's eyes bulge and she shouts, "I THINK MR. WHISKERS LIKES THE STORMBURST, *REALLY* LIKES IT!"

Leroy yells, "OR AT LEAST IRELAND!" and gives his thigh a slap.

I'm still on top of the demo case, with the hairs standing up on my arms. I shout over the StormBurst, "I DON'T THINK I'VE EVER SEEN A—A *REAL* PRARIE DOG BEFORE!" I try to step down gracefully, but my knees are still shaking.

Meanwhile, the house smells more like Ireland than anywhere I've ever been.

I take a deep breath. "Okay, Mr. Whiskers. It's time to come on back from Ireland now…" the kids laugh as I shut off the StormBurst. In a furry flash, Mr. Whiskers retreats to the back of the house again.

I take a long, deep, soothing breath of Ireland.

"So," I smile, "a *real life* prairie dog?"

Leroy stops laughing long enough to say, "Yeah, they don't normally live in this part of the country. We just got him on our last visit out to my sister's. She lives in Kansas, god help her!"

I'm not sure if he's referring to Kansas or the mastectomy. "Let's see, where were we then?"

They all agree that the StormBurst is a pretty amazing machine.

They all agree that they'd rather dump all that dust and dirt and *oh-my-god-look-at-that-pet-hair* outside.

"Hey look! There's fleas!" Gregory inspects the Pot O'Water thoroughly.

They all agree that their family's health—and Jesus—are the greatest gifts of all.

And they all agree that if I can make it possible for them to own a Storm-Burst, they'd be pretty interested.

But it takes another hour and five phone calls to Brenda Sue, to figure out a way to comfortably fit a StormBurst into the Fletcher's budget. In the end, they go with the sixty-month payment plan and their DirtDragon as a down payment.

As I fill out their warranty paper, Polly rubs her belly, pensively. "You know what, Diana?"

I pause, "Yeah?"

"Well, I think I know someone who could really use this kind of thing—for the health benefits and stuff."

"Oh, you do?"

She gives me the name and number for her old friend Henry. "He's a musician. He used to play the cello, with the symphony, you know? He's really talented!" She tells me to make sure I mention *she* suggested I call.

I shake seven hands and thank them for their time and their referral. And I go home with an earthenware toothbrush holder, an original watercolor painting by Jenna Jean and twelve fresh fleabites.

❀   ❀   ❀

The cat food dish is empty and the water bowl is dry. But still no White Kitty. I cluck and call as I hold the grocery bag against my hip and unlock the door.

Holy snots is it hot inside. And the carpet could stand some vacuuming, too. Look at that that filthy stuff. I hate to think of what I'm going to suck out of this old cottage.

I latch the screen door behind me, then search out every window that hasn't been painted shut. Not a screen on one of them. I'd like to take a cold shower. But then: what if an axe-murderer climbed in through the window? I look out at the ivy-thick fence, the trees and the overgrown shrubs around the cottage, all of it somehow not so beautiful at 11:30 at night, alone and with the windows open.

I'll have to buy a fan tomorrow. And make sure I have a StormBurst with me when I head for home.

I dig my pepper spray out from the bottom of my demo case and stick it in my pocket. I grab a Green Hornet from the fridge and head to the front porch. It's much cooler out on the front steps. The stars up between the treetops sparkle. Maybe I'm just overreacting. Paranoid. Heck, most people would be terrified of meeting with strangers—in their homes, every day of the week. But not me. So why on earth would I be afraid of being alone in my own home?

Gulp. Ahh.

I'm not even afraid to go swimming alone.

Gulp. Gulp.

Naked.

Ahh. Maybe I just haven't spent enough time here to feel like it *is* my home.

Gulp. Gulp. Gulp.

Really. I've still hardly unpacked, and I don't have single poster up on the wall. When am I even here—and awake?

Gulp. Gulp.

Weekdays I'm with the retired old couples. Weeknights I'm either with young families or in the telephone room. Saturdays I'm with the lonely singles that have nothing better to do. And Sundays I see the atheists.

Gulp.

But then: what else would I do?

Gulp. Gulp. Ahh.

Christina has been gone for a month now. The dorms, fraternities and sororities are all empty for the summer. Everyone with somewhere to go has gone. I might as well be making money. But it might not hurt to enjoy myself a little now and then.

Gulp. Ahh. Gulp. Ahh.

Maybe tomorrow I'll pick up a little TV, too. I can definitely afford it now.

Gulp. Gulp. Gulp—

"YEE-OWL!"

The silhouette pauses at the edge of the path.

"White Kitty!"

He slinks toward me straight down the center of the path. I try to stand to greet him, but my head spins.

"Where have you been, you clever boy?"

"Vvvr-vvvr."

"I see you've been eating well, at least."

"Vvrr-vvr."

"Oh, dear. Let me get you some water!" I stand up, slowly, and he follows me to the kitchen and back out again. He laps the water as I as I twist the cap off of Hornet number two. "I'm a little thirsty tonight, too."

White Kitty flops down beside me, right against my hip.

Gulp. "You out for a moonlight stroll?"

"Vvvr."

"It's a nice night for that."

The moon pushes up, full and fat between trees, as the Green Hornet buzzes in my brain.

❋   ❋   ❋

"Hello?"

"Debbie?"

"Yes?"

"Have you got a minute?"

"Who is this?"

"This is Diana—your friend Clare suggested I give you a call."

"Clare didn't mention anything to me."

"Well, she probably just hasn't had a chance yet—"

"What is this about?"

"Oh, well, you see—"

"You aren't selling something, are you?"

"*Selling*? Oh, no. I just demonstrate this little machine—Clare thought you'd like to see it too."

"Well, I don't think so—"

"You don't have to buy anything, and you get FREE steak knives just for watching and giving my company your input."

"I do?"

"Well, yeah. Are mornings or afternoons better for you?"

"Oh, well I work all week, so—"

"Great, I have some time on Saturday afternoon, would that work for you?"

"I suppose so—how long does this take?"

"Well, it partly depends on how many questions you have for me, but usually no more than 45 minutes. Okay?"

"Well, okay."

"So, would you prefer two o'clock or three—oh, and are you married?"

"Excuse me?"

"Do you have a husband—or a significant other?"

"What does *that* have to do with anything?"

"Oh, I'm just asking because to get credit for my demonstration, I'll need both of you to be there."

"Why?"

"Um, so in case you like it and decide you *do* want to buy one after all, I won't have to come back and show—"

"You know what? I've changed my mind. Don't call here again."

❦   ❦   ❦

I pull into the parking lot, and there it is: the best parking space in the lot, with my name on it. I pull into it, one space closer to the door than Brenda Sue's green Cadillac, and leave the windows down.

"Hey there, Berta! What, no fries this morning?"

"Nah, I'm on a new diet, kid. No fries until *after* noon!" She grins and sinks her teeth into the toes of a bear claw.

I grab a custard bismark and a cup of coffee, then head upstairs to the ice-cold meeting room. Ed greets me with a smile.

"Hey, man."

"Hey."

We exchange respectful nods.

"So I heard you got a sale last week."

"Yeah, man. It was kind of intense though."

"What happened?"

"Well, the lady's husband came home in the middle of it."

"Oh, well, it can be tough to make sure they're both going to be home."

"Well, but she'd kind of told me he was dead."

"Oh?"

"Yeah, so it was pretty freaky when he showed up and everything."

"I'll bet. But you made the sale anyway?"

"Yeah, with a credit card bonus, man."

"Right on."

Bruce, James and I each get a giant, green "2-in-1" mug, though I've sold more than two StormBursts in a single day, and more than once over the past month. But then: a mug is a mug.

Brenda Sue clasps her hands and squeezes her knees like she has to pee. "AND! We have a new Dealer of the Month to honor today! Diana step up here."

Please let it not be another bumper sticker.

"Diana, as you all know, has been selling like a *demon*! And in just her first month of being a certified StormBurst dealer, she has not only earned the honor of Dealer of the Month here at Chin's StormBurst...Diana Jensen is also our new REGIONAL DEALER OF THE MONTH!!!"

Harold plugs his fingers into his mouth and gives a shrill whistle. The dealers stand and applaud. Ed's fist is going a mile a minute, punching the air, then circling back, punching, circling, punching.

Brenda Sue hands me a small, golden plaque. The engraving on it reads "Chin's StormBurst Dealer of the Month. Diana Jensen." And I glance over at the bulletin board to admire my row of shamrocks, stretching the furthest of any dealer's, running off the bulletin board and rounding the corner onto the next wall. But tomorrow the shamrocks will all be gone, and I'll have to start all over again.

"Diana!" Harold reaches for the inside pocket of his sports jacket and pulls out a green cellular phone. "*This* is for you!" I slip the plaque under my arm and he places the cell phone in my hand. "And for every month you maintain your Dealer of the Month status here at Chin's, *we* pay your phone bill! Does that sound good to you?"

"Sure!"

Brenda Sue beams, "Well, the *president* of the StormBurst Northwest Regional Division is also going to honor you at the next quarterly meeting—that's in three weeks, people! So you'll be sure to be there now won't you, Diana?"

"Of course!"

"And as for the *rest* of you…there will be a FREE all-you-can-eat gourmet BREAKFAST BUFFET! Do you like good food?"

"Yes!"

❧   ❧   ❧

I park at the curb in front of the light blue doublewide mobile home. Mr. and Mrs. Grindle are already on their way out the door to greet me. I point at the plastic chrysanthemums along the edge of the carport as I approach. "How pretty!"

They hug me and promptly seat me at the kitchen table, where a pot of tea and lemon sandwich cookies await. I'm not sure if they understand why I'm there, but I don't want them to stop adoring me. So I sit down a few minutes, and munch a cookie, recalling Harold's latest A.D.T. advice: "Always accept food or drinks when they're offered—it means that the customer is investing more than just *time* in you." I watch them across the table, as she stirs a lump of sugar into his tea, then one into her own.

Mrs. Grindle comments, "You're such a tiny little thing! You must be working awfully hard."

"Oh, I am. I have to pay for college next year and that's not cheap, you know?"

"My, my. Can I fix you a sandwich or something? We have split-pea soup—would you like some, dear?"

I think of Harold, again, but politely decline.

After a couple of cookies, I excuse myself to bring in the rest of my things. When I return, they've already settled into his and her recliners in the living room, and Mrs. Grindle is smoothing the skirt of her dress evenly across her legs. I start casually as I plug in the Ray O'Sun. "Well, you know how people can tell you a lot of things nowadays…?"

Nods.

"You've got to be very careful these days," Mr. Grindle shakes a finger at me and continues to nod his head.

"But you can't always take their word for it, now can you?"

Nods.

"It's just terrible what this world's coming to," Mr. Grindle shakes his head with disgust. "But one day, that will all change."

Mrs. Grindle smiles and reaches over to squeeze his hand.

I sit down on my demo box. "In fact, the only way you can really be sure of anything these days is if you *see it for yourself…*" I shake my finger at Mr. Grindle, then smile. "Wouldn't you agree?" It doesn't come out as smoothly as I'd hoped, but they're nodding just the same. "That's why I'm here to show you something I think is pretty amazing, so you'll know for yourselves just how terrific the StormBurst is. Sound good?"

"Yes!"

And they offer a loud and cheerful "yes!" for every question I ask—except: "Have you ever been to Ireland?"

They blush, "Oh, no, not us, dear."

"Well, I'll just see what I can do about that!" I wink. "Okay?"

"Yes!"

"Would you like your air here at home to be as fresh as it is in the *Irish* countryside?"

"Yes!"

It's so easy, in fact, I find myself adding new questions to the demonstration, just for the sheer fun of it. "Don't you just love it when you discover new things that can save you time—and improve your health?"

"Yes!" They both nod.

"Haven't you always wanted to rid your home of pollen and dust mites?"

"Yes!"

I could push them over with one finger.

"Yes!"

And when I ask them if they could get their vacuum cleaner for me, Mr. Grindle says "Yes, indeedy!" and he returns with a shining, silver bullet in his hands.

Gulp.

His steely eyes gleam just as brightly as the machine he cradles in his arms. He pats it gently with his hand, just over the etched name: "Sputnik 5000."

Harold mentioned something about the Sputnik during training. He ranted about its charcoal filters, cursed its 50 Amps of power, and then mocked its slim, aerodynamic body. He said it's the only vacuum on the market that costs more than a StormBurst. I plug it into my extension cord. "Boy, your air-conditioning sure is nice on a hot day like this, isn't it?"

"Yes!"

But I'm suddenly breaking a sweat. I begin to explain the critical difference between suction and airflow, while trying desperately to remember what Harold said about demonstrating against a Sputnik.

Its chrome casing hardly has a smudge on it. When I ask how long they've had their Sputnik, Mr. Grindle explains that they bought it last summer, and that they "know it's the best one money can buy."

I smile politely and think of Harold. "I can tell you folks like quality, don't you?"

"Yes, we do!"

Mr. and Mrs. Grindle smile and nod to each other. Mr. Grindle extends the footrest of his recliner.

"These Sputniks certainly do have a lot going for them—what with the charcoal filters and all. Why that tells me right there that you guys don't just care about keeping your carpets clean, but your *air* as well. Is that right?"

"Yes!"

"That's great. You know, there's only one kind of filter I know of that works better than a charcoal filter. Do you know what it is?"

Mr. and Mrs. Grindle look confused.

I take a deep breath. "Water!"

They exchange surprised looks.

"Now, Mrs. Grindle, what picks up the dust better—a dry dust cloth or a damp one?"

She still looks confused.

"The damp cloth, right?"

"Oh, yes!"

"That's because, just like everybody knows, water is Mother Nature's little helper! Right Mrs. Grindle?"

She smiles. "Yes, that's right!"

Mr. Grindle smiles too. "Yes, indeedy!"

I still can't remember what Harold told us about the Sputnik. I can't even figure out where its exhaust vent is. "And to prove that to you, I'll show you right now, with a little help from the Ray O'Sun. Just watch as I shine this light on the exhaust from your Sputnik—which has a *dry* filter, right?"

"Yes, it does." Mr. Grindle nods.

"Here we go!" I flip the switch and the Sputnik rages louder than a Storm-Burst. 'There! Can you see that?"

"Yes!"

I run my hand over the glistening Sputnik, but I can't feel air coming out of it anywhere. I smile. "Can you see all that dust blowing out of there?"

"Yes!"

I move the light over the machine from end to end, desperately searching for dust, but I can't see any. "Wow! That's a lot better than the other vacuum cleaners I've seen, but still! Can you believe that?" I shut off the motor. "I'll bet your Sputnik dealer didn't show you that, did he?"

Mrs. Grindle's face is as gray as her hair.

Mr. Grindle's face is as red as his ears.

"But now I want to show you something truly amazing. Are you ready?"

"Yes."

"Right now, you're looking at the exhaust of a StormBurst. If you don't believe me, you can stick your hand out right here and feel it." They remain seated, nodding. "Now, if you don't object, Mr. Grindle, I'd like to invite you to *smell* the exhaust of the StormBurst—oh, I know that may sound crazy. You'd never smell the exhaust of a regular vacuum would you—not on purpose, right?"

"No way!"

"Probably not even if it had charcoal filters!" I grin and widen my eyes for impact.

They chuckle.

Growl—grind—whoosh.

There seems no limit to their amazement, from trapping dust mites to shrinking cushions to touching down in Ireland,

"Well, doesn't this Breath O'Ireland smell good?"

"Yes!"

They're either mystified or mortified by everything I show them—or try to show them. No matter what I say,

"Yes!"

The Grindles believe me. And if they believe in me,

"Yes!"

They surely believe in the StormBurst.

"Yes!"

I grab my clipboard. "And, Mr. and Mrs. Grindle, isn't good health the greatest gift of all?"

"Yes!"

"Indeedy!"

I rise to my feet. "Indeedy indeed."

They beam.

"So then, if I could make it *possible* for you to own a StormBurst today, you'd be pretty interested, now wouldn't you?"

Silence.

The Grindles stare at each other. Then at their hands folded neatly in their laps. I can hear the clock ticking in the kitchen, where my tea has surely grown cold beneath the air conditioning vent.

Finally, Mr. Grindle clears his throat and says, "Well, Diana, we'll be honest with you. I think that Mrs. Grindle and I would both love to buy this amazing machine from you, but the truth is, well," he and Mrs. Grindle exchange an uneasy look, "we spent most of our savings on this Sputnik last summer."

My stomach gurgles loudly enough for all of us to hear. I smile and wait.

Mr. Grindle puts his footrest down. "And you see, well, I think we just wish we'd known about the StormBurst back then." He shakes his head in disgust.

I shake my head too. "Oh, well, I see that is rather, uh, unfortunate, the timing and all…but you know…" I try to think of what Harold would say. They're looking at me, sadly. "Well, sometimes we're able to, um, give credit for the old vacuum, you know, like a trade-in for the StormBurst, and…"

Mrs. Grindle sits up, "Oh, really!"

Mr. Grindle adjusts his belt. "Well, about how much credit do you think we could get for it?"

"That's a good question. I'd have to call my boss and do some negotiating, but I think we might be able to work something out." Mrs. Grindle clasps her hands together with delight. "Uh, just out of curiosity, how much did you pay for the Sputnik last year?"

Mr. Grindle pipes up, "Seventeen seventy-four, oh-five."

Holy snots. That *is* more than a StormBurst. "Okay." I force a smile. "Do you mind if I use your telephone?"

"Oh, go right ahead, dear, it's right there behind you."

"Thanks." They watch as I wait for Brenda Sue to pick up. "Hi, Brenda Sue. This is Diana. I'm over here at Mr. & Mrs. Grindle's lovely home here in Live Oak Park…Yes, they have a lovely double-wide home here, with vaulted ceilings and everything! It's just lovely." I smile at the Grindles who nod approvingly. "You know, they just love the StormBurst—they've never seen it before, and well, we were just talking about how they wish they'd seen it *before* they bought their Sputnik 5000 last summer…Yeah, isn't that just tragic?" I glance at my watch. "Mmm-hmmm."

Mr. Grindle reaches over and pats Mrs. Grindle on the knee. "Well of *course* they'd rather have the StormBurst…mmm-hmmm…Well, yes, I believe they paid—excuse me Mr. Grindle, did you say you'd paid *cash* for your Sputnik? Yes, they took it straight out of their savings account…seventeen seventy four, oh-five…yeah…okay," I try to give them a reassuring smile, "ah-ha, okay…" I scribble down some notes meant more for me than the Grindles, "okay, I'll run that by them and see if that will work. Okay, thanks a *lot* Brenda Sue. We sure appreciate it." Gulp.

The Grindles are waiting.

My stomach is growling.

"Okay, thanks for waiting. Well, according to my boss, we should still be able to get a resale value on your Sputnik for about $900—you see, unfortunately, they already have a newer model out."

Mr. Grindle clears his throat, then nods for me to continue.

"Now, normally we'd give a customer a little bit less than that to make a profit or something—you know how sales work, of course."

They both nod. Then wait.

"But my boss must be in a really good mood today or something, because she told me I could just *give* you the whole $900 credit—if you want to go ahead and get that StormBurst today."

They smile at each other for a moment. Then Mrs. Grindle scoots forward in her seat, "Oh, that's great news, isn't it?"

My stomach growls. "Well, I think so!" I smile and nod and wait.

Mr. Grindle smiles, "Well, that's real kind. But tell me, Diana, how much does that leave us with?"

"Well, let me get my calculator out. Okay, well…first of all, the StormBurst with all of the attachments you see here is just $1437—"

Mr. Grindle interrupts, "Why that's *less* than we paid for the Sputnik!"

"It sure is—isn't that amazing?"

"Yes!"

"So, minus the $900 credit for your Sputnik, that comes to…only $537! That sounds pretty good, now doesn't it?" I smile victoriously.

Mrs. Grindle clasps her hands together, "Oh, yes!"

Mr. Grindle thinks this over a moment while rubbing the crease on his forehead. "Well, $537 certainly sounds like a great deal, I know the machine's worth far more than that…only problem is, Diana, we don't really have $537 right now."

Mrs. Grindle's face fades to gray.

"Oh, I see. Hmmm. Well, we do accept Visa, MasterCard and Discover?"

Mr. Grindle shakes his head, "No Diana, we don't keep credit cards—too easy to get into trouble—s'pecially if somebody steals your wallet! Why a total stranger could ruin your whole credit history—even land you in jail!" He shakes a finger at me.

Mrs. Grindle nods, wide-eyed.

"Yes, well I see what you mean. Hmm. Well, you know we do have a number of different payment plans available. Maybe we'd have one that would work for you?"

And, not surprisingly, we do.

I call Brenda Sue to get the final figures and she groans that we have to set up financing for a $537 balance—she was sure they'd just pay cash. "Well, they paid cash before! What, did they spend their *life savings* on a Sputnik? Good lord." She informs me that my commission for this sale will only be $45.

"Excuse me?" I smile at the Grindles, sitting across the room.

She tells me that, by her watch, I've wasted two and a half hours on these people. "Oh, but don't worry, too much. You're still learning. Pretty soon you'll know how to see the signs—you'll recognize these kinds of situations from the minute you walk in the door."

But then: a sale is a sale.

"Diana, we're having turkey pot pie this evening and we'd just love it if you could stay for—"

I explain I don't have time to stay for dinner, so Mrs. Grindle insists on making me a bologna sandwich for the road. As we stand beside the Rabbit, the Grindles thank me again for the fine demonstration—and for making it *possible* for them to own a StormBurst.

"My pleasure. Thank *you* for your time!"

"You know, any time you're going to be in this area, you're welcome to stop by!"

"Oh, thanks."

"You do still have our phone number, right dear?"

"Uh, yes I do!" I smile and open the door of the Rabbit. But before I can get in, Mrs. Grindle clears her throat. I turn to see a funny smile on her face.

"Dear, did you say you're in college?"

"Yes, yes I am."

"Oh, then you must like to read!" she clasps her hands together.

"Oh, I always have. Last year I was even an English major!"

"You don't say? Well, you've been so sweet, I'd like to give you something—you see, I have some literature I think you'd really enjoy. I'll be right back!"

I stand there with Mr. Grindle, trying to think of something to say. "How about this heat, eh?"

"Yes, it's really something. Over a hundred yesterday."

"Today, too, feels like."

"Yes, indeedy."

"Say, those chrysanthemums sure don't seem to mind the heat." I nod at the polyester blossoms lining the curb.

Mr. Grindle gives them a glance, "Oh, I wouldn't know. Those are the Mrs.'s."

Mrs. Grindle returns with some kind of a leather-bound book, a couple of pamphlets and an issue of *The Watchtower* magazine. "These just have some wonderful articles you might find interesting—you've got two copies there so you can give one to a friend." She smiles sweetly.

I read the quote on the cover of the pamphlet: "If you can find a truly good wife, she is worth more than precious gems…Proverbs: 31.10" The title is printed in big, block letters:

"THE IMPORTANCE OF
BEING A GOOD GIRL
IN A BAD WORLD."

"And this book—" she pats the hefty volume with much affection, "this book here is to keep next to your bible when you read from it. You see, it explains what each part of the bible *really* means."

"Well, isn't that helpful?" I smile and turn toward the Rabbit.

"If you have any questions about anything, don't hesitate to give us a call!"

"Oh, I certainly will!" And before I can get my leg into the Rabbit, she reaches out for a hug. "Well, thank you both, that's, uh, very thoughtful of you. And thank you for your time this evening." I roll down the window so I can close the door without seeming too abrupt. She hands me the book through the open window and I quickly set it on the passenger seat. "We sure had fun today, didn't we?"

"Yes!"

I wave as I pull away from the curb, with the Sputnik, the "literature," and six postdated checks by my side.

PART III

❀

"BUT THEY COME WITH A LIFETIME WARRANTY."

"Hello?"

"Hi, is this Frank?"

"Yeah, who's this?"

"Hi Frank, this is Diana, and I'm—"

"Do I know you?"

"Well, no, but you met a friend of mine last week who signed you up for our speedboat drawing. Does that ring a bell?"

"Oh, yeah. Did I win?"

"As a matter of fact—well, you didn't win the boat, but you did win another great prize—congratulations!"

"What'd I win?"

"You won a new set of steak knives!"

"Steak knives?"

"That's right—and I'd like to deliver them to you personally—"

"I don't want any goddamned steak knives!"

"But sir, they come with a lifetime warranty and they're made of—"

❀   ❀   ❀

No one wants to see a demonstration for a small household appliance the first week of July. Something about a three-day weekend. Lucky for me, most of our dealers are taking advantage of the holiday too, leaving the fishbowl full of speedboat drawing entries to those of us who choose to stick around—and don't have anything better to do. Or anyone to do it with. So I talk a Harveston housewife into a set of steak knives,

"Well, what *kind* of steak knives?"

"The best, ma'am. They're stainless steel, with ergonomic comfort-grip handles. And they come with a lifetime warranty!"

"Well, that sounds pretty good. We could use some steak knives."

"*Everybody* could use some steak knives. When's a good time for me to drop these by?"

So I show up the next morning at 9:30 sharp. It's another 3-bedroom ranch house in the development off Magnolia Ave. I knock and knock and knock and think maybe she had to run to the store or drive the kids to school. Something. I look over at the station wagon in the driveway.

Surely she couldn't have forgotten overnight. Unless she's got multiple personalities. Or Alzheimer's. I guess anything's possible. I head back down the driveway toward the Rabbit.

THUNK.

A little boy appears in the big front window, standing on the sofa and sticking out his tongue at me. In the background I can hear a woman shouting.

"Get down from there! Stop it or she'll see you!"

I smile at the boy, hopefully.

"NA-NA-NA-NA!" He jumps up and down on the sofa.

"Michael, you get down this minute!"

I knock again and smile at the boy.

"Michael, don't you look at her—don't you!"

I finally retreat to the Rabbit, parked at the curb in front of their house. According to my watch, I've got three hours until my next demo. So I sip my Big Gulp until it's dry and listen to the radio. After about twenty minutes, the boy stops jumping. I watch as he leans against the glass with his mouth and blows so hard that his cheeks puff out like a gorilla.

I can't help it. I flip him the bird.

The boy jumps up and down on the sofa again, grinning with delight. He flips me the bird too, on both hands, and continues jumping.

I flip open my green cell phone and call Brenda Sue to tell her the demo's a bust.

"Oh, Diana, thank god!" She explains, "We just had a call from some people out in Huntsville who said that *butt*-brain Bruce was supposed to be there an hour ago—but the *moron* seemed to forget he'd be in *Idaho* today, for Christ's sake!"

"Oh, dear."

"Can you cover it, Diana? Please? It's a *buyer referral?*"

"Well, I suppose it's the least I can do."

"Good girl!" She gives me their phone number to call for directions and to let them know I'm on my way.

I hang up and pause a moment to pretend I'm digging for deep treasure in my nasal cavity. The boy jumps up and down on the sofa, flapping his hands in the air and grinning. Then all at once he stops, carefully stands on the back of the sofa, turns and drops his pants.

I call.

"You'll turn left on Farmington, then drive 1.3 miles down to Alburg Lane—watch your odometer. Then turn right. It's a gravel road. Go all the way to the end, where it runs into another gravel road—that's a left. Just after you turn, you'll see a group of fir trees there. Go to the right. Then you'll see the driveway about a mile and a half down. There are red reflectors and a wagon wheel on each side. Got it?"

"Oh, well, I think so. Say, what color is your house?"

"Oh, well it's not a house—it's a trailer! Beige, I guess you could say."

The boy presses his bare cheeks against the window, then rubs from left to right.

"All right, I'm on my way!" I hang up and turn the key in the ignition. "Oh, your mom's gonna have some fun cleaning *that* window."

Sure enough, I find the wagon wheels and reflectors, then drive on around another group of trees to discover not just one trailer, but eight trailers. And not the mobile home type like the Grindles had. These are real trailers, as in 'travel trailers.' The kind that retired people pull down to Phoenix in the winters. However, these trailers don't look like they'll be traveling any time soon. They have grass growing tall around the wheels, and some even have lean-to's and porches built onto them. I ease the Rabbit off the gravel and onto the short grass. I see a pit bull bolt from behind the first trailer and race toward the Rabbit. He jumps against my door, barking and snarling at me. I can hear his nails scratching the paint.

A young man, shirtless, with green army pants, jumps out through the trailer door.

He approaches us both with a devilish grin. And a belt.

WHACK!

He sends the dog whining back into the trailer and gives me a wink. "Hah there." He leans against the Rabbit.

"Yeah, uh, I'm looking for Bob and Renee—"

"Oh, sure. They're in th'Terry down there'n the corner." He runs his belt through the loops on his pants. "I was jus' talkin' wi'them. They been waitin' fer you fer a while, huh?" He winks again and his pectorals twitch. He finishes the buckle.

"Yeah, I'd better git down there, huh?"

He winks and reveals a missing front tooth.

I nod and drive on.

I'm relieved to see that the Terry is the newest of the group—and the grass hasn't grown nearly as tall around it as it has around the other trailers. In fact, it looks like it's in pretty good shape. It even has a redwood deck along the side, with large cactus plants—real ones—arranged in clay pots. A couple in their early forties steps out on the deck to receive me with smiles and a wave. "We're so glad you found us—sorry for all the trouble!"

They look nice enough. And clean. They even have their shirts tucked into their shorts. "Well, thank you fer waitin' fer me! I'm just sorry 'bout the mix-up, folks!"

They inspect the Rabbit. "Can we help you carry anything in?"

"Oh, uh, sure. I have a couple boxes in th'back." I look back at the slim trailer door and wonder if all of my gear will fit inside—with us.

"So what do you call this machine again?"

"It's called a StormBurst, ma'am."

"That's the one that uses water, right?"

"Yep, it sure is."

We have a little trouble fitting the StormBurst box through the door, but once inside, I'm absolutely positive there won't be enough room to do the demonstration. They sit in the two rocking recliners at the end of the "living room," while I sit poised on my demo case, which fits perfectly between the kitchen cabinets, lengthwise. The carpet, upholstery and cabinets are surprisingly nice. As nice as they are in Mom and Dad's house. But then: I should learn to see the signs, as Brenda Sue said. And this is clearly a sign—I hear a dog yelp outside—in neon.

Renee sits up, "Oh, Diana, can I get you a mineral water? You must be thirsty after that long drive in this heat!" She sneezes. "Excuse me!"

Bob raises his eyebrows, "And I'll bet you don't have A-C in that Rabbit, do you?"

"Oh, well, I sure don't. Do you have any Pepsi?"

She smiles with her lips together, "No, I'm afraid we just have mineral water." She sniffles lightly. "We're overdue for a trip into town." She smiles at Bob.

"Okay then, I'll take a mineral water!"

Renee grins and I stand and she reaches around me to open the little refrigerator. I lean back as she grabs a small glass bottle. She twists the cap off and hands me the bottle.

"Oh, thanks!" I take a swig. It tastes just like Alka Seltzer. "That *is* refreshing." I smile and take another sip. And muffle a burp. "So, do either of you suffer from any allergies or asthma?"

"Renee does."

"Yes, I get hay fever every spring." She runs a pendant back and forth along the gold chain around her neck.

"Oh, so the pollen from the grasses and flowers bother you?"

"They sure do."

"Well, the StormBurst can actually help your allergies while it cleans your—home."

They smile.

"What tools do you currently use to clean your home?" I look around the trailer and quickly deduce that no vacuum cleaner could ever possibly fit inside.

Renee pipes up, "Well, you know, just the usual, I suppose!"

Gulp. "Well, speaking of, could you get your vacuum cleaner for me for just a minute?"

Renee and Bob giggle. "Well, of course…but I'll have to get around you there, Diana." I stand up and press myself against the door as Renee steps over my demo case and pulls the CrumBuster out of a drawer. "Here you go—knock yourself out!" They giggle some more and settle into their chairs.

"Uh, thanks."

To my delight, they even have electricity. I'm not sure how it works exactly, but they have real outlets and I'm able to do everything—except for shrinking a cushion. My elbows get a little bruised, but their enthusiasm and humor more than make up for it. And all the while, I just think of the story I'll tell Bruce and James at the next Monday morning meeting. And I arrive at the close in a record twenty minutes.

"So, if I could make it *possible* for you—" and I unplug the Ray O'Sun, "to own a StormBurst today—" and I start winding up the cord, "you'd be interested, wouldn't you?" I detach the Storm Chaser.

"Absolutely!" Renee squeals.

I turn my head. Bob is smiling. "Great! That's just…fantastic." I fumble with the demo case and sit back down again. I glance through the window beside me and study the "Good Sam" sticker on the neighboring trailer. "Well, we have a number of, uh, payment plans available."

"Well, excuse me for interrupting, Diana, but how much does this Storm-Burst cost?"

"Oh, right. Well, it costs, with all of the attachments you see here, and a couple you don't, it's, uh, fourteen thirty-seven."

They glance at each other. I glance at the CrumBuster.

"But we have some, you know, payment plans." I set the Ray O'Sun in the demo case and wait a moment to be polite.

Bob inquires, "Well, what kind of interest rates do your payment plans offer?"

"Well, it all depends on the plan, you know. The faster you can pay it off the lower interest rate you get." I reopen the demo case and get my towel out to start polishing the machine for my next demonstration.

"Renee, honey, can you hand me the calculator?" Bob pulls his glasses out of his shirt pocket. "Well, Diana, if *you* don't mind, I think I'd like to know more about your payment plans." He gives me a goofy grin.

"Oh, of course. Can you give me just a ballpark figure of what your monthly payments would need to be in order to make this work for you?"

Bob scratches his head a moment. "Well, how about something around one-fifty a month or so?"

Snots almighty.

"Oh, we can definitely do that!"

"Now what kind of an interest rate would we be looking at there?"

"Oh, well I'd have to call in for the exact figure, but I believe it would be somewhere around, oh, twenty-four to twenty-six percent."

Bob chuckles out loud, "Twenty-four percent? Whew! That's pretty steep, isn't it?" Renee smiles and nods. He punches some numbers into the calculator. "Tell me Diana, how much would the interest rate go down if we went up to, say, $200 per month?"

"*Two hundred* per month?"

"Yeah, do you have a plan around there?"

"Well, Bob, I'll be honest with you. It probably won't drop much. That's just how our payment plans work out, I'm afraid. I guess that's why most people put their StormBurst on a credit card, if they can."

"You guys take credit cards?"

"Oh, yeah. Didn't I—sure, we take Visa, MasterCard and Discover."

"Oh, that's super! Bob get your card out, honey. We sure do like this machine!"

Bob presents me with a Visa *Gold*, shining brightly as my eyes.

"So we get to keep this one—it's ours today, right?"

I tilt the card slowly to the left, then to the right, then to the left again, and I can almost see the flecks of *real* gold that must be there beneath the plastic coating. "Yeah sure."

Bob snickers, "So, Diana, have you been doing this long?"

I look up from the card. "Oh, well, not really. Oh! I'm supposed to call my boss!"

"Here, use our phone." Renee hands me a cellular phone.

I think of Harold and accept her offer.

"Hi, uh, Brenda Sue, this is Diana. Yeah, I just finished my demo for Bob and Renee Slecher out here in, um, the countryside, and, well—they just love the StormBurst and would like to buy it with their Visa…*Gold*." I can't stop grinning. "Yeah, I'll see you back at the office."

"So, will you do this year-round, Diana?"

"Oh, uh, no. I go to college the rest of the year."

"Really? Well what an unusual summer job!" Renee takes her pendant between her fingers and runs it back and forth on the chain a couple of times.

Bob asks, "So what are you studying to be?"

"Well, to be honest, I'm not exactly sure yet."

"Well, you probably hear this all the time, but you know that anything related to computers is a pretty safe bet these days." Bob returns his glasses to his shirt pocket.

"Yeah, that's what Bob did. And after just sixteen years—well, and two bypass surgeries—we were able to retire!" Renee pats Bob on the shoulder.

"Yeah, and get the heck out of Silicon Valley." Bob rolls his eyes. "My brother thought we were crazy when we sold our house and bought *this*," he grins and looks around the trailer. "But we love it. We can live anywhere we want now! And whenever we feel like a change of scenery, or if we want to go back and visit friends, or travel south in the winter, we're all ready to roll!"

"No kidding?"

"Yeah. We were getting pretty tired of the rat race…and the cardiac ward." Renee rolls her eyes. "But we sure like it around here, with the beautiful scenery, the friendly people—and it's such a relaxed pace. It's great!"

"It's pretty relaxed, all right." I date the sales receipt.

"And no sales tax!" Bob raises his eyebrows.

"You don't even have to pump your own gas here—it's actually *against* the law!" Renee shakes her head in disbelief. "But most of all, it's just so beautiful." She sighs.

I glance out the window beside Bob, where the scrub oaks sprawl and the blackberries bramble. I see a purple SUV parked in the shade. "Yeah, I suppose it is kind of beautiful, in a way."

"*Kind of beautiful?* Oh, Bob, would you listen to her?"

I just smile and finish filling out the receipt.

❧   ❧   ❧

After several attempts at calling, Henry finally answers his phone. Right away I mention that his friend *Polly Fletcher* suggested I give him a call. This pleases him immensely.

"But you know, I live a ways out. I'm in a cabin, just outside of Sweetwater."

"Not to worry, Henry. I could find a needle in a haystack, and I practically have. But tell me, are the roads labeled?"

I pull off the highway at the rusty mailbox reading "Fitzpatrick 24337." The gravel driveway curls around some firs and up in front of the cabin, which appears to be made of real logs and very, very old. I laugh to see the other car parked in the driveway: a blue Rabbit, just a year or two newer than mine. And to the left of the cabin, I see the hood of an orange Karmann Ghia sticking out from under a tarp.

I pull the screen door open and tap on the door, but the solid wood muffles my knock. I hit it hard a couple of times, and a roundish woman opens the door.

She wears white pants, a long white jacket, heavy duty white shoes, and smiles heartily when she sees me. "That's right, Henry said he was expecting company today."

"Hi, I'm Diana."

"Hi, I'm Debbie. Come on in."

I step into the front, and only room, to find a man propped up in a hospital bed, smiling at me. His knees are elevated, and there's a green and yellow stocking cap on his head. His face is as white as the pillowcase behind him, except for a dark red scar on his cheek.

"Henry?"

He says softly, "Hi there. Thanks for coming out."

I walk over and reach out to shake his hand. "I'm Diana. Nice to meet you."

He slowly reaches out and takes hold of my hand, and I see a long red sore on the back of his hand. He gives my hand a gentle squeeze and there's a flash of something behind his blue eyes, which makes me smile, though I can't be sure why. I set my demo case on the floor beside him and take a seat.

"So how do you know Polly?"

"Oh, well, kind of like you, I suppose." I wink. "Someone sent me over to see her and her family too."

"I see." He smiles gently, and covers his mouth to cough. I see a small sore forming on the back of his other hand.

Debbie calls from the kitchen area of the room, "Would you like a cup of tea? I've got water boiling in the kettle."

"That sounds great." I look back at Henry, who still smiles at me, and then around the room. It's completely quiet. And dark. The walls are simply the other sides of the logs I saw outside.

"So you said you have some kind of a machine?" He coughs softly.

"Yes I do—let me go get the rest of my gear out of the car and I'll show you what it's all about, all right?"

Dear god, what am I doing here?

I stand up and he nods. I walk across the wide planks of wood back to the door, then turn to look around the room again. There's no carpet in the room. Not even a rug.

It turns out that Henry has been to Ireland, several times. He's played cello over there, in concerts that sound pretty serious.

"That's funny, I always think of the Irish as listening to fiddles, not cellos."

Gulp.

I hope I haven't offended him.

Henry winks, "Well the Irish are full of surprises."

He goes on to tell me how his favorite performances were actually at the local pubs. "Oh, Diana, you'd love how they sing and dance over there. Everybody does, the old ones right alongside the young ones." He smiles at something behind me. "The pubs—that's where the *real* music is. That's where the real people are, too." He gives a nod and a smile.

I tell him my parents went to Ireland once for their 25th anniversary.

He tells me that's where his parents came from. "Waterford—did your parents go there?"

"No, but my mom bought a vase that was made there—it's her pride and joy."

He smiles, "No, I'll bet that's what *you* are."

Debbie presents him with a glass of water and a handful of pills.

I smile and take a sip of my tea, and look around the room again. There are some beautiful watercolor paintings hung on the wall behind Henry. Landscapes and flowers. He swallows the last pill and Debbie takes the glass away.

"Well, I suppose I should get on with my demo." I smile.

"By all means," he nods.

Instead of asking him for his vacuum cleaner, I just show him the hardwood floor attachment and explain how "Water is Mother Nature's little helper."

"Makes sense to me!" He winks.

But the best part is when I fly us to Ireland. "Brrrrrrrrrrriiiiiiiiiiiiiiiiiig-a-doooon!" Henry laughs so hard he goes into a coughing fit. But he's still smiling, so I am too. Debbie rushes over with a glass of water and props him up with one hand while she holds the glass with her other. He still smiles, with eyes that sparkle at me like Waterford crystal.

Debbie looks at me, and smiles softly, "He'll need to get some rest soon."

I nod and say, "I'm almost through—is it okay if I finish?"

"You bet." She smiles and leans Henry back against his pillows. "Well, I'll be off to the store now to get the groceries—are you *sure* there isn't *anything* that sounds good for dinner?"

Henry flashes his eyes toward me. "Do you have any suggestions, Diana?"

"Oh, well, I…"

Debbie quickly says, "You're not having a dinner guest."

He smiles, "I know. I'm just looking for inspiration."

I smile back at him, "Well, there's nothing like a good steak to get my mouth a'watering!"

His smile breaks into a wide grin. "That's it! Debbie, I'd like a steak for dinner."

Debbie sighs and shakes her head. "All right, I'll buy you a steak, but the day I see you eat one…" she stops shaking her head and smiles. "Well, it was nice to meet you Diana."

"You too."

She picks up her purse off the kitchen counter and goes out through the front door.

"Now, where were we?" Henry lifts his eyebrows.

"Right. Well, now you've seen the StormBurst. Wouldn't you agree it's a pretty amazing machine?"

He smiles. "Absolutely."

I lift the StormBurst up and reveal the Pot O'Water. "And wouldn't you agree you'd rather have all of this dust *outside* your home, instead of inside it?"

Henry laughs. "But of course."

"Because if you don't, you know, I'd be happy to dump this out for you—right here!"

Henry chuckles and coughs a little.

"But seriously, you can see how the StormBurst can make your life easier all the way around, can't you?"

He lifts his eyebrows and sighs. Then he winks.

"Because it doesn't just keep your house cleaner, it can keep you healthier. And isn't good health—the—um,"

Gulp.

My smile slips off my face and lands in my lap with a thud, "the greatest gift of all?"

"And don't you ever forget it." Henry smiles.

I put the smile back, gently. "So, then, you know, if I could make it *possible* for you to own a StormBurst today—would you be interested?"

Henry lifts his head and coughs, then settles back into the pillow. He stares at me with a small, smug smile. "Well, perhaps in my next life!" He winks. "Although I fully expect to come back as a Leprechaun."

I shoot a look over at the droid. "That's *not* funny." But I can't help smiling at Henry.

My stomach grumbles. I look at his thin, white cellist hands lying on the blanket, and their deep rouge scars.

"Polly didn't tell you much about me, did she?"

I look down at the Ray O'Sun. "Uh, just that you're an old friend of hers."

"I see." Cough.

"Well, I suppose I should let you get some rest now." I stand up and start gathering the accessories.

"Hey, Diana."

I look at Henry.

"Don't sweat it." He grins. "This is the most fun I've had in months." Something flashes again, miles behind his watery blue eyes.

I have to grin too. "I'm glad, Henry. I had fun too."

He tells me more about the Irish as I pack up my gear. "It wouldn't surprise me a bit, Diana, if you had some red roots down under that blond hair of yours!"

I laugh and tell him that it wouldn't surprise me either. "Anything's possible!"

I reach out to shake, then squeeze his hand gently just before I go.

He holds onto it. "Thanks again for stopping by."

"My pleasure, Henry," and before I know it, I'm giving him a peck on the forehead. I wink at him and head for the door.

"Ah, you've got a bit of the Irish in you for sure! Ha-ha!" he chuckles.

I laugh and pull the door shut behind me.

The sun is low enough that it shines sideways through the fir trees. Outside the cabin, the air feels unnaturally hot, even in the shade. I roll down the windows on the Rabbit and realize I didn't call Brenda Sue. I flip open the green cell phone and stare at the display screen, which reads "Ready," and at my hands, my beautiful hands, that hold the green object before me.

Flip.

I toss the phone onto the passenger seat beside me. It's only five o'clock and my next demo isn't until tomorrow morning. And I know it's not worth hitting the phones until seven o'clock at the earliest. I can't help it. I peel out in the gravel driveway and race toward the road. As I pull onto the highway, I lean out the window and scream, "WAHOOOOOO!!!"

The Rabbit drives right on past Chin's and take a sharp right into the parking lot of Landor's Steak and Seafood. The hostess smiles at me from under a stiff swath of brunette, then she stares at the door behind me and waits.

"Oh, no, it's just me—table for one." I smile.

She seats me at my own booth with a menu. "You travellin' honey?"

"Yeah, kind of." I smile up at her.

"Well, your waitress will be Rebecca tonight, and she'll be with you in just a moment." She pats me on the shoulder and walks away.

Rebecca arrives with a bright pink smile. "Will anyone be joining you tonight?"

"Not that I know of." I grin.

"Okay. Well, do you know what you want yet?"

"I think so…Give me the prime rib dinner, medium rare, with bleau cheese dressing on the salad, and a baked potato with *real* butter and plenty of sour cream—and chives."

She scribbles my order down quickly. "Anything to drink?"

"Yes. A glass of your *reddest* wine."

She pauses, "Well, we've only got one kind."

"Good. I hate making decisions!"

She gives a half smile. "Okay, I'll be right back with your wine."

I lean against the back of the booth, marveling at how she didn't ask me for I.D. This must be the first time ever. I stare out the window, across the parking lot, across the street, and take note of the red Corvette perched up high on the corner of the used car lot.

The waitress reappears at my table. "Oh, did you want water, too? We're not just putting it out on the tables anymore, you know, 'cause of the drought."

"The drought?"

"Yeah, but if you want some—"

"Water? Oh, no thanks." I tell the Corvette, "I think I've had enough for today."

Florescent pink stickers scream across its windshield: "1992, Low miles!" I look over at the sales office where a banner stretches across the front windows: "WE'LL FINANCE ANYONE!"

❋   ❋   ❋

Barbara Buchman is a buyer referral of a buyer referral of a teacher who was a buyer referral from Mom. But she might as well be a cold call from the speedboat drawing.

"Well *your company* might want my opinion of this thing, but what do *I* get for my time?"

It's a Drakesville address, off the main highway, off the old highway, off the main road there and then some. But given my shrinking stack of referrals, I figure it's worth the gamble—and the drive time. Naturally, there are no road names, and to make matters worse, she said she lives at the end of a long gravel driveway. It's already after two o'clock as I pull over onto some kind of tractor entrance to a field. I think about calling her up for more specific directions, but I couldn't begin to tell her where I am. There isn't a road sign in sight. I pull the Rabbit over and get out to stretch my legs. I pull up my T-shirt to let my skin breathe. Ahhh. If only there were a small lake or a pond nearby.

But there isn't the slightest hint of water. Or a breeze. Just a dust devil in the distance, redistributing rows of cut grass. I pull the aquati-bra away from my skin to let the heat escape.

Every time I think it can't get hotter this summer, it does. And this drought isn't helping anything.

A blue pick-up appears at the top of the hill in front of me and I pull my T-shirt back down.

The pick-up slows, then stops beside me. A kindly man, with two kids at his side and two dogs in the back asks, "Need some help there?"

"Yes! But I don't know if you can help me—I'm looking for a lady by the name of Barbara Buchman?"

He chuckles a moment, then points to a gravel road beginning about one hundred feet behind me, with no mailbox, no numbers, no nothing.

"Well, how do you like that?"

He rubs the sweat off his forehead with his shirtsleeve. "Well, you know, some folks live out here so long they forget how hard it'd be to find 'em!"

I thank him. "What with this heat and all, you may have just saved my life!"

I head up the gravel drive to find an old mobile home, complete with a covered patio and a molting German shepherd.

The dog barely lifts his head as I open the car door. He just continues to lie there, with his tongue surrendered to Astroturf.

I scramble up the steps to the patio with my demo case in-hand, praying for air conditioning.

Barbara greets me at the door. She looks about 50. Or maybe 60. It's awfully dark inside her trailer. "So you said you're a college student?"

"Oh, yes I am—well, the rest of the year, anyway."

She pulls her pants up at the knees and sits down on a black or brown couch across from me. "So what do you plan to do when you finish?"

I squint my eyes and try to moisten my mouth with what little saliva is left. "I'm not sure yet." There's a large picture of something hanging on the wall behind her. It looks like a cluster of white marshmallowesque blobs.

"Not sure? With tuition as high as it is these days?"

I think I might see an outlet—white—in the dark paneling beside her couch. I run my extension cord across the room to it. "Well, I've narrowed it down a bit."

"Narrowed?"

"Sure, so far I've tried Anthropology, Physical Education, Religious Studies and English. And now I *know* those aren't for me!" I smile.

Barbara frowns. "What year are you?"

"Well, credit-wise, I'm a senior. I just haven't finished all the requirements from one department yet."

She grunts. "Well, why don't you?"

"Well, I guess I just don't want to end up stuck with a job I don't really like."

"Ha! What makes you think *anybody* likes their job?"

My throat feels raw inside. I try to swallow some saliva.

"Well, I think I might like teaching. I just have to figure out what I want to teach first. And then I'll have to go to school another year after I graduate to get a certificate."

"Teach? Why would you want to teach? Don't you want to make any money?"

I roll my tongue inside my mouth a moment.

"I taught for thirty-three years, putting up with those miserable brats, their incompetent parents, and all that bureaucratic bull! Even went on strike—not once, mind you, but *twice*! And what do I have to show for it? Not much! That's for sure!" She reaches over to the end table and picks up a can of beer. I watch as she takes a long, deep, soothing sip of genuine draft.

"Say, could I get a glass of water?"

"Oh, the well's about dry. How about a Coke?"

"Sure, thanks."

"It's in the fridge. Help yourself." She takes another sip.

The refrigerator light blinds me momentarily. I see a bag of grapes, a carton of milk, and two six-packs of Coca-cola. The shelves in the door are solid with beer cans, save for one bottle of ketchup.

I guzzle half a can of Coke right there in the darkness of the kitchen, then retrieve the rest of my gear from the Rabbit.

"So Janet told me this thing does a good job—it really surprised her, she said. But just so you know, there's no way in *hell* I'm buying one of these things. I'm just watching your presentation to help her get some blasted carpet shampooer."

"Right, I understand." All of the drapes are pulled shut, and all of the indoor lights are turned out. My words make way through the darkness of the mobile home, "Barbara, have you ever been to Ireland?"

"Just cut to the chase for me."

I have to run my hands over the carpet before I can find the Ray O'Sun. But then: look how the dust shows up when I turn on the golden light!

"Do you see that?!"

"No."

"All those particles of dust and pollen, and the pet dander?"

"No."

"All right." I feel for my Coke on the end table and take a sip. "Could you get your vacuum cleaner for me?"

"No."

"Oh. Well, could I get it for you?"

"I already know what *my* vacuum cleaner does. I thought you were here to show me this other one."

"Okay, well, the way *regular* vacuum cleaners work is by—"

"I suppose you're going to tell me they blow dust all over the place."

"That's right!"

"And yours doesn't because it uses water."

I take the last sip of Coke and let it linger on my tongue a moment before I swallow.

I force a smile, "Okay, then! I'll just need to fill this with some, uh, water."

"Well, you'll have to get it from the rain barrel out back."

"No problem!"

By the time I'm shrinking her cushion, she grunts "You know, if that doesn't go back the way you found it, I can sue your company!"

I smile, "Well, it's going to go back *better* than I found it!"

She scowls, and crosses her arms.

Barbara Buchman must have had formal training in the art of not-being-sold; I never once see her head nod. But then: it's pretty dark.

Halfway through I notice I'm sweating more than I was in the car. By the close, I'm feeling weaker than the dog outside, and just as thirsty.

But then: I'd hate to have to pack up that StormBurst and Storm Chaser now.

"So, you'd have to agree this machine does a lot of good work, doesn't it?"

No response.

I hold up the Pot O'Water and shine the light up into its murky depths, but no light penetrates the sludge. "And wouldn't your rather have all of this dirt outside your home rather than in your carpet?"

No response.

"So if I could make it possible for you to own a StormBurst *today*, you'd be pretty interested, wouldn't you?"

"No."

I smile weakly, and set the lamp and Pot O'Water on the carpet. "Well, thanks for watching anyway. I hope you enjoy the steak knives."

I begin dismantling the StormBurst, anxious to get on the road back home, where there's a new sundress, a cold shower, a Green Hornet, and maybe even a white cat waiting for me.

"Do you want me to dump this outside or down the toilet?"

"I'll go dump it for you. I know just the place." She takes the Pot O'Water and walks out the front door.

"I'll just bet you do." I stand up and stretch. I flash the Ray O'Sun at the picture on the wall to confirm: it is a pack of wolves.

Barbara returns with the Pot O'Water still full.

"Say, come over here a minute, will you?" I half-way expect her to dump it on my head, but instead she turns on the light above the dining table and sets

down the pot beneath it. A mass of tiny, black, *dead* beetles floats on the surface. "Have you ever seen anything like this?"

I catch my balance on the back of a dining chair. "No...I can't say I have."

"These came out of my carpet, didn't they?"

I stare at the ebony corpses glistening beneath the spotlight. "I...uh...yeah,
they must have." We both look down at the dark brown or navy blue carpet
beneath our feet.

"You said fleas and dust mites don't die in regular vacuum cleaners, right?"

"Yeah, that's right."

"So the same's probably true with carpet beetles, huh?"

Gulp. "Yeah."

"Well, these guys sure look dead to me!"

I think I might feel something crawling on my ankle. "Yeah, me too."

"So how much are these things?"

"Oh, well, with all of the, uh, stuff, it's fourteen thirty-seven."

"What?!" She leans in closer to look me straight in the eye. "You mean to tell
me that this *vacuum cleaner* costs more than a *thousand dollars*? Why I—"

"Look, I'll just pack up and be on my—"

"And I thought gas was getting expensive, but a *thousand*—"

"Actually, fourteen thirty—" I whisper the "seven," and I'm packing up as
quickly as I can.

Barbara rants and rants and curses god and Mary and the government. She
finally picks up the Pot O'Beetles to take it back outside. This time, she's gone
longer. Maybe a minute and a half. She comes back in with the bowl still full.
"I'm guessing you've got some kind of payment plans?"

"Several. Let me get my calculator."

❧   ❧   ❧

"Hello?"

"Hi, I'm calling to congratulate Dorothy on her winning entry and fabulous
prize—is she home?"

"Oh, yes, just a minute—Dorothy! You won a prize! Hurry up—they're
waiting on the telephone!"

"Hello, this is Dorothy?"

"Hi, Dorothy, this is Diana over at Chin's StormBurst. I wanted to congratulate you on your new set of stainless steel steak knives that come with a life-

time warranty, and let you know that you're now a semifinalist for our speedboat drawing—congratulations!"

"Oh, well, goodness. Did you say steak knives, honey?"

"That's right! And they come with a lifetime warranty!"

"Well, oh, pardon my asking dear, but what is the catch?"

"Oh, ha! Well, the only catch is that I'm going to deliver them in person, and before I go, I want to show you a brief demonstration of our product—"

"Are you some kind of a *salesman*?"

"A *salesman*? Oh, no ma'am, I'm not a *salesman*. I'm sorry if I got you out of sorts there—I'm actually a college student. This is just my summer job. You see, I just demonstrate this product, and—"

"Well, because I can tell you right now that I'm not buying anything!"

"Oh, dear me, you don't have to buy a thing, Dorothy—unless of course you decide you want to! But I, uh, get paid just to show it to you!"

"You do?"

"Sure!"

"Oh, I see. Well what is this *product* exactly?"

"Well, it's hard to describe it over the phone…that's why they have me demonstrate it for people in person, just like I will for you."

❧   ❧   ❧

Chile is warm, the ocean is warm, my skin is tanned and warm, my breasts are bulging out of—

BANGETY-BANG KA-THUMP.

The Cottage is dark, the sheets are soaked, and the clock reads 4:28 a.m.

"YEEMF."

"White Kitty?"

"YEEMF." Thump.

I feel him on my feet at the end of the bed and reach for the lamp.

Click. "AAHHH! Mother of—"

He drops the bloody lump right on the bedspread and sits back on his haunches.

I ease my way up out of the bed without disturbing the gory heap of—is that a mouse? Dear god, that was in the cottage? And how did he catch it, blind?

"YEE-OWL."

The red smear around his mouth looks like lipstick. He waits.

"It's a *gift* isn't it?"

He blinks his eyelids over the holes in his face.

"Did you bring me a little present, White Kitty?" I can't help it. I'm giggling.

He doesn't move. I imagine the blood seeping through my old flowered bedspread, through the sheets, then the mattress.

"You know, I'd really prefer flowers next time."

I gently scratch the top of his head.

"Vvvr. Vvvr."

"Yes, you're a good roommate, aren't you? Where would I be without you, eh fella?"

"Vvvvr."

I reward him with some flakes of tuna on a plate in the kitchen, where a small red smear on the linoleum marks the murder scene.

"You know, White Kitty, I've been thinking about it and it's time you had a *real* name. What do think of Gautama?"

Munch. Munch.

"Tiresias?"

Lick.

"Tiresias couldn't see anything either, except for the truth, of course."

Munch. Munch. Sneeze.

He licks his nose as best he can.

"Yeah, well, maybe that's too much to expect of a cat."

"YEE-OWL."

I wipe up the smear with a paper towel. "You know, Capone isn't a bad name for a tough guy like you." I might as well be talking to the mouse. "Fine. How about…Kerouac?"

Munch. Munch.

"Well, I like Kerouac. I think it's a cool name for a cat, so that's what I'm going to call you."

Munch.

As Kerouac feasts in the kitchen, I carefully roll up the bedspread around the deceased and deposit both in the trashcan on the alley.

❧   ❧   ❧

I wish Ed well in his new career as a children's shoe salesman at Harveston Mall. Bruce, James and I divvy up his referrals—which make for some great stories at the Monday morning meetings. Like James's demo that turned out to be for an Alzheimer's patient in a retirement home. Security guards escorted him and all of his StormBurst equipment to the parking lot. Then Bruce called on a transvestite couple that lives in a school bus. We laugh as he tells us, but Bruce is quite proud of his sale; he hasn't had one in a while and he got a *cash* bonus to boot.

I inherit Ed's referral for the Holmesbys. Mrs. Holmesby seems almost too anxious to see my demonstration. I figure she must really want the steak knives. It takes three passes to determine which house is theirs, but unfortunately, out of all the houses on Arboretum Road, theirs is the old, white, clapboard number, with a sagging barn in the back and a couple of shutters dangling from their hinges. I pause a moment to take in the scene. One of the upstairs windows has the side of a produce box filling in where glass should be. A rusted tractor rests in peace on the sparse lawn, as a pack of semi-feathered chickens pecks at the dirt. I punch the air with my fist.

WHACK!

A hefty boy bounces off the passenger side of the Rabbit. He pulls up his pants and keeps on running. "MOTHERFUCKERS!!!" he screams as he disappears around the side of the house.

I make my way through the chickens and feel my sandal slip in something moist.

"LITTLE SHIIIIIIIIT!!!" Two older boys disappear around the side of the house.

The porch steps rock beneath my feet, and threaten with creeks and groans. But I persevere. Beside the front door sits a cardboard box, where a mama cat nurses her kittens. Oddly, she appears to be balding on the top of her head.

I knock softly on the frame of the screen door, hoping nobody inside will hear me. But then: slow, heavy footsteps approach the door, and I'm greeted by one of the largest people I've ever seen. "Mrs. Holmesby?"

She smiles upside down, then reaches through a strategic rip in the screen door to twist the knob from my side. "You must be that StormBurst gal!"

"That's right, and I brought your steak knives just like I promised."

"Oh, that's so sweet, honey." She takes the knives from my hand, "Why don't you come on in?"

I step through the doorway and into an odor that could only be death. Or bad hygiene. I follow her, slowly, into what must be the living room. Strips of gold-flowered wallpaper cling to the walls here and there, and a lifetime, or two, of cigarette smoke browns the walls up near the ceiling. I study the room quickly to figure out where I should set my demo case, and where the outlets might be. Mrs. Holmesby settles into a sturdy recliner draped with a beach towel. I watch as her sides settle on top of the armrests, and her arms settle onto her sides. She emits a heavy sigh, and then a wheeze. With much effort, she smoothes a plate of salt-and-pepper hair off of her forehead, and reveals a face as large and round and white as the moon, with just as many craters.

I continue looking around the room, around my feet, and—everywhere I think of setting my case, there's something. A beer can with cigarette butts overflowing onto the carpet. Stacks of newspapers. A half-deflated basketball. An ashtray. A stack of TV Guides. A crumpled bag from Taco Land. A headless Barbie Doll. Half a dog biscuit.

"Oh, just throw that junk on the floor over there, and make yourself comfortable!" She cackles twice and begins to wheeze.

The stench of decay closes in on me. I think of the coroners on TV who always smear something under their noses before they work. I force a smile and slide a stack of newspapers over with my foot, revealing a patch of gold shag wide enough for my demo case. "So, were those your boys I saw playing out front?"

Mrs. Holmesby chuckles. "Yeah, those little bastards get into more trouble—why I can't hardly keep up with them!" Wheeze, wheeze.

"I can see what you mean!" I scratch my neck, "They sure run fast, don't they?"

She coughs into her hand. "Yeah, my husband can't hardly keep 'em still long enough to give 'em what's coming, neither!"

"Oh, dear."

"Their teachers call on us nearly every day with some damned story—I'm just glad I don't have to watch them little shits the rest of the year like they do! Ha!" She coughs.

"Me too!" I laugh with Mrs. Holmesby but it only seems to make the stench worse. Now I *taste* it. "So, where is *Mr.* Holmesby?"

"Oh, yeah. He's out getting' the wood."

"Oh, really? Will he be back soon, do you think?" My stomach grumbles. I try holding my breath.

"Um, well, he's just gonna be a little while. Had t'run out t'Sweetwater. You can go ahead though—you don't have to wait for him!"

"Oh, well," I pick up my demo case, "that's awfully sweet of you to offer, Mrs. Holmesby, but the truth is," I step backwards into the entryway, "I only get credit if you're both here." She sits up in her chair, perplexed, coughs, and I continue. "And since I know you two are both going to want to see this, I'll tell you what…" she raises her thin eyebrows and coughs, "I'll just give you folks a call later, and we'll figure out a different time when you're both here, sound good?"

She's reaching for her pack of Marlboro as I feel for the rip in the screen door. She looks up, "What about my steak knives?" and sticks the filter between her lips.

I step one foot over the threshold, still smiling at her. "Why don't you just go ahead and keep those, kind of like collateral or something, all right?"

Both feet are on the porch, but my upper body is still inside with Mrs. Holmesby. "All right, I guess."

As I descend the steps, I holler, "Great! I'll talk to you later!"

Two boys run screaming from the Rabbit. My front tire is half-deflated.

I return to the office by way of a service station, then my apartment and a cold shower. Rather than try and explain what happened to Brenda Sue, I slip Ed's referral card into the stack of speedboat entries.

❧   ❧   ❧

A week later, Bruce returns to the office in high spirits, explaining to James, Brenda Sue, Harold and me that although he "couldn't make it possible for them to own a StormBurst *today*, he did find a way that they might own a StormBurst *soon!*"

Brenda Sue clasps her hands together and squeals, "Bruce, you got a recruit!"

Gulp.

Bruce shakes his head and straightens his tie, "And you know, it's the luckiest thing, too. They said someone was supposed to give them a demonstration a couple weeks ago and never called back! Then I happened to call!"

Harold shakes his hand, "Great job, Bruce. You know what this means?"

Bruce's cheeks flush and he tells his shoes, "I'm on my way to the big time now."

We all laugh for a moment.

Then Harold continues, quite seriously. "So for every eighth StormBurst they sell, Bruce, you'll get a *free* machine."

"That's how you make the big bucks, Brucee!" Brenda Sue squeezes his arm and stamps a gold boot on the carpet. Then she turns to narrow her eyes at James and I. "Now, you've both done well with your own sales, you two, but you know that *recruiting* opens up a whole new world of possibilities—you can see how with just a few recruits of your own, you could work *half* the hours you do now, and make *twice* the money!"

Yes, it's easy to see how that would work. But not with the Holmesbys.

James and I promise to try and bring in some new recruits within the next two weeks.

Harold tells Bruce to invite the Holmesbys to our Monday morning meeting. I think about calling in sick, but I just can't believe Mrs. Holmesby could make it to a meeting in town, let alone up the stairs.

But then: there he is.

Mr. Holmesby sits in the front row next to Bruce. Brenda Sue's nostrils flare as she smiles and says, "Let's all welcome the newest member to our Storm-Burst family, Arnie Holmesby!"

We all shout, "Welcome Arnie!" and watch as he stands to wave at us all, then anxiously wiggles his fingers through his beard.

Harold steps toward Arnie and reaches out to shake his hand. Arnie pulls his fingers out of his beard and slips them into Harold's hand. He smiles but there's nothing there. Just gums where a row of teeth should be.

Harold's eyebrows rise up into triangles. "So, Arnie, you've seen the demonstration already…what do you think of the StormBurst?"

Arnie faces the dealers and shouts, "It's pretty goddamned friggin' fantastic!" He sticks his fingers back into his beard and grins.

Harold's eyebrows stay put. "So, then, Arnie…I believe Bruce told you about your special perks for joining—"

Arnie runs his tongue across his upper gum and grins.

Harold pulls a stack of bright green cards from the pocket of his sports jacket. "So then, would you like to draw a lucky card from the StormBurst New Dealer Deck, or just take the $20 cash for gas this week?"

Arnie adjusts the strap of his overalls. "Oh, uh, huh-hum, I think I'll up'n take that cash!"

Someone mumbles, "You bet he will."

Harold smiles with his lips pressed together as he returns the deck to his pocket, then reluctantly pulls the wallet from his back pants pocket. He presents Arnie with a crisp twenty and tells him to go ahead and sit back down.

Arnie takes his seat and carefully inspects the bill in his hand.

Brenda Sue's hand smoothes over her bubble of blond hair. "Now for last week's—"

Arnie shouts, "Hey, this ain't funny money is't?"

Harold chuckles, "No, Arnie. It's just the new twenty-dollar bill. It's perfectly legal." He looks at Brenda Sue and gives his nose a good rub with the back of his hand.

Brenda Sue fidgets with a gold chain and continues, "Actually, Bruce was telling us your wife will also be joining StormBurst. Is that right?"

"Uh, yeah. She's down in th'back of the pick-up!"

Brenda Sue's eyes bulge.

Bruce explains, "They're going to work as a team, right Arnie?"

"Yeah, okay." He puts the bill in his pocket.

After the meeting, Harold explains to Bruce that he will be driving out to the Holmesbys' house each day to train them personally. I hear Harold clear his throat and say, "Of course it might cut into your demonstration time a little, but I'm sure the investment of your time now will pay off in the end. Right Bruce?"

Bruce looks puzzled. "Right."

Harold pats him on the shoulder, "Fantastic."

Bruce scratches his scalp. "So *I'll* be training them?"

And each day for a week, Bruce drives out to the Holmesbys. Only once does he find Arnie at home, and he's "pretty liquored up" as Bruce puts it. And if that's not bad enough, the Holmesby kids scratch a four-letter nickname in the side of his car. I feel kind of sorry for Bruce, but I figure he should have known better. After all, I did.

❧   ❧   ❧

"Hello?"

"Hi, is this Bill?"

"Yeah, who's this?"

"Hi Bill, this is Diana. How are you doing?"

"Better now that you called!"

"Oh, wonderful! So, I'm calling—"

"Yeah, I didn't think you'd really call me back."

"Well, of course I called—you're a semifinalist!"

"Semifinalist? What the hell is that supposed to mean?"

"Excuse me?"

"So you haven't left that bastard yet? What? You just want to jerk me around some more?"

"Uh, I want to bring you your FREE steak knives—congratulations!"

"Who is this? Is this a joke?"
"No, I'm calling from Chin's Storm—"
"Ahhh, shit. Listen, bitch—"

The good news is I haven't done a demonstration for a teacher or a professor in a while, which means that most of my demos are closer to home. But every so often I get a referral down in Cottage Glen or out in Sweetwater. I try my best to enjoy the drive and stop off for a tax-deductible burger and fries or something else along the way, like today.

I stuff the receipt for my Hoppin' Jalapeno Burger and Mochamania shake into the ashtray of the Rabbit and pull back out onto the highway.

I haven't seen Mom and Dad since I delivered their shampoo wand just after the kick-off weekend. But it's not too much of a problem because I've taken to sink laundering—and buying new clothes. I like to think of all the water I'm conserving during this drought. And it makes much more sense financially to hit the Harveston Mall between demos than to waist a whole afternoon of demonstration time sitting in a laundromat. My time is worth a lot these days. And besides, I could use some new clothes.

Oh dear, we missed you again—this is Mom and Dad calling.

I have at least two appointments every day of the week. But some cancel, some have to reschedule, and some don't open the door.

We just wanted to check in and see how our successful daughter is doing!

To keep such a full schedule, I have to plan strategically. That means setting aside enough time for calls, in addition to my demonstrations.

Well, you're probably out making a sale right now!

The best time to get people is between 7:00 p.m. and 8:30 p.m.

At this rate, it won't be long till you're making more than your old Mom and Dad!

Except that's when people expect telemarketers to call. So I make a separate stack of referrals for everyone who hangs up on me or doesn't answer the phone. I save these referrals for what I call "The magic hour," which is 10:00 a.m. to 11:00 a.m.

I do evening calls Monday, Wednesday and Friday, and magic hour calls on Tuesdays and Thursdays. Saturday nights, I order a pizza and watch whatever's on my new TV. Sunday nights I get Chinese take-out. And watch my new TV.

Mr. Trevor Jackson's house is just outside of Cottage Glen. I follow a gravel road off the old highway and wind around until I see the wooden bridge that must be the start of his driveway. There's nothing but scrub oak, blackberry brambles and tall summer grass until finally I see a long, stone wall—with a black wrought-iron gate. As I pull up to the intercom, the gate doors pull to the sides and reveal a very large, very grand white house with double front doors and white pillars framing the porch, just like the White House, and—

Gulp.

A wolf bolts through the front door and heads straight for the Rabbit.

The gates close behind me in the rearview mirror as I roll up my window, fast as I can, recalling that dogs can smell fear. Slobber and snot wash over the glass as the weight of the wolf-dog shakes the Rabbit.

Holy snots almighty.

And suddenly he appears before me, in a shimmering red Speedo swimsuit. Mr. Trevor Jackson stands perfectly framed in the front window, holding a phone to his ear and waving in my general direction. He has more muscle, and more tan, and more more than I had anticipated.

He disappears for a moment, then materializes at the front door, still speaking into the phone. He snaps his fingers in the air, and the dog retreats into the house behind his mostly-bare body. He signals at me to come in, then disappears into the house. I take a deep breath and try to exhale sans hoppin' jalapeno. As I step out of the Rabbit, I discover my stomach has cramped so badly I can no longer stand up straight.

From this day forward, I'll avoid all foods with verbs in their names.

The front doors are taller and wider than they'd appeared from the driveway. I step into the circular entryway, with a black and white checkerboard floor and wide, open doorways lining it: one to the living room, one to the dining room, one to the kitchen, and one to a hallway with several other doors along it. Trevor's voice bounces out from the center doorway, and I approach with care, trying to muffle the clip-clop of my sandals.

And the gurgling of my stomach.

The kitchen is also black and white, with a smaller checkerboard pattern on the floor and a red and brown stripe of man pacing back and forth in the middle of it all. He's still speaking on the phone, but he turns to smile at me. He snaps his fingers in the air and points toward the doorway to my right.

I step down into deep, white carpet. There is some kind of a lopsided sofa, white and reaching toward the fireplace. To the left of the fireplace sits the wolf-dog, eyeing me cautiously.

I set my demo case on the carpet gently, and the dog snorts.

"Hi, puppy!" I smile. "Aren't you a *good dog*?"

He grumbles, motionless.

Trevor's voice echoes through the doorways and off of the high ceilings: "Have it there by eight, but not before seven forty."

Sensing the stomach cramps moving south, I make way back toward the kitchen door where I mouth the words, "Where is the bathroom?"

He wrinkles his brow and points to my left.

I find it just in time.

The bathroom is lined with black marble and I have to giggle as I sit atop the black toilet staring at the black telephone installed above the roll of paper.

The most magical hour of all, perhaps.

As I make my way back through the house, I can still hear Trevor talking on the phone.

"No, I told you no. It's no good. No good. They dropped there the last time…No, Pooky's not talking, I'm sure of it…Jack, I'm telling you, just leave it in the wheel well like usual, behind the laundromat!"

Wheel well?

I pause before the entrance to the kitchen, and consider going back to the bathroom and making more noise to announce my coming down the hallway. But then: I can't seem to move my legs.

"Jack, I'd hate to have to remind you who's in charge here."

I hear a quick, deep snort, but it's nothing like the dog's. The sound repeats.

I tiptoe back to the bathroom to open and close the door.

Clop-clop-clop-clop.

Cough.

He nods at me from across the kitchen as I pass.

I leave the case shut, and slowly sit down on top of it, watching the dog watch me.

Two minutes?

I glance at my watch.

One.

Finally, I get up and slowly walk to the kitchen doorway.

Clop-clop-clop.

Trevor holds the phone between his ear and shoulder and pulls the cork from a bottle.

He sets the corkscrew on the butcher's block, beside a little mirror of some kind, and turns his bare chest toward me.

Everything about him is golden brown—his short, wet hair; his perfect skin; his dark nipples; his glistening eyes. He winks and points to the bottle of red, then to me, and raises his eyebrows.

Gulp.

I mouth the words "No thanks," and smile.

"I'm going to have to call you back. Someone's here—no, no, it's no one you know," and he hangs up the phone. He walks toward me, slowly, one bare brown foot at a time, with the glass of wine in his hand and a tremendous grin on his face. "So you must be Diana." He watches me over the top of his glass as he takes a long, slow sip.

"Yeah, that's me!"

He sips, then swallows, then smiles. "So you are a…" he takes another sip, "college student trying to make money for tuition and *books*?"

"Yeah—" the word barely comes out. I clear my throat.

"And Reggie suggested you give me a call?" He winks a brown eye.

"Uh, yeah. Marcie and Reggie gave me your name."

"You're sure you don't want some wine? It's a great year—I just pulled it out of the cellar." He sips, watching me over the top of the glass.

"Oh, thanks anyway, but you see I—"

"Yes, you…?" He leans toward me with a perfect smile and raises his eyebrows.

Gulp.

"Miss Jensen, surely you're old enough to have a glass of wine?" He grins and leans against the edge of the countertop.

I watch the muscle bulge on the outside of his thigh.

"Oh, I am! Of course I am!" I can't help it. I have to giggle. I look at the checkerboard floor, trying to think of why it is I shouldn't have a glass of wine with the most attractive man I think I've ever seen in my life, who is smiling at me, and already told me on the phone that he's not married…"Well, you know," I try to look at anything else in the room but him. "I'm not supposed to drink on the job." I smile.

"Too bad." He takes a long sip, eyeing me over the rim of the glass.

I turn and walk toward the living room.

I'm telling you, just leave it in the wheel well like usual, behind the laundromat!

My stomach gurgles loud enough for Trevor to hear. I press my hand against my abdomen and take a seat on the demo case, then glance up at the stranger who greeted me practically naked.

For a vacuum demonstration?

"And besides!" I give him my broadest smile and slap my knee, "I'm a *good girl*!"

We chuckle together a moment.

He cocks his head toward the fireplace. "It must be difficult to stay a good girl when you're on your own at *college*." He crosses his arms and smiles.

I chuckle alone. And think. And chuckle.

"Yes, well it's a *Christian* college, you know?"

"I thought you said you went to Harveston?"

"Me? No…" I look to the dog. "So what's his name?"

"Killer." His smile broadens and he reaches for his glass.

"Really?"

"Yeah, he has a thing for squirrels and rabbits. Cats too, actually."

I glance out the window toward the driveway. "Yeah, I noticed—well, about the rabbits anyway."

Trevor laughs and takes a long, slow sip. "So what do you do when you're *not* working, Diana?"

"Oh, I go to school."

He grins, "That's not what I mean."

"Oh, right…I, uh, read a lot."

He shakes his head a little and settles back into the sofa. For just a second, light glares off of something—a diamond in his earlobe.

"You don't by any chance swim, do you? I was just about to—"

"Oh, well, I never really learned how—I'm even afraid of the bath tub!" I try to laugh.

Killer whines.

"Too bad, on a hot day like this." He watches me over the top of his wine-glass.

I glance out the window at the closed gate.

"Yeah, well, I know." I turn my toes in, awkwardly. "My *church* group is always going up to the reservoir to swim, and stuff like that. All I can do is just coordinate the, uh, psalms."

"*Psalms*?" There's a crease between his brown brows.

"Yeah, you know, for Sunday School." I clear my throat, "For YAAAY!!!"

He jerks back on the sofa.

"Though I walk through the shadow of the valley of evil…" I throw my arms out to each side, "I shall FEAR NOT!" I fall to my knees on the carpet, lift my hands to the ceiling and shout: "AAAAAAAAAAAAAAAAAY-MEH-HHN!"

My chest heaves in the silence. Until my stomach growls.

I raise my eyebrows. "Do you read the Good Book, Mr. Jackson?"

"Oh, well, I…"

"It's like I always say, Mr. Jackson: My family's health and *Jesus* are the greatest gifts of all! Wouldn't you agree?"

He takes a gulp of wine.

"Shall I start the vacuum cleaner demonstration now, Mr. Jackson?"

He clears his throat. "*Vacuum cleaner?*"

I flip open the demo case.

"Well, uh—"

I raise up the Ray O'Sun and grin. "This is what we call the Ray O'Sun because it's just like a Ray O'Sun shining straight out of heaven! Wait 'til you see, Mr. Jackson!"

"Uh, Diana, so how long does this *demonstration* usually take?"

I look out at the closed gate. "Oh, just a couple of hours or so, Mr. Jackson."

He sits up. "A couple of hours?"

"Yeah, give or take. But don't you worry, Mr. Jackson, it's so entertaining you'll hardly notice the time passing by! Do you know that the average home collects one point six eight seven nine tons of dust in a calendar year?"

"What, are you kidding me?" His brown nipples shrivel into tiny raisins. "*Two hours?*"

"Well, of course, if you have a lot of questions for me, Mr. Jackson, then it might go a little longer." Killer sits up, anxiously, and watches Trevor. "And then there's the paperwork when—I mean, if you decide to buy it from me." I cock my head toward the fireplace. "If this is a bad time, Mr. Jackson, we could reschedule?"

"Oh, well, yeah. You see, I have some friends coming over for dinner, and I—that's just *too fricking long*. I wasn't even planning to buy the damned thing—I—"

I shrug my shoulders. "Well, I understand, Mr. Jackson."

"I mean, do people actually sit through this thing for *two hours?*"

I stand up and reach for my demo case. "Sometimes. I guess a few people might get bored with *parts* of my vacuum cleaner demonstration, but they're usually polite about it. Good Christians, you know?" I set the Ray O'Sun back in the demo case. "And like everybody knows, cleanliness is next to godliness right? And who doesn't love the lord?" I wink.

He tilts his head back and slurps the last bit of wine from his glass. "You know, I just don't think I'm going to have time for this after all—uh, Diana."

I walk across the living room and into the entryway. For a moment, I think I feel his warm, smooth hands pressing on my shoulders, his breath on the back of my neck. But I turn and he's vanished. Every inch of him. "Okay. Well…thanks anyway." I walk through the front door and see the gate standing wide open.

❧   ❧   ❧

I don't know if I'm more disgusted by Trevor Jackson or by myself for walking right into that situation. But how could I have known? How can I ever know, for that matter?

But then: maybe I overreacted. I mean, one incredibly handsome man with loads of money flirts with me and I automatically assume he's the devil. No wonder I never get beyond the first date. Maybe I should have just done the demo anyway. He definitely has the money. And besides, a sale is a sale.

I open the glove box and take a swig from the little bottle of Mylanta, then flip open my phone and speed dial Brenda Sue.

"Oh, he was a total freak."

"Well, honey, freaks spend money too!"

"Yeah, I know. Hey, listen, I must have eaten something bad—can you get someone to cover my 5 o'clock today?" I give her the information.

"Now go home and rest up 'cause I can *just feel* that tomorrow's going to be a big day, honey!"

"Yeah, me too."

"And don't forget—you still need to get yourself a recruit!"

Kerouac is curled up on my doormat in the shade. "Long time no see—no pun intended, of course."

"YEE-OWL." He stretches with his white butt in the air and gives a quick clawing to the doormat.

"Back at ya." I crouch down and give him a thorough head-scratching, careful not to touch the eye-holes. "So what did *you* do today?"

"Vvvrrr."

"Yes, eating, sleeping, sunbathing, napping in the shade—it's a rough life, isn't it?"

I sit down Indian-style and look out across the sagging porch, then across the dried up lawn and brambles of old climbing roses with not a leaf or bud left on them. Just thorns where beautiful blossoms should be.

"You know, it's a funny thing, Kerouac. Mom always said roses were a lot of hard work. But those right there, why they probably haven't been trimmed, or fertilized, or even watered in years."

"Vvrr."

"Yes, I know it shows. Well, I suppose it's a fine time for a Hereford Valley Heffeweizen. What do you—"

There's a small face peeking around the fence at the end of the path.

"Hello?"

A little boy wanders up the path, in a striped shirt and Spiderman under-wear.

"Well, hi there."

"Hi."

He grabs onto the railing and climbs the steps to sit down by Kerouac.

"I'm Diana."

"Hi."

He pets the cat affectionately.

"What's your name?"

"Kenny."

"Hi, Kenny. It's nice to meet you. That's Kerouac."

"Kenny *Deh-veh-gah.*"

He continues petting the cat and smiles.

"Do you live around here?"

He points toward the fence.

"Oh, we're neighbors."

"Him's Blanco!"

Pet, pet.

"That's his name?"

"Mmm-hmm. Him's blind."

"Yes, I know he is. Is he *your* cat?"

Kenny looks up at me and beams. "Mom says him's everybody's cat!"

"Oh, I see."

❧   ❧   ❧

The ad runs on a Thursday, the office fills with applicants on Friday, and Monday they all begin their FREE weeklong training session to become certified dealers. The following Monday, most of them return their equipment to Berta. The ones who stick around roll their eyes at Harold and snicker at the rest of us when we sing at the morning meeting. They usually check-in their equipment before the following Friday, when the office fills with applicants all over again. But Bruce, James and I have remained, James for five months and Bruce for nearly a year now.

According to Brenda Sue, who bobs her hair at us over her coffee cup, we three "have the stuff true salesmen are made of."

Bruce, James and I nod as we chew our bismarks, then head upstairs for the meeting and, more importantly, our paychecks.

Brenda Sue shouts at the newest dealers: "Remember the magic four!" She smiles. "And what do I mean by that, Diana?"

I take a swig of coffee and clear my throat. "According to the national StormBurst average, one in every four demonstrations is a sale."

Brenda Sue looks at each new dealer, one at a time. "That's right..." She nods her head and looks a couple of new dealers in the eye. "So if *you* want to get a sale, how many demonstrations should you expect to do?"

The new dealers look at each other.

Bruce, James and I answer, "Four!"

"And if you want to get TWO sales, how many demonstrations?"

Everyone answers, "Eight!"

I still prefer to think of each demonstration I do being 25%—or more—of a regular commission. That way I really am getting paid just to show it to people. If I were Brenda Sue, I would explain it to the dealers *that* way. But then: I guess she already did during their interviews.

"How many demos did you last week, James?"

James runs a comb through his hair, transforming the gel-crisp waves into a bristly hedge above his face. "Well, about three I guess."

"Well no wonder you didn't make a sale! Now after this meeting I want you take these new dealers out and get us a whole new goldfish bowl filled with speedboat entries!" She stamps a purple cowboy boot and smiles. "And don't come back until it's filled to the BRIM with new names and phone numbers!" She winks at James.

James groans.

Brenda Sue turns to pick up the stack of shamrocks from the tray below the whiteboard.

In the back, someone whispers, "Where are we going?"

James mumbles, "Straight to hell."

"Diana, how many demonstrations did *you* do last week?" She beams.

"Oh, uh…"

"Ha! Did you hear that? She has to take a minute to remember all of those demos!"

"Well, I think it was about twelve, or thirteen maybe. No, fourteen, I guess."

"Ah-ha! And how many sales did *you* get?" She holds up my new paper shamrocks in her hand and spreads them like playing cards.

"Eight."

"That's right! Pay attention to Diana, now—she's one of the best salesmen in the *state*!"

Brenda Sue excuses herself and Harold takes over for A.D.T. Today's topic is "The *psychology* of a sale." He takes the green pen and writes across the top of the board "THE HIERARCHY OF CUSTOMER NEEDS." Harold's shirt comes untucked as he writes, exposing his bulging sides.

"We all have needs, don't we? We all need to eat—"

Someone muffles a giggle.

Harold clears his throat. He proceeds to draw an enormous triangle, then divides it into four sections. In the bottom section of the triangle he writes "SAFETY." Harold faces us with a grin.

"All right, now as salesmen, we already work to *solve* our customers problems, right?"

"Right."

"But we also have to meet their needs—*all* of their needs, or the sale might never happen. Now here, we have the first 'rung on the ladder,' if you will: The customer's need for safety. If we can't make him feel safe about his investment, we might as well pack up and go home, okay?"

"Okay."

"Great. Now, how can you make sure your customer feels safe about his investment? It's really very simple. Just mention what a fantastic, reliable product the StormBurst is—which we already do in the demonstration, right?"

"Right."

"And if your customer still isn't sure it's going to be a *safe* investment, you can mention the two-year renewable warranty plan and even the StormBurst's long, successful history. You all remember Brenden P. Callahan, right?"

"Right."

FART...

Harold clears his throat. "Now then, your customer may be convinced it's a safe investment, but..." on the section above safety, Harold writes "PRES-TIGE."

Someone shouts: "Oh, god! Who let that one out?"

The dealers giggle.

Harold turns to us with a fresh smile, "Let's face it, who wants to spend a thousand dollars without feeling like it's going to make them cool? Ha-ha! Am I right?"

"Yes."

"So how can you make sure your customer knows the StormBurst will give them *prestige*?"

No one has a clue.

"Well, maybe your customer is a guy who likes to have all the cool new toys, right? Like a big TV or a speedboat. Or maybe it's a housewife and she needs to feel important and good about the work she does in the home. So you've really got to pay attention *early* in the game. Then you'll know exactly what your customer *needs*..." Harold points his pen at the word "needs" and takes a deep breath, "to hear."

"Dude, it REEKS in here!"

Harold begins writing on the next section of the triangle. "SELF-ESTEEM." Harold turns to us and clears his throat. "So how do you know if your customer has a problem with self-esteem?" He waits a moment. "Well, maybe he's a little defensive!" Harold raises his eyebrows. "Or maybe she wears a lot of baggy clothes to hide her figure, you know?"

We nod.

"But how do you know if their self-esteem will be a problem for *you*? You probably won't until the very end when you're trying to close, right?"

"Right."

"So watch for the clues! Maybe the man drives a fancy sports car or has a wife that's half his age! Does he look like he might be wearing an artificial hairpiece?" Harold crosses his arms and nods at us as we absorb this new information. "Is the woman a neat freak? Or anorexic? Does she wear too much makeup? Ah-ha!"

My stomach gurgles.

"These are the people who don't want anybody telling them they aren't good enough. So what do you want to make sure they know about the *Storm-Burst*?"

James raises his hand. "It's good?"

"No, it's not just good—it's the *best* money can buy! Does that make sense?"

Bruce's eyes are shut and his mouth is open a little.

"Okay, now if you can meet all of these needs for your customer, do you know what you're going to have?" Harold smiles and turns to write at the top of the triangle "A HAPPY STORMBURST CUSTOMER!" Harold turns to us with a serious face, "BUT! What's going to happen if you take away one of these?" He taps the pen against the lower sections of the triangle.

A gentle snore emanates from Bruce.

Harold shouts: "You won't have this!" He slams his pen against the happy customer. "You have to make sure you meet *all* of their needs. Does that make sense?"

"Yes."

"Great. Now who would like to come up here and give this a try?"

❉   ❉   ❉

"Hello?"

"Hi, Lois?"

"Yes?"

"Hi, this is Diana. A friend of mine was over in your neighborhood last week—"

"Are you one of those StormBurst people?"

"Excuse me?"

"How many times do I have to tell you people to quit calling me?"

"I'm sorry, ma'am, I had no—"

"Don't call again!"

❉   ❉   ❉

Maev Bola is the professor of Women's Studies at Cornston U. She just got back from a sabbatical in Egypt and returned Mom's call about helping me get started with my summer job. I met her once, in person, at a fundraiser dinner where I heard her speak about the dramatic rise in teen pregnancies in the U.S.

And here she is again, tall and beautiful, with her long braids and ebony eyes. She wears some kind of loose, flowing pants and a top that drapes just over her shoulder, and I follow her into the living room wondering if I could ever dress like that.

"Thanks so much for having me over."

I've seen a lot of black people at Harveston, but Maev Bola makes them all look brown. And she isn't African-American; she is African-African-American.

"Hah-nee, can I get you something to drink?"

I could listen to her speak for days, like music.

"Sure, what have you got?" I try my best to sound casual.

She brings me unpasteurized apple juice in a tall blue glass and curls up on one end of the ivory couch.

"Thanks. I've got your steak knives, too—"

"Oh, hah-nee, you can keep them. I don't eat meat."

"Right."

I take my time setting up for the demo, partly because I just wish I were there for any other reason than to sell her a vacuum cleaner. I pause by the patio doors and look out onto the large wooden deck that looks into the tops of fir trees.

"This sure is a beautiful house!"

"Oh, thank you. Actually it was designed by an architect friend of mine. He lives in Shih-cah-go."

She is Maev Bola, the woman who traveled through Pakistan alone—on foot. The woman who sponsored three families from Cambodia to immigrate to the U.S. The woman who hid in the hills of Bosnia to provide first aid to wounded soldiers and those fleeing for their lives. The woman who wrote the forward for Linder B. Tillerman's latest book of poems. The woman who appeared on Opal Whitman's talk show, not once but twice. The woman who was nominated for a Nobel Prize *and* a Pulitzer.

"Have you ever been to Ireland?"

"Certainly, hah-nee. Once to the north and twice to the south. And have you been there, dear?"

"Oh, no. Not yet, anyway!" I smile.

Maev Bola smiles back at me.

I apologize for having to shrink her couch cushion. I apologize for having to show her the dust blowing out of her Kirkstone F-10.

"It's okay, hah-nee. I know that you are just do-ing your job."

"Now this part is my favorite. Just close your eyes for a moment…"

"Oooooh, yes, I could get used to that I think!"

When I hold up the Pot O'Water, I can't bring myself to shine the light through it.

"Hah-nee—you mean to tell me this thing picked up all that *dirt* out of my carpet right after my Kirkstone cleaned over it?"

"Well, yes." I set the Pot O'Water on the carpet.

Maev Bola is not happy. "Have you eh-ver lifted one of these Kirkstone machines up the stairs? I have been breakin' my back—lit-rah-lee, and—"

If only I were there for any other reason. Any reason at all.

"Well, Di-ah-nah, tell me, can I buy this thing from *you*?"

"Okay." And she does with her MasterCard.

As I fill out the paperwork, Maev Bola offers to make me a pomegranate salad and of course I say yes. We eat on the deck, looking into the tops of the trees.

"My pahr-teh-ner, Sarah, is gone today. I'm sorry you couldn't meet her."

"Oh, me too."

"She is speaking on the East Lawn of the White House today."

"Really?"

"Yes."

She is Maev Bola and she is eating a pomegranate salad. With me.

"Um, my, uh," I take a sip of apple juice and clear my throat, "you know, my *partner*, Christina, is in Chile right now."

"Oh, real-ly?" Maev raises a thin eyebrow. "And what is she do-ing in Chile?"

"Oh, she's studying Spanish."

"I see."

We concentrate on our salads for a while and listen to the birds flitting through the forest.

"So, Di-ah-nah, you go to the Harveston U.?"

"Oh, yeah. Well, I probably would have gone to *Cornston*, but you know, with Dad there and—"

"And what do you study at Harveston?"

I try to laugh. "Oh, you know, a little of this and a little of that!"

Maev Bola stops eating her salad.

"But what is your ma-jor?" She sets her fork down so the prongs rest just on the edge of her plate.

"Oh, well, I'm kind of between majors right now."

She raises her eyebrows.

I feel a warming trend in my cheeks. "I guess I can't make up my mind."

"I see." Maev Bola folds her hands in her lap and waits for me to say something more.

"Well, so far I've tried Biology, Anthropology, Physical Education and…English."

"And?"

"And I didn't really *like* any of them." My cheeks continue heating up.

"What do your parents say?"

"They say that if I don't graduate this year, I'm on my own!" I grin.

But Maev Bola looks concerned.

"Doctor Bola, how did you know what you wanted to do?"

"Call me Maev, hah-nee." She looks into the trees. "Well, I just did what I was passionate about and it turned into a career, I sup-pose." She smiles at me. "What are you passionate about, Di-ah-nah?"

I smooth the napkin across my lap. "Well, to be honest," gulp, "I really don't know." I look up at Maev Bola. "I mean, I really don't."

"Well, just think about it for a mo-ment."

"Yeah, okay." I look out at the green tree needles arranged against sky like brushstrokes on a canvas. "I am passionate about…maybe…making *money*." I grin.

Maev folds her arms on the edge of the patio table and doesn't smile. "You can make mah-nee doing *anything*." The muscles of her face relax, at last, and Maev Bola picks up her fork. "Well, then I guess you will just have to keep trying new things until you find some-thing you *are* passionate about." A smile sweeps wide across her face like arms offering a hug. "But when you find it, hah-nee, listen to me: don't give it up no matter what people tell you. Not for the whole damn-ed world."

"Okay." I take a sip of apple juice.

We have to lean the passenger seat back and lay the Kirkstone across it. Maev Bola fastens the seatbelt over it and says, "Hah-nee, you can never be *too* careful."

I am smiling at Maev Bola and Maev Bola is smiling at me. She reaches out to shake my hand. "If you are eh-ver in the neighborhood again, I hope you will stop by."

"Thank you, Maev."

"You are welcome, Di-ah-nah. Good luck."

It's been a long time since I've driven down Fish Farm Lane. Since high school, I suppose. The houses and barns and outbuildings still look the same, but the fields are unusually brown. I take a right on Schoolhouse Road and follow it out toward Hidden Springs. The Rabbit stirs up a cloud of dust as we roll over the gravel. Happily, we don't see another soul traveling in either direction.

Just past milepost 12, I ease over onto the shoulder. There are still no cars in sight. I start down the path, careful not to brush against the poison oak. There are the usual wads of toilet paper in the brush and an occasional beer can. But otherwise, nothing appears to have changed. I step out between the trees and onto the rocky beach. I look into the clear, deep water, then out at the boulders jutting up from the water and into the sun, just perfect for sunbathing. I kick off my sandals, slide out of my clothes, and unhook the aquati-bra.

SPLASH.

"Wahoo!" It's as cold as I remember, and every bit as refreshing. I dog paddle out, then duck my head under and roll onto my back. I kick my way out to the best rock-island in the stream and climb onto its smooth, flat top. The fir trees, brush and moss all glow, so incredibly green. I take a long, deep soothing breath,

"SHOOO."

My goose bumps melt against the sun-warmed rock as I settle onto my back. I let my hand dangle over the edge of the rock and find its way into the water, still springing up from somewhere deep in the earth where even a drought can't touch it.

I rub the referral card between my thumb and forefinger. On the off chance that this woman agrees to a demo, I'll have to drive two hours each way. Whether she buys or not. But then: she is the referral of a buyer, who was referred to me by a buyer, so I figure I should at least call.

"I want the steak knives."

"Terrific."

So I'm winding my way down Highway 4, between the firs and the maples, thinking about how much easier sales calls would be if I drove a certain '92 Corvette instead of this '86 Rabbit.

Holy snots. What happened to the reservoir?

I ease onto the shoulder and set the parking break. There's nothing but a field of stumps where water-skiers, fishermen and, well, water should be. And there, in the middle of the wasteland, snakes a thin river of green.

I can't help it. I have to get out of the car.

At the edge of the gravel, brown swords of fern still stand, dying but not yet dead.

HONK!!! HONK!!!

A log truck passes a little too close, leaving me breathless in its wake. I look back out at the field of stumps. An osprey makes its skilled descent into the little water left, then rises, its talons empty.

I get back into the Rabbit and drive on. Another hour.

Mailbox #58790 is decorated with red and blue reflectors, and the other side of the driveway has a wooden sign reading "Organic Garlic." There's a second sign about five feet behind it reading "Great Wines!" I roll down the driveway and up in front of the big green farmhouse. The porch steps are dappled in sunlight, and I look up to discover the roof above me is made of lattice—and grapevines hung with clusters of *real* grapes almost close enough to reach.

"Hellooo!" I turn to see a sun-bonneted woman standing in the flowerbed behind me. She's waving a gloved hand while holding a basket of pink and yellow roses in the other.

"Hi, I'm Diana. I brought your steak knives."

"Oh, fantastic. I've been needing a set."

"This is a lovely place you have here…Mrs. Du-*bwah*."

She chuckles. "Oh, no dear, it's Du-*boy*!"

"Really?"

She leaves her gloves and clippers on bottom step, and proceeds toward me. I hold out the steak knives and smile. "Oh, thanks. And you can call just me Chloe! Would you like a tour of the place?"

She explains how she and Mr. Dubois had modernized the kitchen in '68. "Oh, we bought it from an eighty year old woman—funny, that used to sound *old* to me! It'd been in her family generations, and so had the oven!"

"Oh, dear!"

"I told my husband I'd sooner leave the country than gather up wood to fry his eggs!"

There's a tuft of long white fur beneath the avocado-colored dishwasher.

As we make way through the "public rooms," as Chloe calls them, she explains how they carpeted over the old wood-plank floor with this lovely lime green shag—except for in the master bedroom, which has been done entirely in pink.

"You see, the *master* bedroom is a place of repose. And it's the most personal space in a home." She lowers her voice, "A feminine touch goes a long way in the master suite, dear." She nudges me with her elbow. "Yes indeedy."

Gulp.

I smile. "I can see you guys have put a lot of yourselves into this place."

Chloe beams.

"Who's that?" I point to large white cat lounging across one of the bed pillows.

"Oh, that's *Sue Ellen Antoinette!*" She rushes over and strokes the cat, adjusting the pink bow on her head. "She's a purebred, pedigreed Persian—albino!"

The cat licks its scrunched face and blinks its colorless eyes at me. "Well, how unusual."

Chloe shakes her head regretfully. "The poor thing has been deaf since birth…" Then she drives that elbow into my arm, "That's how we got her for free!" She smiles.

"Well, shall I set up in the living room?"

"That would be *perfect*."

"Okay then, I'll get my things!"

"Can I get you a glass of fresh-squeezed lemonade?" She pulls off her sunbonnet, and runs her fingers through the curls of white-blond hair.

"Oh, that sounds delicious!"

And it is. A little puckery, but anything's good on such a hot day.

So I get all set up, take another long, deep, soothing drink of lemonade and wait. I'm poised on my demo case, with my Ray O'Sun in my hand, ready to go as soon as she walks through the door again. I finally start coughing to remind her I'm there, and then she returns. "Is there some problem, dear?"

"Oh, no, not at all. I'm ready when you are!" I smile.

She looks around the room, then back at me, where I sit on the case.

"I figured you'd want to sit on the couch?"

"Well, but, surely you don't expect me to *watch*!"

"Well…that is why I'm here," I try to maintain my smile.

"Trust me, honey. I'll be able to tell how well that thing cleans carpets when you're done—I don't need to watch it in action!" She winks and retreats to the kitchen.

My stomach gurgles.

I flash the Ray O'Sun on, then off. On, then off. I look at my watch again, but it hasn't even been a minute. On, then off.

Chloe pokes her head in the living room again. She asks in a rather stern voice, "Is there a problem, Diana?"

I take a long, deep sigh. "Well, Chloe," I set the lamp down on the carpet, "I think we got our lines crossed. You see, I'm not in the business of cleaning houses—I'm in sales. Actually I'm just a product demonstrator." I clear my throat. "And I came out here, and brought you these steak knives as a thank you for *watching* my demonstration." Her mouth slowly opens, "I'm sure you can understand that, since that's what I get paid to do, that's what I need to do here, or else, perhaps, I should be on my way."

She fluffs out a curl on her temple. "Oh, honey, I'll cover for you. You don't have to worry about that! If anybody calls me, I'll—"

"I'm afraid I'll have to go now. Thanks for your *time*." I wind up the cord on the Ray O'Sun and do my best to ignore her. But she lingers in the doorway until she finally says, "Well, I'm sorry honey. I thought you were coming out to clean a room for free."

Gulp. "I think that's the carpet shampooing company that does that."

"Oh, I see. And you don't do that?"

"No, I'm not a cleaning woman."

"Oh, dear." She shakes her head. "Well, so what does your machine do then?"

"Well, you could say it's an air-purifying-vaporizer-shampooer-vacuum cleaner-in-one. That's why it's so much *fun* to show people in person," I say without smiling.

She adjusts her skirt.

"But of course, not everyone has the time, I suppose, to watch a complete stranger—"

"Well, how long does it take?"

"About an hour."

"And I just sit there on the couch and watch?"

"Yep."

"And then I can keep the steak knives?"

"Yes, *then* you can keep the steak knives."

She glances at the kitchen door a moment. "All right, let's do it then."

"If you're sure…"

I do my best to put the whole demonstration on fast forward, but Chloe isn't much help. "So you said that attachment does lamp shades?"

"That's right."

"Oh, well my lampshades are a rather unusual texture—raw silk, you see. Could we try it out on one to make sure it will work?"

"Sure."

And then there's, "My goodness, that cushion really does look fluffier now, doesn't it?"

"I'd say so!" I reposition it with a smile.

"Oh, dear. Well now the other one looks dreadful next to it, doesn't it?"

"Oh, well—"

"Oh, would you be a dear—I'm sorry to be so much trouble, but you know I really can't have one cushion looking new while the others, oh, thank you so much…"

And it doesn't end there.

"Do you think that would take the kitty-smell out of Sue Ellen Antoinette's favorite pillow?"

"Oh, I don't know about that."

"I'll go get it!"

"Great."

"So that's what I would use on my linoleum, then?"

"Yes, this is the one. Genuine horse-hair bristles and—"

"Oh, could I see? I just want to be sure it fits underneath my cabinets—it'll just take a second, follow me."

Two and a half hours later, I'm mopping my brow with the tail of my shirt as I sigh, "So if I could make it possible for you to own a StormBurst today, you'd be interested."

Chloe draws her lips up like she's about to kiss the air. "Well, I don't know." She sits down on the fuzzy pink stool in front of the bathroom vanity.

I unplug the StormBurst and leave her electric hair setting kit unplugged. I wind up the cord. I detach the Pot O'Water and it is filled to the rim with tufts of white fur. I cross in front of her, flip up the toilet seat, dump it in, and flush.

"Did you say this comes with a carpet shampooer?"

I rinse the Pot O'Water in the bathroom sink, splashing the sludge on her faux marble countertop. I don't wipe it clean. "Yes, you can get a shampooer to go with it."

"Well, now that's the only real reason I'd buy something like this."

"Oh, is it?"

"Sure, you see I already have a vacuum I'm happy with, I have a vaporizer, I have a top-notch Swedish air filter, and frankly, I have plenty of space to store my sweaters."

"Well, that's too bad." I pick up the StormBurst and exit the master bathroom.

Chloe follows me down the hall, "But like I said, a shampooer would be—"

"Well, that's nice of you to say, but I'm sure the StormBurst's price tag is more than you'd want to pay for just a shampooer. Thanks for watching though." I head down the stairs into the living room.

"Oh, but, now you never know until…you see it for *yourself*, right?"

I turn and Chloe is smiling at me, enthusiastically.

"You did bring it with you, didn't you?"

I take a long, hard look around the living room.

"Didn't you, dear?"

I take a look at my watch. "Oh, sure I did, Chloe. But you see, I'm afraid I've used up all my time here."

"Oh, that's okay, dear, I don't mind if you stay a bit longer."

"Well, I'm sure *you* don't, but I really must be getting back."

"But what if I want to buy it?"

"Do you?"

"Well, I can't be sure until I see the shampooer."

I look over the StormBurst and all of its attachments sprawled across her living room. "I see." I look at my watch again. It's already 4:30 p.m. Well, I'll tell you what Chloe, I have just enough time to pull one stain, just *one* stain, out of your carpet to show you how well the StormBurst shampooer works."

"Oh, that's wonderful!" She clasps her hands together under her chin.

"But I'll warn you Chloe, this shampooer will work so well on that one, *little*, stain that it's bound to leave the rest of your carpet looking dingier than you ever imagined."

"Oh, well that's just fine!"

"And I'm warning you because once I pull that stain out of your carpet, I won't have time to do any more. I'll have to leave no matter what."

"All right, dear."

I look at my watch again. "Okay then. Why don't you pick out one, small stain in your carpet while I get the shampooer ready."

"Sure!"

I dig the StormBurst shampoo bottle out of my demo case.

She doesn't move. Or stop smiling.

"Well, aren't you going to find a stain?"

"I already know which one! Right here behind the coffee table—it's an '82 Bordeaux!" She's beaming.

I feel a bead of sweat trickle down my temple as I head for the Rabbit.

She follows me. "Yes, it's a *red* wine. I haven't been able to get it out in all these years!"

"Fine." We return to the living room and she helps me move the coffee table aside. Sure enough, there's a dark red stain about the size of my foot. I try to smile, confidently.

Chloe smiles back and clasps her hands beneath her chin. "If your machine can get *that* out, I just might buy this thing!"

"Fine, fine." I try to force a smile and start running the hose into the kitchen.

Chloe follows me anxiously, alternately fidgeting with her skirt and twisting curls between her fingers. "Does it use steam?"

"No."

"Do you have to run a hose outside?"

"No."

"What kind of shampoo is that?"

"I don't know."

At last, we're standing before the Bordeaux. I rehearse Harold's words and study the long strands of green shag.

"Are you ready now?" She rocks back and forth on her feet in anticipation.

"Now you saw me attach this to your sink—it has adapters for both kitchen and bathroom faucets. Then you just pour a little of our special StormBurst shampoo in this cup here, then click it back into place…"

Chloe asks, "Are you sure you don't know what's in that shampoo? It's not going to damage my carpet, is it? This is top-notch carpeting, you know?" She looks at the stain and shakes her head.

"First you just pull this little trigger here, very gently—see how that sprays a nice, even mist of shampoo over the surface?"

She looks back at me. "Oh, yes, I see."

"Then just give it a gentle rub with the patented rub-and-release bristles at the tip there…and only now do you turn on the StormBurst…"

Growl. Grind. Slurp.

"And as you press down gently, just pull the shampoo wand toward you and watch—watch!" It's already lifting the stain. "Can you see it pulling all the dirt—and the *wine* through the window?" We both stare in awe as brownish-red, then pink streaks flash across the window. "And, uh, when you finish pulling the shampoo up, you use the, uh, the second trigger like this, and spray a nice even mist of clean water over the area. Then you pull out the rinse water…" More dirt and pink flash through the window, not simply erasing the stain, but leaving behind the brightest patch of green carpet I've ever seen.

I turn the StormBurst off, take a deep breath and hold it.

Chloe is pale. She holds her chest.

I sigh. "Well, thank you for your time." I bolt for the kitchen to detach the hose.

"So how much is it?"

"Well, the StormBurst, with all of its standard attachments is just fourteen thirty seven. But the shampooer is extra."

"Oh, well, how much extra is the shampooer?"

"One seventy-five."

She adjusts her skirt. "And I can't use the shampooer without the StormBurst?"

"No." I detach the hose and head back to the living room.

I'm polishing the gold buckles on the StormBurst with my shirttail when she asks, "Well, will you take a check?"

Gulp.

"I have a guarantee card and everything…"

I turn slowly, waiting for her to laugh, but she doesn't. I take a long, deep and soothing breath and smile. "Well, of course you can write a check, Chloe!" I pat her on the shoulder. "Let me just write up a receipt for you and fill out the warranty card."

Chloe gives me a bottle of carrot brandy and a wreath of organic garlic as a bonus for being such a "delightful vacuum cleaner demonstrator!" She smiles.

I put the check inside my demo case and hit the road.

The Myrtlewood Inn is bigger than I'd imagined. The parking lot wraps around it on three sides, and there's a striped awning over the entrance where taxis, limousines and shuttles drop off hotel guests. A man in a red uniform opens the door to the lobby and waits as I make my skillful ascent up the steps on the front half of each foot.

Just inside the lobby, I see a sign directing "STORMBURST REGIONAL CONFERNECE THIS WAY" with an arrow to the right. And sure enough, through double doors, is the start of the grand buffet.

"Hi there, can I help you with your name tag? Which office are you with?" The woman smiles from across the table loaded with nametags.

"Oh, I'm Diana Jensen. I'm with Chin's StormBurst, in Harveston."

"Of course, let me see...yes, here you are. You'll be at table fifteen—your table number's there in the corner of your tag if you forget."

I enter the ballroom and take my plate. Scrambled eggs, poached eggs, hard- and soft-boiled eggs. White toast, wheat toast and powder-sugared French toast. Sausage patties and sausage links. Bacon and ham. Hash browns. Honeydew. Pancakes and waffles. Crepes and crème puffs. Strawberries, whipped cream, pineapple sauce, chocolate sprinkles and tapioca pudding. Yogurt, granola and—holy snots, there's another table across the aisle.

I carry my full plate along the length of it just to see what else is there: Quiches, crab legs and shrimp cocktail. Danishes and donuts. Fruit salad, fondue and flaming—bananas?.

I scan the room for a familiar face, and there, not three rows from the podium, is Brenda Sue's beehive. She's already waving at me.

"There's our girl!" Brenda Sue beams.

Harold rises from his seat and shakes my hand as I take my seat next to the two of them, across from Bruce, James and Berta.

"Where are all the new dealers?"

Brenda Sue nods toward table sixteen behind us, "We let them have their *own* table."

"Can I get you some coffee, fresh squeezed orange juice or champagne this morning?"

I stare at the young man in the tuxedo. "Oh, well," I glance around at the table and the five bubbling glasses, "champagne would be lovely."

"Very well."

BURP.

Brenda Sue shoots a look at Berta.

"What? It's a compliment to the chef!" She grins at James. "That's what the Japs say, right?"

He belches back, "RAAAAAHT."

A roundish man in a pinstriped suit approaches the podium. He taps the microphone twice and clears his throat. "GOOOOOOOOOOOOD MORNING STORMBURST FRIENDS!"

"GOOD MORNING!"

He smiles. "I hope you're all getting enough to eat this morning."

We all laugh.

"I see some new faces around the room, so allow me to introduce myself a moment, I'm Ted Kinnedlicky, president of StormBurst Northwest Regional Division.

Harold, Brenda Sue, Bruce and most of the people around the room stand immediately to applaud.

Ted nods his head and smiles, "Thank you." He waits for the applause to die down and clears his throat again. "Now, first off, I'd like it if we could go ahead and honor this quarter's REGIONAL STORMBURST DEALERS OF THE MONTH!"

Applause fills the room once more.

"COME ON UP HERE!" He smiles and looks around the room, waiting.

Brenda Sue prompts me, "Go on, Diana, that's you!"

I navigate my way between round tables and hurried waiters to the front of the room where Ted and two other men stand beside me.

The applause continues as Ted whispers, "Now which of you is which—you *guys* I mean—not hard to tell which one you are, little lady!" He winks at me.

The woman who gave me my nametag approaches with large plaques in her arms, each shaped like a flat, silver cloud.

Ted glances at his notes on the podium. "For the month of April, with twenty-six sales, coming all the way from Spokane, let us congratulate MR. OMAR SHANE!" Ted shakes his hand and the woman hands him his plaque. "Now, for the month of May, with THIRTY-FOUR sales, coming to us from the Woodburn office, let's give a hand for MR. URI PETRANOVICH!" Uri shakes Ted's hand and accepts his plaque, and shakes the woman's hand, then Ted's hand again. "And let's not overlook one of StormBurst's most *attractive* sales *men…*" Ted pauses while the room fills with laughter—and a whistle. He winks at me. "For the month of June, with thirty-eight sales, from Harveston: MISS DIANA JENSEN!"

I shake his hand and accept the plaque with my name engraved on it.

He kisses my cheek.

Harold shakes my hand and Brenda Sue gives me a hug, just before setting my plaque in the center of our table.

Ted adjusts the microphone. "Now, I'd like to introduce our motivational speaker for today. Please give a warm welcome to Medford's Dealer of the

Month for *sixteen months straight*, RICH DAVIES!" He shakes hands with the man in the camel-colored suit.

"Hi there, how are you doing this morning?"

Everyone mumbles.

He clears his throat. "I'd like to take you back through time, to a time when I, well," he breathes hard into the microphone, then looks up at us, "I was just a shell of the man you see standing before you today." He nods and takes a deep breath. "You see, I used to drink—oh, not a little bit!" He grins. "I couldn't keep a job, and finally, my wife left me—who can blame her, right?" He shrugs his shoulders. "And it just seemed like no matter what I did, I couldn't win. Have you ever felt that way in your life?"

"Yeah!"

"Yep!"

"Ah-haw."

"But I know that one day, one glorious day, the good lord must have been smiling down on me. He brought someone into my life who would change it for the better—forever." He gestures toward table five, "Larry Hillman, would you please stand up? Come on, Larry!" Rich starts the applause.

The man stands with scarlet cheeks and smiles and nods at the rest of the room. He waves briefly and sinks back into his seat.

"Larry Hillman showed up, literally, on my doorstep one day. One *very rainy* day. You see, his car had broken down on the highway, just a little ways from my house. Well, while we sat there waiting for the tow truck to arrive," he gestures toward table five again, "I was feeling sorry for Larry the same way I'd been feeling sorry for myself for years. And that's when I told Larry, I believe I said, 'man, if isn't one damned thing, it's another, isn't it?' I hope you'll pardon my French, ladies." He smiles. "But do you know that Larry didn't seem bothered by it at all? Here he was, with his car broken down on the side of the highway, having no idea what it would cost to get fixed, and soaked to the bone to boot. And do you know what Larry said to me?"

He looks around the silent room.

"He said, and I quote: You won't hear *me* belly-achin!"

Laughter rolls across the room.

"And then he smiled at me. He smiled this big, incredible smile that I'll never forget. I was so impressed—I mean, I was *stunned* by this man's sheer positivity. I couldn't speak!" He blinks toward the ceiling a moment. "I mean, I just knew that if that was *me* in his shoes, well, I'm not proud to say it but I'd be cursing like a sailor!" He raises his eyebrows, then smiles. "That's when

Larry told me about the thing that had transformed him into the positive person that he is, that had changed his life for the better, had given him a real sense of purpose, a sense of pride, had brought comfort and security to him and his wife and children. And can you guess what that thing was?"

Everyone shouts, "STORMBURST!"

Rich nods, "That's right. And I knew that just from looking at Larry and seeing the way he conducted himself, and the true happiness there was shining in his eyes, I knew that if this company could turn his life around and bring him such—such absolute *joy* in just being alive, there was a chance that maybe it could do something for me, too."

Rich takes a sip of water.

"Well, people, that was five years ago. And this man, this man right here," he gestures to himself, "has made a complete turnaround! After I joined Storm-Burst, I began to take some responsibility for my life. I saw that it was all up to me if I was going to succeed, and they taught me how to do just that. Instead of being a guy who just let life *happen* to me, and complained when I didn't like the outcome, I became the *master* of my own destiny…" He nods. "I'll bet a lot of you out there know exactly what I mean, don't you?"

We nod.

"Today, I am a recovering alcoholic."

Everyone claps and cheers.

"I own a brand new car, paid for with *cash*…I go to church *every* Sunday, without fail. And…"

He waits for the room to quiet down.

"And I have a beautiful wife, of four months now," he gestures to table eight.

The room fills with applause, cheers and whistles.

He shouts to the ceiling, "And I LOVE MY LIFE!"

Everyone stands and claps.

Ted Kinnedlicky approaches the podium and shakes Rich's hand, then pulls him in for a big bear hug. "Let's hear it for RICH DAVIES!"

Rich leans in toward the microphone, "And Larry Hillman!" He takes his seat back at table eight and kisses the woman beside him.

Ted readjusts the microphone. "Now, to lead us in a song this morning, would you please welcome the lovely Miss Natalie Jenkins!"

She bends the microphone down a little further. "Good morning. Most of you out there should be familiar with this song, but for anyone who isn't, just listen a little while and you should get the hang of it." She smiles gently, then moistens her lips. Natalie Jenkins opens her mouth wide and takes a deep breath as she closes her eyes:

> Show…them the wah-ter.

Half the people in the room join in:

> Show…them the wah-ter.
> Show…them the wah-ter,

Natalie drops her chin as her voice sinks lower,

> And close…the…sale…

She shouts, "Everybody!"

> Show…them the wah-ter.
> Show…them the wah-hah-hah-ah-ter.
> Show…them the wah-ter,
> And close…the…sale…

"A little faster now!"

> Show them the water.
> Show them the water.

"Oh-ho lord!"

> Show them the water,
> And close…the…sale!

We continue singing as Natalie begins to rock back and forth at the podium. Her eyes have closed, her nose wrinkles up, and she begins to improvise:

> Show the water…ooh!
> Show the water…ooh!
> Oh, oh, baby, I said show-show the water!

People begin to clap and stomp in syncopated rhythm. Natalie's hands reach high into the air and she rocks side to side as we sing another round of:

> Show…them the water.
> Show…them the wah-hah-hah-ah-ter.
> Show…them the water,
> And close…the…sale.

"Now listen people!"

> If there's one thing that you…
> You got to do now!

We respond:

> Show…them the water…

She cries:

> Let those people
> SEE what it's all about!

We shout:

> And close…the…sale!

"Let's sing it now!"

> Show…them the water.

"LOUDER!"

> SHOW…THEM THE WAH-HAH-HAH-AH-TER!
> SHOW…THEM THE WATER,
> AND CLOSE…THE…SALE!

We rock and sway, clap and stomp, and table six breaks into harmony. Ted Kinnedlicky raises his hands toward the ceiling and closes his eyes as he sings. The party at table twenty-three begins to dance in a circle as they sing.

"Lord almighty!"

> Show…them the water,
> And close…the…sale.

"This side of the room now!"

> Show…them the water.
> Show…them the wah-hah-hah-ah-ter.

"Now this side starts!"
At table four, there's a woman lifting her skirt and clambering up onto a chair. She regains her balance atop the table and shouts, "Hallelujah! Amen!" Natalie smiles, "A little softer now."

> Show…them the water.

"Softer still…"
We whisper:

> Show…them the wah-hah-hah-ah-ter.

She gestures for us to slow down.

> Show…them the water,

Natalie cues us to stop. She tilts her head back and cries out an octave above:

> And mah-hay-aaaake…
> Thah-hah-hah-hah-hah-hah-haaaht…

She gasps for air.

> Say-hay-ay-ay-ay-ay…

Her fingers flicker through the air.

> That say-hay-aaaaaaaaaaale…

Her chest heaves in the silence; her head sinks down toward the podium.

Somewhere in the back of the room a pair of hands slaps together.

Slowly, the rest of us begin to applaud, then cheer, then raise our glasses to Natalie Jenkins, who smiles and nods and finally takes a deep bow.

Ted shouts into the microphone, "CAN THIS GIRL SING, OR WHAT?" There is even more applause as Ted hugs Natalie, then kisses her on the cheek.

PART IV

❀

"DOES THAT SOUND GOOD TO YOU?"

"Hi, is this Delores?"

"No, you've got the wrong number!"

"Wait! I'm sorry, *Doris*, you see, your friend Carrie wrote your name on the back of my card—"

"I don't know anyone named Carrie!"

"Oh, really?"

"Good night!"

"Well—isn't this Doris Green?"

"Yes."

"Oh, what a relief! I'm sorry to bother you this evening, ma'am, but I did want to let you know that, although you didn't win the grand prize of a fabulous new speedboat, you were selected for another great prize: a set of heirloom-quality stainless steel steak knives. Congratulations!"

"Steak knives? Well, I—oh, are you the little girl who stopped by here last week?"

"No, that was my *friend* Carrie. She's on vacation right now but she made me promise to call you if you won anything."

"Well, you tell Carrie thank you very much. Will they be coming in the mail?"

"No, but I'll tell you what, Doris. I'll deliver them to you in person!"

"Oh, you don't have to do that."

"It's no problem at all. But you know what…oh, I hate to put you on the spot like this, Doris, but you see, I'm doing this new job to help pay for my college tuition next year, and if you could do me just a small favor…"

"Well, what is it?"

"Oh, well, I know it sounds a little silly, but you see, this company is *paying* me just to show people this little demonstration—a household gadget of sorts. It doesn't take very long, but as you can imagine, every time I can get somebody to watch, well, it all adds up, you know? And with tuition getting so high these days—"

"Well, I suppose I—say, I don't have to buy anything do I?"

"Oh, no. Not at all!"

"Well, I guess that would be all right."

"Great! Then I can drop off your steak knives and show you my presentation at the same time! Say, when would be a good time for you and—oh, I don't mean to be rude, but I'm supposed to ask if there's a Mr. Green too?"

"Oh, well, there *is* a Mr. Green, dear, and we're both retired people—so just about any time, I suppose."

"Oh, super. Let me see, would Thursday at two work for the both of you?"

"Thursday? Oh, sure, dear."

"Fantastic! Thanks a lot, Mrs. Green. I really appreciate it."

"Oh, it's no problem at all."

"I'll see you folks on Thursday at two!"

❧   ❧   ❧

It's a cold call from the latest round of speedboat entries, so I already know the neighborhood—it's James's favorite development where he claims, "The housewives practically bend over the minute you knock on the door." I assume he means he's made a lot of sales in the area; I know I have.

The houses look just the same except that the garages are on opposite sides. Two front doors are side by side, then two garage doors, then two front doors. I roll along down Magnolia Street. Pick-up truck. Station wagon. 4-door sedan. Pick-up truck. Sedan. Station wagon. Pick-up truck.

I side step along the driveway between the juniper hedge and the pick-up truck, careful not to scrape the paint with my demo case. Marcie sits on the step on the front porch in a cloud of smoke. She can't be a year older than me. I note the black T-shirt with big red lips and a tongue stretched across her chest.

"Hey." I reach my hand out toward her. "I'm Diana."

She takes another drag, blows the smoke aside, and shakes the ashes off her cigarette before finally shaking my hand. "Hey." She nods over toward the toddler playing silently in the bark dust. "That's Lily. You got any kids?"

"No, not yet." I grin.

"Well, enjoy your peace and quiet while you got it, man." She half-smiles and takes another drag.

"Yeah, I know what you mean. My, uh, sister's got two already, and I don't think she's slept in like four years."

Marcie walks over toward Lily and stomps out her cigarette in the brown grass. "You need some help with that stuff?" She lugs Lily up onto her hip.

"Nah, that's all right…you've got your hands full already." I follow them both into the living room. "Hey, Reggie, the StormBurst Lady's here. Can you help her get set up—I've got to change the brat again." She disappears down the hall. I set my demo case between the playpen and entertainment center.

Reggie greets me from the sofa with a nod. "Oh, hey, you want something to drink? We got Coors and Bud Light?" He pulls at the threads of his fraying cut-off jeans.

"Nah, I'm all right. Thanks."

WHOOG.

"Jesus Christ! What's that?"

Reggie laughs, "Ain't you never seen a St. Bernard before?" He takes a sip of beer.

The grizzly bends the patio screen door with the weight of his snout. He backs up a little and spills a puddle of drool onto the cement patio.

"Looks like he's good in a drought—got his own water supply and everything!"

Reggie snorts and sets down his beer.

I study the framed poster of a red Ferrari on the wall above Reggie's head. "So what's your dog's name?"

Reggie scratches his nuts and stares at the sports channel.

"I just have to get a few more things from my car. I'll be right back."

Scratch. Scratch.

But then: as soon as I'm ready to begin, Reggie turns off the TV. And Marcie, Lily and Reggie all quietly watch from the couch. Saint Bernard watches from the patio.

"So when somebody tells you to believe them, you want to see the proof *first*, don't you?"

Marcie and Reggie grin at each other a moment, then Marcie says, "Yep, definitely."

And I'm off and selling, like a hot knife through the small-town butter of their lives. SLICE—and I make them say "yes". SLICE—and I make them both nod. SLICE—and I have them shrieking with surprise and delight.

"Ain't that freakin' amazing?"

"Yeah!"

And when I ask them to get their vacuum for me, Marcie's already on her way. I could sell these people anything, but I try not to look too confident. After all, I'm just there to demonstrate. I can hear Marcie fumbling with something down the hall.

"Oh, I should tell you to like brace yourselves for this next part, 'cause everybody totally freaks out when they see what I'm about to show you, man." I bulge my eyes for emphasis. "It's pretty intense."

Reggie waits on the couch, holding Lily on his knee. He grins, sips, and scratches with anticipation.

Here she comes down the hall.

SLICE—

Marcie rolls a StormBurst across the living room carpet and beams.

Reggie removes Lily from his lap and sets her on the couch beside him. "Dude, it's like the coolest vacuum, man." He nods.

Gulp.

"Well, I'm, uh, glad you like it." I stare at droid number two.

Marcie sits on the sofa with a grin. "Yeah, so when you offered to come show us the new model, and bring the steak knives and everything, we couldn't wait to see it!"

I look at their StormBurst, then at mine. "Right!" I look at their StormBurst again. I take a deep breath without dropping my smile. "Well then…here it is! Now you've seen it! And you've got your steak knives!" I stand.

Reggie sets his beer on the coffee table. "So what new features does it got?"

"Oh? Well…" I look back and forth at each machine again. "Um, if you liked the *old* StormBurst," I point to the machine on my left, "you'll *love* the new one," I point to the StormBurst on my right. "For example, the, uh, Storm Chaser, yeah, the *Storm Chaser* has been changed, as you can see." I point out the gold-colored wand. "Yeah, and the new Storm Chaser practically drives itself…man!"

Marcie takes a swallow of Reggie's beer. "That sounds good to me!" She looks at Reggie.

"It does? Oh, great." I try to recall where I left off in the demonstration. "Hey, Reggie! Why don't you take this bad boy for a test drive—"

Growl—grind—whoosh.

"Here you go, yeah, squeeze the handle, just like that. Do you feel how it propels itself?"

"Oh, totally!"

"It's like driving a vacuum cleaning *Ferrari*, isn't it?"

"Dude, that's fuckin' awesome!" His eyes twinkle like Christmas lights.

"Yeah, it's like the most powerful one you can buy! The best, man. And look! If you want to stop all of a sudden, like to pick up one of Lily's toys or something, you just let go, go ahead for a second, yeah, and you see, it stops completely. Isn't that cool?"

"Totally!"

Marcie beams. "Yeah, the old one doesn't do that!"

"It doesn't? Oh—yeah, right."

Marcie and Reggie sit back down on the sofa, on each side of Lily. Reggie pulls a Marlborough out of the pack on the coffee table and lights up.

"Let's see, what else is new…"

"I like the gold buckles too!" Marcie offers.

"Oh, yeah, the old ones were, uh, green weren't they? Hmmm…yeah, this is the *Gold* edition."

"And it's a lot more powerful than ours, isn't it, hun?" Marcie pulls out a Marlborough for herself, and Reggie offers up his lighter.

I glance at the new StormBurst. "Yeah, well, I suppose so—"

"Oh, it totally is." Scratch, scratch.

Marcie holds the cigarette between her lips as she pulls Lily onto her lap. "So how much are they now?" Lily reaches up for her mom's cigarette.

"Oh, it's fourteen thirty-seven." I nod my head and wait.

Marcie taps the ashes off the cigarette and Lily reaches toward the ashtray. "Mine!"

Marcie takes another drag and blows the smoke aside. "And that includes all these extra attachments, right?"

"Yep."

"Well it hasn't gone up too much, has it?" Reggie finishes off the beer.

"No, we got this one two years ago, and it was, I think, twelve sixty, right? We just finished paying it off a couple months ago."

"Oh really?"

"Yeah, talk about good timing." Scratch.

"Right."

Marcie clamps the cigarette between her lips and carries Lily over to the playpen. "And this new one is so much better."

"Yeah. Well, you know…if you guys decide you want to go ahead and get the new StormBurst today, I should be able to get you some credit for your old model."

Marcie wipes something out of the corner of Lily's eye. "Really? Like trading in your used car or something?"

"Used car? Yeah, something like that." I feel my stomach gurgle.

"Can we get the shampooer too?" Marcie stubs out her Marlborough. "I didn't think we needed it last time, but now we can totally use it."

Reggie squeezes the empty beer can in his hand. "Yeah, how much is it for the shampoo head?"

"Well, it's one seventy-five…or I can give it to you for FREE. Whichever one you prefer." I shrug and smile.

They both grin.

"Well how do we get it for *free*?"

"It's really easy—all you have to do is just give me the names of four different friends of yours—but they all have to live in different homes and be the heads of the household, right? Like they could really buy this thing if they wanted to—'cause I'd *hate* to make anybody feel bad who couldn't qualify for a payment plan."

They nod.

"And after I do all four demonstrations, I'll swing by and drop off your shampooer FREE. Isn't that easy?"

"Totally!" Reggie grins at Marcie.

Marcie nods as she exhales smoke to the side.

"Cool. Now let me call my boss and see what kind of a deal I can get you guys, all right?"

"Phone's in the kitchen!"

"Right on—oh! And how do you guys want to pay for your new StormBurst?"

"Well, we got a really good payment plan last time—what was it, Reg? Well, it was a two-year plan. Can we get something like that this time too?"

"I'll see what I can do. Oh, and how much do you want to put down today?"

Marcie looks over at Reggie, who scratches and thinks. "Fifty bucks okay?"

"I think that'll work."

The kitchen sink is filled to the rim with dirty Tupperware containers, baby bottles and spoons. Flies buzz above the enormous dog dish labeled "Bear."

"Hi, Brenda Sue. Here's the deal: they have an old StormBurst and they'd like to upgrade to the new one, on a two-year payment plan with fifty down." I can hear Brenda Sue writing down the information. "So what kind of a credit should I give them for the old machine?"

"Well, see if they'll take three hundred…if they're willing to go with that, well, hold on, let me double check the figures for the payment plan…"

I write her final numbers on the clipboard.

"So guys, how does a *three hundred dollar* credit sound?" I grin as wide as I can.

"Right on!" Reggie punches the air with his fist.

WHOOG.

The heavy tail whaps against the screen.

They give me seven different referrals and we agree that, statistically, four out of seven ought to cooperate. I'll promise to give them a call in case there's a problem. "So, I'll see you soon with that FREE shampooer, all right?"

"Definitely!" Marcie waves and Reggie scratches his nuts as I load their old StormBurst—with the green buckles—and the Storm Chaser—that doesn't drive itself—into the Rabbit.

I enter the lobby and casually set down the old StormBurst, then walk over to wave at Brenda Sue through her office window. I return to the reception counter, where Berta gnaws away at a burger, and in the time it takes me to ask if I can have a fry, and for her to respond, "HELL NO!" Brenda Sue is at my side.

"Oh my GOD!"

"Yes, my child?"

"But Diana, that model can't be more than two years old."

"Two years and a month."

"But the only difference between that one and the one you just sold them is the Storm Chaser!"

"And don't forget the buckles." I wink.

There's a flash behind her green eyes, but the smile is slow to come.

Berta peers over the edge of the bar and sees the StormBurst parked on the carpet. "Hot damn!"

I cock my head to the side. "Got any ice you need sold to Eskimos, darlin'?"

Brenda Sue giggles and snorts. Her eyebrows raise and she lifts her hand in the air, snapping her fingers in as she cackles: "You go, girl! Wahoo!" She pats me on the shoulder. "See, I *told* you I had a good feeling about you!" She wraps her arms around me and squeezes me hard against her soft bosom.

Berta laughs too and says, "All right, I'll give you a fry—" then she sticks out her tongue, coated in a layer of half-chewed fries.

❧   ❧   ❧

A few days later, Harold asks me to join him in Brenda Sue's office. Brenda Sue is waiting behind her big desk with her little hands folded under her chin.

"Have a seat, Diana."

I sink into the big, padded chair.

Harold boosts himself onto my side of the desk and sits facing me, just to the right of Brenda Sue.

Brenda Sue rubs the palms of her hands over the writing pad on her desk. "Diana, what I'm about to share with you is not to go beyond these four walls, understood?"

I look out the window at the end of her desk and see no one standing in the hallway. "Okay."

"Great. Now you know that Harold and I are *business* people, don't you?"

"I certainly do!" I smile at them both.

They smile back. "Good."

"Now as *business* people, we always have in our minds a *long term business plan.* Do you know what I mean?"

"I think so."

"Terrific." She folds her hands. "As part of our *long term* business plan, Harold and I have been considering opening a second office—in Cornston."

Harold crosses his ankles, "That's your hometown, isn't it, Diana?" He rubs his nose.

"Oh, yes it is."

"Well, as savvy business people, we know that a second office is nothing to rush into. So, you see, Diana, we've been waiting for the right time..." she picks up her pen and taps it on the writing pad, "and the right person."

Gulp.

"Diana, what would you say if I told you that you could make $70,000 a year without doing a single demonstration?"

"Heh-heh." She raises her eyebrows at me and I feel myself sitting up in the big, padded chair. "Really?"

Brenda Sue pulls out a clean sheet of paper and begins writing as she says, "That's right, Diana. With just ten *average* salespeople working under you—"

"Did you say *seventeen* or *seventy*?"

Harold snickers, "Seven-O, Diana."

And before I know it I have all the statistical evidence in front of me that I can—without a doubt—make $70,000 a year without even doing demonstrations.

Harold chimes in. "Now, we're not prepared to make you an official offer *today*—"

"Holy snots! I could never make that kind of money teaching!"

Brenda Sue's eyes flash up from the paper. "Well, that's why I wanted to let you know ahead of time, so you'll know what your options *really* are, Diana."

"Right." I sink back into the big, padded chair. "My options."

❧   ❧   ❧

Kerouac is waiting for me, sprawled across the doormat. "Hey, there, fella!" I scratch the top of his dirty head. "Kenny's *again*?"

"Vvrr."

I check the mailbox and find my water bill and the first postcard from Christina. "Well, it's about time—it's a letter from our elusive roommate."

"Vvrr. Vvrr."

> Hey, Diana!
>
> Santiago is spectacular, the people are super friendly, and guess what? I'm in love!!! Will tell-all in September. Still returning the 12th, hopefully, as planned. See you then!
>
> Love ya,
>
> Chris

I look back down at the cat. "Well, how do you like that? Not even a return address."

"YEE-OWL."

"Hey, I've been saving something for you—come on." I open the screen door carefully above his long, lax body. I hold it a moment and wait.

He sits upright, stands, stretches, yawns, claws the doormat a couple of times and walks straight through the living room to the kitchen, no longer rubbing his gray side against the walls to find his way. He sits on his haunches in the middle of the linoleum, waiting as I latch the screen door.

I put some treats in a bowl on the floor and he wolfs them down. I fill a bowl of cold water for him, and he laps it with zeal. "Too bad I don't have some real food for you…"

"YEE-OWL."

"I know. I have to go to the store."

"YEE-OWL." He sits back on his haunches, not-staring straight at me.

"Ah-ha!" I open a can of tuna and put half of it into his bowl. And while he's hard at work on his tuna fish, I mix my half with a little mayo and relish and smear it across a slice of bread. I set the bread in the new Italiamatic Toaster Oven and set the dial to auto-sense. "Well, it's not steak dinner, but it's something. Tell ya what, later I'll pick up a pizza for me and some cans of that Classy Cat wet food you like."

Kerouac works on the bowl until it looks empty to me. Then he licks the invisible layer of oil from the sides of the bowl until he's convinced it's thoroughly clean.

"Good job." I scratch his head. "I need a bath—a cold bath." I pull my sweaty T-shirt over my head and grab a McClanahan's Amber from the fridge. "You know, you look like you could use a bath, yourself, fella."

He sneezes.

"Ah, don't worry, I wouldn't do it to you." Kerouac follows me to the bathroom and sits beside me while I wait for the tub to fill. I take a couple of Tums from the bottle by the sink, chew a few times and wash them down with the amber. "Well, Kerouac, it's like this: I know a lot of people could never pull it off—just look at how many dealers have come and gone in the three months I've been there."

I take a new towel from the cabinet, plush with Egyptian cotton and embroidered with a purple letter *D*, and set it beside the tub.

"But then: look at me. I've broken every record at that office. And I'm still out-selling every dealer there." I step out of my shorts and underwear. "And it's not like James said—it doesn't make any difference if they know who I am or not!" I unhook my aquati-bra and drop it on the floor. "And it's not like I really want to teach or anything, or be an archaeologist. I just didn't know what else I might do—and make a living at, you know?"

"YEE-OWL." Yawn.

"I mean, maybe this *is* my passion."

Kerouac inspects my pile of clothes and curls up in a strategic spot.

"I guess I never really understood what my options were before."

I toss a purple bath bead into the water and watch as it floats away from the faucet.

"To think, with just an average team working out of my office—and let's face it Kerouac! With my guidance and support, they would be way above *average* because you know I could give them way better training than Harold gave us—my sales staff would break every record known to StormBurst because I'll give them *real* tips, on everything from their clothing and hair to how to relate to different kinds of people. And there sure are a lot of different people out there, Kerouac!" I take another Tums from the bottle on the counter and chew. "Yes, indeedy. My sales staff will be genuinely happy because they'll be genuinely successful, and they'll stick around for a long time because I'll teach them how to do their jobs with integrity—"

"YEE-OWL." Sneeze.

The tub is full.

"I'll even provide donuts at *all* of the Monday morning meetings, not just the ones with new dealers. And most *importantly*, I'll recruit lots of college students from right there in Cornston, and I'll teach every one of them how they too can make *good* money while they're in school—and not have to wear polyester pants and plastic visors, working for minimum wage. They'll just have to say the magic words: 'I'm not a salesman. I'm a *college student*. This is just how I'm earning my tuition...and paying for books.' And they'll get rich, like me. And then I'll just keep getting richer and richer. And I won't even have to go on a single demonstration. Or call for appointments."

"YEE-OWL." The cat paws at the closed bathroom door.

"And the customers! After while, we'll develop such a great reputation in Cornston that the customers will call us up and even come in off the street asking for demonstrations. Not even demonstrations! They'll just come in to buy a StormBurst—it will be like a regular store, where the customers *choose* to come and shop because they've already heard so many good things about the StormBurst. It will be so...different."

I step into the tub.

"Holy snots that's cold!"

Kerouac sits on the pile of clothes, not-staring at me with his two eye-holes.

❧   ❧   ❧

"Hello?"

"Hi, is this Dave?"

"Yea, who's this?"

"Hi, Dave. My name's Diana and your friend Reggie thought I should give you a call—"

"Oh did he?"

"Well, you see, I'm a college student and, well, I'm trying to earn some extra money for my tuition next year—"

"Are you?"

"Yeah. And I'm working for this company that will *pay* me just to show their product to you—and demonstrate it right in your home!"

"Oh?"

"Yeah, can you believe it?"

"Sounds pretty good. So, uh, what do you want to show me?"

"Well, it's kind of hard to describe, but I think you'll *really* like it—"

"Oh, heh-hey! Like I always say, I'll try anything once."

"Great. Now in order for me to get credit—"

"So do you wear anything special when you do this?"

"Excuse me?"

"Oh, just tell me what you're wearing right now."

"Right now?"

"You're not *blond* by any chance, are you?"

"Well, actually—"

"That's all right—blond wigs do it for me too!"

"Look, Reggie *and Marcie* both wanted me to call you because—"

"Any chance you got a little nurse's uniform? I'd *love* for you to come on over and *nurse* me back to health!"

"Look, *pal*—"

"Will you take my temperature, too?"

"That's not—"

"Yeah, with a skirt so short, I can almost see your—"

"I've got to go."

"Oh, don't stop now, honey, I was just getting—"

Everything about her is purple: Her dress, her shoes, her earrings, her finger-nails—the highlights in her hair.

"What a fun summer job!"

"Yeah, it sure is. Say, your dahlias are magnificent!"

We contemplate the lavender dinner-plate-sized blossoms surrounding her porch.

"I know. Can you believe I got them on the Internet?"

Geraldine Kemper sets the tray on the coffee table and pours the iced tea into our glasses. She sets my glass on a purple cocktail napkin beside the Hummel music box.

"So you collect these—*sculptures*?"

"Oh, yes! Aren't they just darling! It's amazing what bargains you can find nowadays on the Internet! If you're good at bidding, of course."

"I'll bet."

I run the extension cord across the living room, quickly analyzing the Berber carpet for tread and wear patterns.

"So, what do you do, Mrs. Kemper?"

"Oh! Call me Geraldine! I haven't been married in fourteen years!" She snorts.

"Okay, Geraldine."

"So you're a college student, Diana?"

"Oh, yes I am." I test the Ray O'Sun.

"Heavens! What's that?"

"This is what we call the Ray O'Sun. Because it's just like a ray of sunlight shining in through your window, now isn't it?"

"Well, you're right! Look at that!"

"Say, have you ever been to Ireland, Geraldine?"

"Oh, no! But I would give anything to go."

"Well," I grin, "say no more because before we're through here, I'm going to take you to Ireland! Does that sound good to you?"

She chuckles, "Does it ever!"

"Terrific." I click on the Ray O'Sun once more, "Now, would you believe that the average home accumulates 40 *pounds* of dust *per year?*"

She clutches her chest. "You're kidding me!"

"I wouldn't lie to you, Geraldine!"

"And did you know that, according to the EPA, indoor air can be as much as a hundred times *more* polluted than the air outside?"

"Oh, sakes alive!" She grins, fascinated.

"Well, my friend, wouldn't it be nice if we could make the air inside our homes as clean and fresh as it is in the Irish countryside?"

"You bet!"

"Do you see all those dust particles, and bits of pollen, and dust, and filth and *everything* floating around in there?"

"I sure do!"

"That's what most vacuum cleaners leave behind! Isn't that *disgusting?*"

"I'll say!"

We chuckle together.

"You're just going to *love* this, Geraldine. Watch!"

Growl—grind—whoosh.

"Do you see any dust coming out of here?"

"I can't say I do!"

Click.

"Now, can you get your vacuum for me?'

I can already see I could push her over with one finger. I speed through the rest of the demonstration, cutting to the most exciting parts.

"Oh, good heavens! Look at that cushion! It's flat as a pancake!"

"Are we having any fun yet, Geraldine?"

"Oh, we sure are, Diana!"

"Do you feel how that glides along—"

"Yes!"

"So smooth and easy—"

"Yes!"

"And how it practically drives itself?"

"I do!"

"It's like a vacuum cleaning Ferrari, isn't it, Geraldine?"

"It is!"

"Did you ever guess there was such a powerful, handy, complete home cleaning device in you life?"

"No!"

"Don't you just love the way that genuine horse hair bristle takes the dust right off of your Hummels?"

"I sure do!"

I sit down a moment on the purple sofa. My head is spinning. I take a sip of iced tea, followed by a long, deep breath.

Geraldine sidles up to me on the sofa. "I had no idea this would be so much fun!"

I smile and take another sip. "Well, we're not finished yet. Are you ready to go to Ireland?"

"You bet, Diana!"

"Now for this part, you'll want to just relax and close your eyes—get real comfortable now!"

"Okay, Diana!" She puts her feet up on the coffee table and leans back against the purple cushions. She can't seem to stop smiling.

Growl—grind—whoosh.

Slurp. Slurp.

"TAKE A LONG, DEEP, SOOTHING BREATH—"

"OH MY GOODNESS! OH MY! WOW! HOLY COW—"

"JUST RELAX NOW! REMEMBER, YOU'RE ON VACATION IN IRE-
LAND!"

She laughs, but keeps quiet.

Click.

"So wouldn't you agree that the StormBurst is a pretty amazing machine?"

"Oh, you bet I would, Diana! It's incredible! Just incredible."

"And you can see how the StormBurst can keep you healthier—"

"Oh, definitely."

"And, Geraldine, isn't your health the most important thing of all?"

"You bet."

"So if I could make it possible for you to own a StormBurst today, you'd be
pretty interested, wouldn't you?"

"Diana, I would absolutely love you to death if you could!"

"Well terrific! We take cash or credit, and we have a number of payment
plans available. Which would work best for you?"

"Oh, well, you take credit cards?"

"We sure do!"

She chews her thumbnail as she asks, "So, well, how does that work though?
Do you have a machine?"

"All I need to do is copy down your information and get your signature!"

"Great!"

But then: Brenda Sue calls me into her office the following afternoon.

"It seems we have a little problem with your good friend Geraldine. Her
card isn't *working*." Brenda Sue's nostrils flare.

"Not working?"

"Not working."

"Oh, that's odd."

"I'd like to think so. You're going to have to call her up Diana, and
straighten this out." She clears her throat.

"Well, but, what do I say?"

"What you say is this: 'Hi Geraldine, this is your good buddy, Diana, here at
Chin's StormBurst, and unless you come up with some money to cover this
fourteen hundred dollar machine I left in your care, there's gonna be HELL TO
PAY!"

Gulp.

Brenda Sue folds her hands under her chin and smiles at me. "And if that
doesn't work, you might ask if she has another credit card she'd like to use, and

we can take the number right over the telephone. Or if she'd like for us to work out a payment plan that will comfortably fit into her budget."

"Right."

I pick up the phone for the third time, this time dialing Geraldine's complete phone number.

"Hello?"

"Hi, Geraldine. This is Diana Jensen, I showed you the StormBurst yesterday?"

"Oh, hi Diana, how are you?"

"Oh, well I'm a little concerned, Geraldine. For some reason that credit card you gave me isn't…going through. Do you have another one you'd like me to try?"

"Oh, dear! How embarrassing! Of course I do, sweetie! Wait just a moment while I get my purse!"

Click.

The line is dead.

I stare at the phone a moment, then press redial.

"Hi! This is Geraldine! Sorry I missed your call! You know what to do!"

BEEP.

"Geraldine, this is Diana—somehow we got disconnected. Please call me back here at Chin's StormBurst with your other credit card number—or we can figure out a payment plan or something like that. Okay? The number here is 596–2444. Thank you."

I take a long, deep breath, but it isn't soothing.

"I left a message. How long do we give her?"

"Well, by law she has 72 hours to change her mind about the sale. If she doesn't have the money, let's hope she *changes her mind!*"

"Well, but she really likes it! I think she'll want to keep it."

Brenda Sue's eyes flash, "That's exactly what I'm afraid of."

I call twice a day for the next two days, in between my demos, and check with Berta, but there's no sign of life from Geraldine.

"Shut the door, Diana."

I sit down in the big, padded chair.

"I was hoping it wouldn't come to this, but that *woman* has put you in a difficult situation, Diana, and there's no two ways about it."

"She put *me* in a difficult situation?"

"That's right. She stole your merchandise."

"Well, but she didn't really *steal* anything. She just—she just hasn't—"

"Diana, you're a smart girl, but you've got too soft a heart sometimes. But your heart's not going to be so soft when you see *one thousand four hundred and thirty-seven dollars* subtracted from your next paycheck, is it?"

Gulp. "What do I do?"

"Well, the best thing I can recommend is you surprise her at home. Real friendly, though, you know. And you don't leave until you've got that damned StormBurst!"

"But—"

"But nothing. Do you want Geraldine to buy this machine or do you want to buy it for her?"

"Well—"

"And you know darn well Geraldine can't pay for it, so find somebody else who can! We're not checking out another machine to you until you get this resolved, Diana. I'm sorry but that's just the way it works around here with this kind of situation."

I reschedule my demos for the later in the week and drive to her neighborhood the first thing in the morning. I sit in the Rabbit, a few houses down from Geraldine's and pretend I'm a cop, undercover, sipping my coffee and waiting. I can't tell if she's home or not.

Gradually, the neighborhood kids line up for the bus at the corner. And then there's a flash of purple and I'm off, jogging down the sidewalk.

"Geraldine! Good morning!"

She doesn't seem to hear me and continues walking toward her car.

"Geraldine! It's me, Diana!" She looks up nervously.

"Oh, hi there! How are you!" She smiles. "I've been meaning to call you—I've just been so *busy* lately!"

"Well, I totally understand, Geraldine." I try to give her a reassuring smile. "Listen, I just need to figure out a payment plan for you or something—for that amazing new StormBurst that I left here the other day?"

Geraldine fidgets with her keys.

"Unless of course you were having second thoughts about it—'cause if you are, I could just take it back with me today. I mean, I know you may have felt a little pressured by my being here, trying so hard to make the sale and everything."

She glances up from her keys. "Well, um…"

"We could just load it into my car right now, and you wouldn't have to worry about it another minute. Does that sound good to you?"

"Well, okay. Yeah, I guess so."

"I understand, Geraldine. People are entitled to change their minds—I change mine all the time!" I chuckle a little as we walk toward her front.

❦   ❦   ❦

The garbage can is already halfway filled with misshapen ice cream cones. I pull another cone from the long, tall box with the smiling cartoon kids. Carefully as I can, I lift the lever for vanilla soft-serve and out it gushes with the force of a breaking dam. I take hold of the cone with both hands, leaning into the oncoming ice cream with all my weight, but it's just too much—

"This is Larry from KPRN reminding you…if it's yellow, let it mellow…if it's not…you decide."

Kerouac is sprawled across my ankles, shackling me to the bed. I try to move my feet, "Vvrr, vvrr," but it's not easy. He's getting fat.

"Let's go, Fat Cat. Monday morning meeting's on its way, and I should be too." I reach over and turn up the radio on my alarm clock.

YEEE-AAAHWN.

"I know, can you believe it, Larry? It's just awful how many of those farmers are losing their crops this year—even their livestock!"

"A real tragedy."

"Say, have you heard about the island in Delmont Reservoir?"

"Yeah, that's right. I'd like to drive out there and take a look at it for myself."

"I mean, I knew the reservoir *had* to be getting low, but—"

"Yeah, they say the last time you could walk out to that island was in 1962!"

"That was a bad drought then, wasn't it—well, you probably weren't even born yet, were you Rita?"

"Now, don't be giving away all my secrets there, Larry!"

"Ha-ha-ha—"

Click.

I pick up the remote for the new stereo and point it toward the open bedroom door, pressing the "random" button. The CD carousel rotates and I step out of bed, singing along with the best of the 60s war protest folk ballads.

The cottage is already heating up, so I walk my bowl of cereal to the front porch. I reach over and pat Kerouac as he munches his breakfast beside me.

Kenny wanders up the path in saltwater sandals and swim trunks.

"Hi, D'ana."

"Hi, Kenny."

"Hi, Blanco."

He climbs up the steps and sits beside the cat and me.

"You going swimming today?"

He nods. "Mmm-hmm."

"That sounds nice." I take a bite of cereal.

His eyes light up. "You want to come?"

"Oh, no, sweetie. I'd love to, but I have to work today."

Kenny sighs.

"I know, sweetie, but thanks for the invitation."

He pets the cat.

❀   ❀   ❀

We have donuts and a fresh batch of dealers in the lobby. Bruce and James and I get our donuts and coffee and head upstairs to sit together, in the front row.

James snorts, "Did you guys hear about my Ed referral Saturday?"

Bruce's forehead wrinkles up, "I thought we were out of Ed referrals?"

"Yeah, well so did I until I met *Mr. and Mrs. Leadbetter*!" James coughs a cloud of powdered sugar as he laughs.

Bruce smiles, "Let me guess, it was really Mr. and *Mr.* Leadbetter?"

James takes another bite and laughs a white cloud as he chews, "No, even better!"

"Look, guys, I'm too tired to guess. Just tell us." I slurp some coffee.

James rolls his eyes up into his head and sticks a donut-crumbed tongue out the side of his mouth. He beats his chest with his free hand and grunts. "They…were…RETARDS!!!"

Bruce half-chokes on his donut, "No!"

"Both of them?"

"Sure as shit!" James laughs and swallows some coffee.

"Well, what did you do?"

"What I was there to do—I did the whole god-damned demonstration!" he grins and washes down the last bite of donut. "They loved it!"

"You didn't!"

"Of course I did. Hey," he raises his eyebrows and mimics Harold's voice, "*at StormBurst we don't discriminate!*" He pats Bruce on the shoulder, "Right, buddy?"

Bruce takes a swallow of coffee.

"But that's not even the funniest part. Are you ready for this?"

"I think at this point we're ready for anything." I bite into the bismark and feel the lemon custard filling ooze into my mouth.

"So when I ask them to go get their vacuum cleaner, they go and get—hey, wait here, I'll show you!" He sets his coffee mug on the floor and runs back to the vacuum graveyard. In a flash, he's pushing the skeleton of an old nameless upright toward us, with just a metal pole and handle where a vacuum bag should be. "They brought this out to me, and they were *dead* serious!"

Bruce adjusts his glasses. "But there's no bag on that!"

"No shit, Sherlock! So I try to keep a straight face and everything, and I ask them if it's been running okay, right?"

"That was diplomatic of you."

"And they say they guess so, but it makes them cough a lot! Can you believe that?" James slaps his knee as he cackles.

"You didn't turn it on, did you?" Bruce waits nervously.

"You bet your sweet ass I did! I never seen so much shit spew out of a vacuum in my life! Chunks of carpet and everything!"

"What, were you pushing it across the rug or something?"

"Of course I was! Do you think *I'm* a retard?"

Bruce removes his glasses and rubs the lenses with his handkerchief. "Well, of course they couldn't *buy*."

"Guess again, my friend!" James' eyes twinkle and he flashes a most unnatural smile. "All we had to do was prove that they get a set amount of money every month from the government, which they do, and badda-bing, badda-boom, the payment plan is approved!"

"No!"

"Oh, yeah…" He takes hold of the skeleton. "Guess I'd better put this back before I scare all the new dealers away!"

Brenda Sue finally starts the meeting, explaining that Harold has a sinus infection and is at home getting some rest. She adjusts the chains on her chest, then passes out the songbooks. Bruce volunteers to lead:

> Go, show another StormBurst,
> over the hills and everywhere!
> Go, show another StormBurst,
> and make that magic four!

"Verse two!"

I'm proud to be a dealer,
I show both night and day.
I ask how I can help folks,
and they show me the way—hey!

Why don't you go, show another StormBurst...

Brenda Sue cues the left side of the room to repeat the second verse, while the other half sings through the chorus. We sing it in rounds, faster and faster, until we finally sit down, exasperated, and the new dealers laugh and shove each other.

Brenda Sue puts on a little smile. "Now, I have a *big* announcement to make."

Bruce, James and I sit up in our chairs, exchanging quick glances.

"Bruce, you may remember last year when we had a special *contest* in September?"

Bruce's eyebrows pop up above the rims of his bifocals. "Oh, yes!"

"*Well*...you see, everyone, each year StormBurst International sponsors a special incentive program. For one month they will be offering *unbelievably* great prizes to honor your efforts as certified StormBurst dealers." She pauses to look around the room at each one of us. "And for each week of September, the dealer in *this* office who gets the most sales for that week will get a FREE StormBurst! And you all know what that means, don't you?"

"Yes!"

"But THAT'S just the tip of the ice burg!"

The room is silent.

"The dealer who gets the most *total* sales for this office for the month of August will get..." she wiggles her eyebrows, "an all-expense paid trip for two to HAWAII!"

Holy snots. I've never been to Hawaii.

The room buzzes with excitement.

Brenda Sue holds up her hands to quiet us. "HOLD ON! HOLD ON! Don't you want to know what the *grand prize* is?"

The room falls silent again.

She beams. "The dealer who gets the most sales for his region for the whole month will get a..." she clears her throat. "The regional dealer of the month for September will get a brand new, forest green, EagleEye® edition SNOW TIGER S...U...V!!!"

Holy snots.

"And it all starts *tomorrow*!"

James gasps, "Fuck me!"

Brenda Sue raises her voice, "So who wants to sell a StormBurst?!"

We all shout: "I do!"

"I couldn't hear you...WHO wants to sell a StormBurst?!"

We shout louder: "I do!"

Brenda Sue screams, "WHO WANTS TO SELL A STORMBURST?!?!"

"I DOOOOOOO!!!!!"

She grins, "Well, then. You'd better get as many demos scheduled as you can! Right?"

We all shout: "Right!"

The new dealers watch as Bruce, James, and I put up our fresh shamrocks, the last Shamrocks for the month of August. A month ago, I had so many shamrocks that they ran off the bulletin board and onto the wall. Now they barely reach the edge of the bulletin board. And tomorrow, these too will all disappear.

But then: I'm still in the lead for now. And I'm still Dealer of the Month for Chin's StormBurst.

James whispers, "Watch out, Diana, you've got your work cut out for you now—those retards gave me referrals!" He cackles loud enough for everyone in the room to hear.

❧   ❧   ❧

I've thought about the business of recruiting and decided I'm not interested. In theory, it *should* work out. In theory, it *is* a brilliant way to earn a much higher income than the one I have now. In theory, it *is* the smartest move I can make in my sales career. But then: based on the average number of demos the average new dealer completes before he quits, I would see an average of zero FREE StormBursts for my efforts. Better to get my customer's referrals and sell to their friends myself.

Of course, that will all change when I'm the one in charge.

As I drive along Highway 22, the corn looks unusually short—and brown—for this time of year. And there's not a chicken, or horse, or cow in sight. I turn up Patereau Lane and see the small, old clapboard house. It looks like the set for a movie about pioneers who get massacred. There's a long narrow front porch along the length of it, just wide enough for a rocking chair. I give a couple taps on the screen door and smell sweet pipe tobacco.

"Hello 'der." The graying man gives me a nod, pulls the pipe from between his thin lips and pushes the screen door open with the stem of it.

"Hi, I'm Diana Jensen. You must be Mr. Nichols."

I smile and reach out to shake his hand.

"Daniel."

He reinserts the pipe, gives a quick shake without smiling and turns to the side.

"Edie! Edie that girl's here. Get on out here now!"

A woman appears, wiping her hands on her apron. She has long silver hair pulled back in a bun. "Hello, I'm Diana. Diana Jensen—we spoke on the phone."

There's a pinkish wart or mole on the tip of her nose. I reach out to shake her hand and she shakes mine back, vigorously, but without smiling.

"Edie."

"Nice to meet you, Edie." I try not to look at the short black hair coming out from the center of the growth.

"Now, like I told you on the phone, we're really just watching to help you out with your presentations, but we're not going to *buy* anything today, you understand?"

I give my warmest smile. "I understand."

Daniel grunts. "Good, 'cause I wear the pants in this family and I also carry the wallet and I'm not spending a penny on anything we don't need!"

"Understood, sir. And I really appreciate your taking some time out of the day to help me out." I wipe the bead of sweat from my temple with the back of my hand.

"We get the steak knives whether we buy anything or not, right?"

"Absolutely. Let me get those for you right now."

They sit silently, watching my every move as I set up for the demo.

"Some heat wave we've been having, eh?"

I hear a hawk screech outside.

If she didn't keep rocking in that chair and he didn't keep puffing on that pipe I wouldn't hesitate to call the undertaker for these two.

"This is what we call the Ray O'Sun."

Click.

"Just like a Ray O'Sun shining through the window, it shows us the dust particles in the air, doesn't it?"

Rock, rock.

Edie directs me to the hall closet where I can fetch the Electro-Sweeper myself.

I smile. "Now, you don't have to be a rocket scientist to know that it doesn't make a lot of sense to blow dust around the house when it's the dust you want to get rid of, does it?"

Rock, rock.

I clear my throat. "That just doesn't make any sense, does it?" I speak up in case they're having trouble hearing me. "NOW I'D LIKE TO SHOW YOU WHAT REGULAR VACUUMS DO!"

Click.

Poof!

Sure enough, there's dust blowing out of the Electro-Sweeper. "WOW! CAN YOU SEE THAT? THERE'S DUST BLOWING RIGHT OUT OF THERE!" I raise my eyebrows to help communicate my surprise.

Rock, rock.

Puff.

I shut off the Electro-Sweeper. "FOR THIS NEXT PART I WILL NEED SOME WATER." I stand with the Pot O'Water in my hands.

"Tap's over there. F'you can get anything out of it it's yours."

"OKAY!" I wink and walk over to the sink.

CLANG. BANG. DONG-DONG-DONG. SPLAT.

The first splash is reddish, rusty and thicker than water should be. Then it clears up a little.

SPLAT. SPLAT. SPLAT.

I decide it's full enough and return to my designated demo-space on the floor. "THIS SHOULD DO JUST FINE!" I reach between the Leprechaun's legs and secure the Pot O'Sludge. I remind myself to smile.

Rock, rock, rock.

Surely their sense of smell must still be intact. "HAVE YOU EVER BEEN TO IRELAND?"

"Heavens no."

"Well, would YOU LIKE TO GO?"

"I don't think so." Rock, rock.

Puff. "Bunch'a drunk micks."

"Well," I force some kind of a chuckle, "I know it's an AWFULLY LONG WAY to go just to get a glimpse of the Irish countryside and smell its FRESH,

SWEET AIR…but I have an easy way to get a whiff O'Ireland right here in your own home! ARE YOU READY?"

Puff, puff, puff.

"YOU'RE GOING TO LOVE THIS!" I bulge my eyes at them and flash a crazed grin.

Growl—grind—whoosh—

"Isn't that WONDERFUL?"

Rock, rock.

Puff, puff.

"CAN YOU SMELL THAT FRESH IRISH AIR? WOW! DOESN'T IT SMELL GREAT?" It smells a little like Irish rust.

Rock, rock.

I turn the StormBurst off and waste no time connecting the hardwood floor attachment. I roll the StormBurst right up to them so they can see the "GENUINE HORSE-HAIR BRISTLES!"

"Good lord, you don't have to shout at us!" She adjusts her collar.

"Right." I smile. "Would you like to take it for a test drive?"

"I don't think so."

Rock, rock.

Puff.

The Breath O'Ireland and pipe smoke mingle in a sickeningly sweet combination.

"How about you, Mr. Nichols? It drives like a *vacuum cleaning Ferrari*!"

Puff, puff.

"MR. NICHOLS? WOULD YOU—"

"Not interested."

"Oh. Well, then." I roll the StormBurst back a respectable distance. "Let's go ahead and take a look at our POT O'WATER NOW AND SEE WHAT WE'VE GOT!" I grin as I shine the light up through the russet water.

Edie grunts: "We'd appreciate it if you'd keep your *voice* down, young lady."

"WE'RE NOT HARD OF HEARING!" Daniel plugs the pipe into his frown.

My stomach gurgles in the silence.

"Oh, certainly…By all means. I…" I look back at the Pot O'Water. "Well, my goodness sakes! It looks as if that Electro-Sweeper hasn't been holding up its end of the bargain—"

Puff.

"I mean, you know, that Electro-Sweeper works really well, doesn't it?"

"You'd better believe it, young lady."

"Right, because I know that otherwise, you never would have bought it, isn't that right, Mr. Nichols?"

"Yep."

"Why, I bet that a lot of time and research went into that decision, didn't it?"

"Yes it did."

"So you know that if there's any machine out there that can still pick up dust after that sweeper passes through—well, that would have to be a pretty amazing machine, wouldn't it?"

Puff.

Edie smoothes her hand over the silver strands of hair. "Is that the end of your demonstration?"

"Oh, well, almost. I just have to ask you a couple of questions."

"Well, go ahead then."

"Great."

I pick up the Pot O'Water and shine the light up through it again. "Wouldn't you rather have this dust and—all this dust and filth out of your home for good?"

Puff.

"Are we supposed to answer?"

"Yeah, you can just say yes or no. Uh, wouldn't you rather have this dust and dirt out of your home for good—instead of *inside it*?"

"Yes."

"Sure."

My arm starts to shake so I set the Pot O'Water on the floor and look up at the two of them. Each stares at the wall behind me. I take a long, deep breath and grin. I raise my voice just slightly. "So, if I could make it *possible* for *you* to own a StormBurst *today*, you'd be interested, *wouldn't* you?"

The chair stops rocking.

Daniel pulls the pipe from his mouth.

I grit my teeth.

"What do you mean—*possible*?"

"Possible? Oh, well, you know, I realize you guys didn't have any plans to purchase a StormBurst today, and especially since you already have that new Electro-Super Sweeper—that looks brand new. Why, how long ago did you buy that?"

"Uh, March, I believe."

"Yes, it was right before they announced we were doomed to have this blasted drought this year."

"Yes, well, I'm sure that, given all those circumstances, it's just not very likely you'd even consider buying a StormBurst today, even though you *clearly* appreciate a good machine and an excellent *value.*"

"Right."

"So, by *possible*, I guess I just mean, well, like if we could roll back the clock and go back to March when you were spending so much *time* and doing all that *research*, and if somebody had shown you the StormBurst then, well, you would have been pretty interested, wouldn't you?"

"Well, I suppose I might have been."

Rock, rock.

"Great! Well, thanks so much for your time. I'm supposed to call my boss now and let her know I've completed my whole demonstration. Do you mind if I use your phone?"

"Oh, well, it's in the kitchen."

"Thank you, I'll only be a minute."

I return to the living room with the biggest smile I can muster. I throw my hands out to each side: "You're not going to believe this!"

"What's that?"

"Well, I think I may have found a way to make it March again."

"Come again?"

"Well, when I was just talking to my boss, Brenda Sue, and I told her about how you guys *do* like the StormBurst and everything but that you already have that brand new Electro-Sweeper and you just wished you'd heard about the StormBurst sooner and—well, I guess she must be in a really good mood today or something because—"

They're eyes are on me now.

"Well, she said that she'd actually let me give you *credit* for your Electro-Sweeper—for the full price you paid in March! Isn't that *wonderful*?"

"Well, yes, but we paid a full hundert and fifty-four dollars for it!"

"One hundred and fifty four dollars? Well, it doesn't matter! She made the offer and I'm going to keep her to it! Now then—"

"So your boss's name is Brenda Sue?"

"Yeah—Brenda Sue Chin."

"A *woman* boss, huh?" Puff, puff. "Did you say *Chin*?"

"Why that's a *Chinese* name isn't it, Daniel?"

"It certainly is. You know it's a Chinese when you hear one of them chink names like *Chin,* 'er *Lo,* 'er *Ping,* 'er *Lee.*"

They stare off through the wall behind me.

"Well, by golly!" I slap my thigh. "My history teacher never mentioned that Robert E. *Lee* was Chinese! Why that adds a whole new dimension to the Civil War, doesn't it?" I grin.

He bulges his icy eyes at me and nurses on his pipe.

My stomach gurgles. "Well, anyhow, let me get my calc—"

"Yep, there's a lot of 'em out there."

"And *too many* of 'em around *here.*" She rocks on, indifferently.

I glance out the window at the acres of short, brown corn and not a house or a soul in sight.

"Well, the good news is, we have a bunch of payment options: cash, credit—"

"Well, now hold on there—how much is't?"

I smile and look at the clipboard. "Well, the amazing StormBurst with *all* of the attachments you've seen here today, is normally fourteen thirty-seven. Now, after we deduct your generous credit for the ElectroSweeper—"

"Yep, that's just like a Chinese, always tryin' to steal you blind or somethin'. They tell you one number, then they tell you they'll give you a *bargain* like you're stupid or somethin'. Like you don't know it ought to cost you twenty-percent less in the first place. Huh, Edie?"

"That's right, Daniel."

"Just like a bunch'a Jews." Puff, puff.

I feel a serious cramping in my bowels.

A blue stream rolls upward from the bowl of his pipe, and he points the stem at me. "You ought to be careful working for the Chinese, honey."

"Yes indeed."

"They'll steal you blind if you don't watch it."

Rock, rock.

"Specially a young *American* girl like yourself."

My stomach gurgles.

Daniel pulls the pipe from his mouth long enough to clear his throat of something that sounds wet and slippery.

"Well, actually, I work for myself..." I pick up the clipboard. "I'm a, uh, *independent* contractor."

"You are, huh?"

"Yeah." I feel my stomach churning. Sweat trickles down the back of my neck. "Well, boy, oh, howdy!" I slap my knee and grin. "You know, I think this heat's really gotten to me—'cause I just realized something!" I try hard to realize something.

Edie and Daniel sit up. They're looking at me now, curious.

Daniel takes his pipe in his hand. "Well, what 'tis it?"

"By, golly, I owe you folks an apology." I shake my head and consult the floorboards. "I'm just so darned *embarrassed* right in this moment…"

Edie sits forward in her chair and stops rocking. "Well, what's the matter?"

"Somehow, well, I completely forgot to deduct the two hundred and seventy-five dollars for that Storm Chaser."

Daniel's eyebrows draw up into the lines of his forehead. "Come again?"

"Well, seeing as you have the wooden floors and everything, you probably won't be needing a carpet power head now will you?" I smile incredulously and shake my head, left-right, left-right.

"Oh, well, no. No, I don't suppose we will."

"No, indeed."

"Well, my goodness sakes. Let me look at these numbers again. Now then…" I punch some numbers in the calculator and scribble on my notepad. "Oh, yes, by golly that's a lot better." I smile and Daniel puffs anxiously. "Oh, yes, I should be able to arrange a nice, comfortable payment plan for you, no problem—say, what kind of monthly payment would be nice and comfortable for you? Don't worry, I can get 'em pretty low, I'm good at negotiating, you know what I mean?" I grin and give them a wink.

Edie cracks a half-smile at Daniel. "Well…"

He removes the pipe. "You got somethin' around $30?"

"Well, let me see what I can do. May I use your phone again?"

"Help yourself."

Brenda Sue reminds me that it won't be much of a commission without the Storm Chaser. But then: a sale is a sale. And most importantly, it will help me keep my Dealer of the Month status.

"Alrighty then. Now, if you can make a $65 down payment today, I can get you *exactly* $30 per month payments. Will that work for you?"

He slides the pipe stem out from between his lips and clears his throat. "You take a check?"

"You bet. Just sign here, Mr. Nichols…Perfect."

I drive on past the dried brown pastures, the sparse green patches of beans and under-sized squash. A red-tailed hawk stares at me from a fencepost, then again from my rearview mirror.

Ah, snots.

Stabbing pains shoot across my abdomen.

I reach over to open the glove box and retrieve the bottle of Mylanta. Maybe I should have said something. Maybe I could have found some subtle, tactful way to show them that I'm more open minded than I'd let on. That racism *isn't* okay with me. That they shouldn't be so free with that kind of talk in front of a complete stranger, just because she happens to have blond hair and blue eyes and a name like Jensen instead of Chin.

I take a sip of Mylanta, and another.

But then: could I really have made any difference? Look at how hard it was for them to even warm up to the StormBurst—and everybody loves the Storm-Burst. They'd have probably shown me to the door the second I opened my mouth about racism and bigotry. Well, yes. I don't suppose anyone likes to be called a bigot, especially by a stranger in his own home.

But then: maybe there's something I could have said, or a certain way I could have said it, that would have changed their minds—the same way I changed their minds about spending money today. I can be very persuasive when I want to be.

I take another swig of Mylanta.

But then: who am I to think I can solve the world's problems in thirty minutes to an hour? After all, my job's not to sell people on the idea of interracial harmony. But if I can sell them on the idea of cleaner living, well, I guess that's something.

The gravel drive ends at the top of a hill. I wait a moment, as the dust clears, but there's not a house or trailer in sight, just some kind of a pole building. It looks like a small warehouse, with a Port-O-Potty on the side.

I park the Rabbit and get out to stretch and take in the brown, dry field that slopes down the hillside. Nope, not a single house in sight. I climb back into the Rabbit to study the directions one more time.

"YOOO-HOOO!"

I turn to see a woman standing in the doorway of the pole building. She waves at me, wiggling each of her fingers in the air.

"Hello?"

"Hi, there, sugar! You must be Diana!"

"Oh, I sure am." My stomach gurgles.

"Well, faaaaantastic! I'm Bonnie Joe!"

I force a smile and approach the doorway. "Well, it's a pleasure to meet you, in person, Bonnie Joe!" I peek over her shoulder and sure enough, there's furniture inside the pole building. And what looks like a plywood ceiling and walls.

"Hi there, young lady!" A man waves to me from the recliner with a remote control in his hand.

"Hello, I'm Diana. Diana Jensen."

"Hank Hallstrom! Pleased to meet you!" His shoulders are as wide as the back of the recliner.

"Can I help you carry something in?" Bonnie Joe smiles and waits.

"Well, sure, if you want to!"

I set up for the demo on the area rug in front of the sofa set, aside from that the floor is entirely cement. Hank turns off the TV and watches me instead.

Bonnie Joe disappears behind a makeshift wall and hollers, "You want a cup'a tea, sugar?"

"Oh, that would be lovely—with sugar, *sugar!*"

Hank busts out laughing and slaps the arm of the recliner with a hand the size of a small pork roast. "Oh, you're a clever one, aren't you! Oh! That's a good one, that is!"

Bonnie Joe peeks around the makeshift wall. Her nose is all wrinkled up, in surprise. "Oh, my goodness sakes, Diana! You're a funny girl, aren't you now?"

I just wink at them as I run the extension cord from behind the TV set. "So, Hank, how long have you folks been out here?"

"Oh, well, let's see, goin' on five years now I suppose!"

I try not to look at the cement floor or the three floor lamps behind the sofa, compensating for the lack of windows. "Nice and cozy in here, isn't it?"

"You bet. Well, but we won't be in *here* much longer! No sir! This," he chuckles, "this is just temporary!"

"Oh?"

"Yes, ma'am, we're building a house out here—gonna be 5200 square feet!"

"My goodness! Sounds like a palace!"

Bonnie Joe sets my teacup on the coffee table.

I click the Ray O'Sun on, then off, trying to capture their interest.

"And we're putting in a swimming pool too—the in-ground kind!" Bonnie Joe beams.

"That's right! Everything's gonna be *top drawer*!" Hank lifts his enormous hands into the air and pulls open an invisible drawer.

"Well, how about that?"

"You see, Diana, it's just been taking us a while to make all the decisions—there are so many decisions when you're having your own home built from scratch!"

I click on the Ray O'Sun. "I'll bet there are! So—"

"And you see, Diana, we've just been so busy making *all this money*! We haven't had time to think twice about anything but going to the bank!"

Bonnie Joe snorts, "Ain't that the truth!"

I smile. "Well, that's terrific. There's nothing bad about making a little money, now is there?" I click on the Ray O'Sun and hold it out at arm's length. "Now—"

"You know, Diana, you look like a smart young lady to me. Doesn't she look like a smart young lady, Bon-Bon?"

Bonnie Joe nods to her husband, "She sure does, Hank."

My stomach gurgles loud enough for the two of them to hear. "Well, thank you. That's a nice compliment. And thank you for taking some time out of your *busy* schedule to see me today! Oh, let me get your steak knives now." I kneel beside the demo case to retrieve the knives.

"Oh, sugar, we don't need your knives! You keep those for somebody else who can't *afford* to buy themselves steak knives!"

"Or a steak!" Hank busts into a fit of laughter and slaps the arm of the recliner.

Bonnie Joe snorts and laughs along with Hank.

"Well, alrighty then." I toss the knives back into the demo case and take a seat on top. "I'll just get started with my presentation then!"

"Just outta curiosity, Diana, about how much time do you spend in a week, just travelin' to and from and doin' these demonstrations?"

My stomach gurgles again. "Oh, well, it keeps me pretty busy! Say, have you folks ever been—"

"Sugar, I hope you don't mind my saying so, but are you really making enough *money* to be worth all this lost time driving around God's country and showing people—a *vacuum cleaner*?"

I casually press my hand against my abdomen. "Well, frankly, I do quite well, and I wouldn't be here today if I weren't." Gulp. "But thank you for your concern." I take a deep breath and smile. "So you've seen the StormBurst before?"

"Oh, we didn't mean to get your feathers all ruffled up there, Diana, did we now, Hank?" Bonnie Joe puts on a warm smile.

"Oh, heavens no. No, no, no." He breaks into gentle laughter.

"No harm done." I wink. "Now, *this* is what we call the Ray O—"

"It's just that you seem like such a smart young lady and all, it just—well, it just breaks my heart to think of how hard you must be working, and to keep that little old car of yours running and what not." Bonnie Joe shakes her head.

"The car's fine. Hasn't even overheated once this summer—in spite of this awful heat!" I force a smile.

"Oh, Diana. You're a real trouper, aren't you?" Hank grins and nods at me.

"Yes, a real trouper, you can see it in her eyes, can't you Hank?"

"You guys must get an awful lot of dust out here, eh? Surrounded by all these dry fields?"

Bonnie Joe clears her throat. "Diana, do you know what the number one cause of fights is among married couples?"

"Excuse me?"

"That leads to *divorce*?"

"Money!" Bonnie Joe bulges her eyes at me, then looks back at Hank.

"And do you know what the leading cause is for world hunger around the globe?"

"World hunger—around the—"

"Money!" Hank's enormous hand slaps the arm of the recliner to punctuate.

"And what causes all the terrible diseases and illnesses to keep on spreadin', killin' the millions of thousands of innocent people all over God's earth? Well…it's not because they got too much in their wallets, now is it?" Bonnie Joe shakes her head from side to side.

I set the Ray O'Sun on the floor.

"You see, Diana, money may not buy happiness, but it can sure help you get there, can't it?"

I smile, "I suppose so, Hank." I stand and begin to open the StormBurst box. "I'll just need some water—"

"Diana, what would you say if we told you that we possess the true secret to happiness?" Hank raises his eyebrows at me.

"Well, I don't know, 'congratulations'?"

He grins and nods, "Would you like to see what we're talking about?"

Bonnie Joe exclaims, "We don't just show this to everyone, Diana, but you seem like a real special girl—"

"Like someone who could really make something of herself if someone just gave her the right opportunity!" Hank raises his eyebrows again. "Isn't that right?"

They both wait, in silence, smiling at me.

I smile back, and say nothing.

Finally, Hank clears his throat, "Would you like to see what we're talking about?"

I look at my watch, "Well, if it won't take too long, 'cause you know I have—"

"That's our girl! Come on!"

I follow Hank and Bonnie Joe around the makeshift wall to where a stove sits side-by-side with a dorm-size refrigerator. We walk around another makeshift wall and there, holy mother of snots, is a pyramid—up to the rafters of the pole building—of laundry detergent boxes.

"Soap King?"

Bonnie Joe beams. "That's right, Diana!"

Hank rocks on his heels and grins, "What's the heaviest thing you lug home from the grocery store, Diana?"

"Oh, well I don't—"

"It's the laundry detergent!" Bonnie Joe nods her head, assuring me.

"What's the number one cause of skin irritation in the US of A, Diana?"

Gulp. "Laundry detergent?"

"You guessed it!"

"And what would you suppose is one of the harshest pollutant's in our nation's water supply today?"

"Oh, well," I smile, "I'm thinking it might be *laundry detergent*?"

"That's right, Diana!" Bonnie Joe squeezes my arm.

Hank places his hands on his hips and looks at me in earnest, "Well, Diana, what would you say if I told you that there is now a product that can solve *all* of these problems…quickly…simply…and inexpensively?"

I look up and down the pyramid of boxes.

"You'd say that's a pretty amazing product, wouldn't you?"

I smile at Hank, then at Bonnie Joe. I smile at the Soap King boxes touching the rafters above us. I smile at the plywood wall behind me. And I smile at myself. "Well, thank you for sharing your little secret with me!" I take a look at my watch. "Oh, dear! It seems we're out of time!" I bulge my eyes at the couple and turn on my heel.

"You know, Diana—"

I walk around the makeshift wall. "Yes, Hank?"

"I'd be willing to guess that you could also make *a lot of money* the same way we have."

I cross the living room area and close the lid on the StormBurst box. "Selling Soap King?"

"Selling? Heavens no!"

Bonnie Joe and Hank break into a brief fit of laughter.

I unplug the extension cord from behind the TV set. "No, Diana, judging by your way with people and your—your business *savvy*—"

"Yes, savvy!" Bonnie Joe squeezes her hands together.

"Well, I'd be willing to venture you're *management* material."

"Management?" I set the Ray O'Sun on top of the demo case. "What do you mean by management?"

"Well, what I mean is, a girl as smart and gifted as yourself shouldn't be running herself ragged seeing every customer herself!"

"No sir!" Bonnie Joe shakes her head.

"You got to *delegate!*"

"That's right, Diana, just imagine—if you could *clone* yourself, how many more sales do you suppose you could make?"

"Oh, well, probably a lot."

"Well, Diana, that's what we're offering to you today—a chance to clone yourself. To make double, triple—heck, a smart go-getter like yourself could probably make a hundred times what you do now with StormBurst!"

"That's right, Diana. Just imagine taking your last paycheck and adding two zeros onto it—what was your last paycheck?"

"Well, it was kind of a slow week, things have been kind of—"

"Oh, that's all right, you don't have to tell us if you're embarrassed! But all the more reason to try something new, right?"

"And if you start now, Diana, you'll still be getting in at the *ground level!*"

Bonnie Joe nods, "Ground level, Diana! It doesn't get much better than that!"

"And all it takes to get started is just a one-time initial investment of, would you believe, *five hundred dollars*?"

Bonnie Joe squeals, "Five hundred dollars for a lifetime of comfort and security!"

"Five hundred dollars, huh?"

"That's right, Diana, just *five hundred* to invest in the business opportunity of a lifetime." Hank nods. "Does that sound good to you?"

I take a long, deep breath, then look at the floor lamps. "Well, I guess it's certainly worth thinking about." I kneel down to put the Ray O'Sun in the demo case.

"Worth thinking about?"

I smile up at Hank, "Well, of course!"

"Bon-Bon, we offer her the secret to *true happiness* and the girl tells us she has to *think* about it?" He forces a light chuckle.

I stand up and brush the dust off my knees.

Hank's face has flushed red. His chest rises and falls, rises and falls.

"Oh, well, I didn't mean to be disrespectful or anything—I just," I glance at my watch, "I was just thinking about how I'm going to be late for my next appointment if I don't skeedattle along here!"

Hank rubs his chin with his porterhouse fingers. A bead of sweat rolls down the side of his face.

Bonnie looks nervously at Hank.

"I mean, you folks, as such successful business people I'm sure recognize the importance of being on time for an appointment—right?" I smile and pick up the demo case.

Hank takes a deep breath, and almost whispers, "We're offering you the chance to be *rich*, girl, rich beyond your *wildest dreams...*" He narrows his eyes at me.

"And I *truly* appreciate it too! Well, why don't I give you folks a call maybe this evening—I've got your number, of course."

Hank stomps across the cement and disappears behind the makeshift wall.

"We can talk all about—about this *exciting* opportunity then, but I really must be—"

"Rich!" He shouts from behind the wall, "A GODDAMNED MILLION-AIRE!"

Bonnie Joe forces a smile and whispers, "He's just so *passionate* about the business, you know?"

"Why, if I'd been given this opportunity at your age—UNGRATEFUL! Some people don't know a good thing when it comes up and BITES THEM ON THE ASS!!!"

"Maybe you could help me with my things?"

"Of course, sugar."

Something crashes against the other side of the wall. Bonnie Joe and I hurry for the door.

I slam the trunk closed and hurry to the driver's side of the Rabbit. "Well, thanks for your time!" I turn the key in the ignition.

Bonnie Joe smiles, "Now don't forget to call us tonight!" She waves, wiggling her little fingers in the air.

PART V

❀

"I'LL BE HONEST WITH YOU."

"Please take off your shoes."

"Of course! You know, I *always* take off my shoes at my house, too." I squat in the entryway, struggling with the buckles on my new sandals.

"Follow me." Mrs. Shojenji leads me down a hallway and into the living room, where a black coffee table sits surrounded by large pillows and a hardwood floor.

"Please sit down. I will get Mr. Shojenji."

"Terrific."

She turns to leave the room.

"Oh, but I need to bring in some things from my car—"

Mrs. Shojenji stops and looks at me. "Please wait."

"Okay." I sit on one of the large pillows and cross my legs, Indian-style. One wall of the room is glass, from the ceiling to the floor, and on the other side is a small bonsai garden.

Mr. Shojenji walks across the polished floor and shakes my hand. "You are Diana?"

"Yes, it's nice to meet you, Mr. Shojenji."

The Shojenjis take their seats across the coffee table from me.

"I will need to bring in a few things from my car."

The couple exchanges looks.

"It will just be a minute, okay?"

They nod and watch as I cross the room.

The unbuckled sandal straps drag along the driveway as I walk out to the Rabbit, then return with my demo case in one hand and the Storm Chaser box under my other arm. I step out of my sandals in the entryway and walk down the hall to where the Shojenjis wait for me.

"These are steak knives?" Mr. Shojenji stares at me.

I smile, "I'll have those for you in just a moment, Mr. Shojenji—I just need one more thing, I'll be right back!" I smile.

They exchange looks and nod again.

I repeat the process and return with the StormBurst box.

Both stare at me with blank expressions.

"Thank you for waiting," I carefully add, "Ahhh-reee-gah-tow," then nod my head in a partial bow to show my respect.

The Shojenjis' eyes bulge.

I smile and flip open the demo case. "Here are the steak knives I promised you." The couple nods at the box of cutlery I place before them on the coffee table.

Mr. Shojenji drawls, "Thaaaaank yooooou," and exchanges glances with Mrs. Shojenji.

I pull out the Ray O'Sun and run the extension cord across the room to an outlet near the entrance.

"What is that?"

"Well, Mr. Shojenji, this is what we call the Ray O'Sun." I click on the light. "See, it's just like a ray of sun shining in through your window, isn't it?"

He stares at the yellow beam, then looks at his wife.

I sit on the end of the demo case, towering above the Shojenjis who are only sitting on pillows. "Now, have either of you been to Ireland?" I smile and wait as the couple consults one another.

"You're—you're serious?" The man raises his eyebrows at me.

"Sure! You just have to answer yes or no." I wink.

Mr. Shojenji looks at his wife, then back at me. "Young lady, I don't *have* to do anything."

My stomach gurgles. I smile, "Oh, no, I didn't mean that you *have* to, I just—oh, what a silly misunderstanding!" I laugh a little.

Mr. and Mrs. Shojenji look at each other, then back at me.

"Well, anyway, I just like to ask that because people who *have* been to Ireland—to the countryside anyway, well, you know I'll bet that the air in the *Japanese* countryside is pretty fresh and nice too isn't it?" I smile and nod my head.

Mrs. Shojenji clears her throat.

"You *are* from Japan, right?"

Mr. Shojenji's eyebrows shift toward a newly formed crease at the bridge of his nose.

"Well, why don't I stop *telling* you about the StormBurst now, and start showing you what it can do?" I jump up and open the lid of the box and remove the Pot O'Water. "I'll just need a little water to fill this—is there a faucet nearby?"

Mrs. Shojenji rises from her pillow and takes the bowl from me. "I will get your water."

"Thank you."

Mr. Shojenji turns from me and stares out the window at the bonsai shrubs.

"Those sure are beautiful, Mr. Shojenji. I just love bonsai. Did you do those yourself?"

He looks at me a moment, then turns back toward the window.

"It must take a lot of patience and—well, one wrong clip and—"

Mrs. Shojenji returns with the Pot O'Water.

"Thank you, Mrs. Shojenji. This is just perfect. Now, let's see…What cleans dust better, a dry cloth or a damp cloth?"

The couple stares at me.

"The damp cloth, right? Because the dust sticks to the water, doesn't it?"

Mr. Shojenji leans back and shifts his weight onto his hands.

"Well, that's exactly how the StormBurst works to trap all of the dust and pollen and dirt in your home—in water!" I reach between the legs of the StormBurst and clamp the Pot O'Water to the machine. "Now watch closely as I shine this light above the air *intake* of the StormBurst. You will see the dust particles going straight into the machine—just from the air."

Growl—grind—whoosh—

Mr. Shojenji puts his hands over his ears and grimaces.

Mrs. Shojenji stares at me, but not the light or the dust particles.

Click.

"Well, if you thought it *looked* like the dust particles were going into the machine, I'd like to show you the proof. Would you like to see the proof?"

Mr. Shojenji uncovers his ears and says snidely, "Yes, we would like to see the *proof*." He leans forward and crosses his arms on the table.

I give him my warmest smile. 'Terrific!" I unclamp the Pot O'Water and shine the Ray O'Sun up through it. "Do you see those—" I walk right up to the couple and hold the water at the level of their noses. "Do you see all those dust particles floating around in there?"

"No."

"No, I don't either."

"You don't?" I look down at the water and can't see a single thing in it. I laugh lightly, "Well, then it's *proof* that Mrs. Shojenji is an excellent house-keeper, isn't it?" I grin.

Mrs. Shojenji clears her throat and turns her head toward her husband.

Mr. Shojenji smiles at me. "Mrs. Shojenji is not an excellent housekeeper; Mrs. Shojenji is an excellent *surgeon*."

Gulp.

"Ha! Well of course she is!" I paste the smile back onto my face. "Well, now, where was I?" I walk back to the StormBurst.

"You were showing us your invisible proof."

I look up in time to see Mr. Shojenji smile at his wife.

"Right! Well, then…" I look down at the floor beneath me, seeing my reflection on the polished surface. "But you see, the StormBurst is *much more* than an air filter. It is a *complete home cleaning device.*" I look around the room again. "Do you have any carpet in your home?"

"No."

"Oh, well, that's okay." I flip open the box. "Here, let me show you the hard-wood floor attachment, made with genuine *horse hair bristles.*" I assemble the necessary parts.

"Horse hair?"

"That's right! Top quality."

"What do they do with the rest of the horse?" Mr. Shojenji raises his eyebrows at me.

I chuckle. "Oh, dear. Well, then, how would you two like to try this out? It's very lightweight and glides—"

The Shojenjis stare at me.

"Well, of course I can just show you here—"

Growl—grind—whoosh—

Both Shojenjis cover their ears and squint their eyes as I work in a circle all the way around the sitting area. I attack a couple of the pillows, too, just to be thorough.

Click.

"Okay! Let's take another look!"

The Shojenjis reluctantly pull their hands down from their ears.

I shine the Ray O'Sun up through the water again, only to find a few pollen particles at the bottom of the bowl. "Do you see those particles there? Those are bits of pollen—they can cause allergies and, well, I suppose Dr. Shojenji is quite familiar with that!"

Mrs. Shojenji glances up at me for a moment, then returns her gaze to the Pot O'Water.

Mr. Shojenji grins. "So, after you clean this whole room—that is all you can show us?"

"Well, but you see, the StormBurst is *much more* than just a home cleaning device!" I pull the Breath O'Ireland out of the demo case. "You're going to love this! Just relax a moment and close your eyes while I take you…to Ireland!"

Growl—grind—whoosh—

The Shojenjis cover their ears.

Slurp. Slurp. Slurp.

The room fills with a pleasant Irish breeze and—

"Oh, my GOSH!"

"DISGUSTING!"

Click.

The Shojenjis stare at me with wrinkled noses.

"You don't like it?"

"It's TERRIBLE!"

Mrs. Shojenji shakes her head in disbelief. "What are you doing?"

I glance down at my reflection on the floor. "I guess I'm going home."

❧   ❧   ❧

Bill Buckley lives in the Live Oaks trailer park near the Grindles, but I can see from the curb his mobile home is nothing at all like the Grindle's place. It's a beige singlewide with brown painted steps going up to the door from under the carport.

I take a swig of Mylanta, pop a Rolaids in my mouth and grab the steak knives as I chew.

He answers the door in a flannel shirt, buttoned clear up to his neck, and miraculously, there's not so much as a drop of sweat on his brow. He has dark circles under his eyes, but a bright smile upon his face.

"Hi, I'm Diana."

"Bill Buckley." He continues smiling as he shakes my hand.

"These are for you."

"Well, isn't that nice? Thank you, Diana."

Without air conditioning, the inside of the trailer feels even hotter than it does outside. I consider the faded, stained carpet as I set up for the demo and can't wait to see the Pot O' Water I'm about to create.

Bill settles onto the threadbare sofa and I hear footsteps in the hallway.

"Maggie, she's here if you want to watch this!"

A pretty blond teenager steps into the living room rubbing her lips together to smooth a fresh layer of pink lip gloss. Her smile is like her father's and she reaches out to shake my hand. "Hi, I'm Maggie!"

I shake her hand, "I'm Diana. Nice to meet you."

"I can only watch for a little while—my friends are coming to pick me up soon." She settles onto the sofa by her dad.

"Oh, that's just fine." I waste no time picking up the Ray O'Sun. "So, have you guys ever noticed the way—when the sun shines in at a certain angle—you can see a million dust particles floating in the air?"

Click.

"Look, Dad! It's just like the sun!"

"That's right! That's why we call this the Ray O'Sun."

"Good heavens, would you look at that dust?" Bill shakes his head.

"Oh, don't you worry about that! Truth is, 40 *pounds* of dust accumulate in the average home each year!" I bulge my eyes, then smile. "Unless, of course, people have this machine I'm about to show you." I wink at Maggie and she smiles. "Would you like to see why?"

"You bet!" Bill grins and nods at me.

They're nothing but smiles and giggles as I show them their dust trapped in the water.

"Say, Maggie, could you go get your vacuum cleaner for me?"

"Sure, Diana! I'll be right back."

As she disappears down the hallway, I whisper to Bill, "She sure is a sweet girl, isn't she? You must be so proud."

He beams, "You'd better believe it!"

Maggie rolls the vacuum cleaner across the floor to me.

"Oh, the VacuViper! That's a *very* popular model." I nod as I shine the Ray O'Sun directly over the exhaust vent of the old vacuum cleaner. It must be about the same age as me. "Now watch closely and you'll see how traditional cleaning methods can actually work against you in the home." Click.

Poof.

"Oh, Dad! Oh, my gosh! That's disgusting!"

I turn off the VacuViper. "Yes, isn't it?"

Bill rubs his eye with a fist.

I push the VacuViper aside. "Well, and the truth is, that's what *all* vacuum cleaners do—*except* for the StormBurst." I nod.

"Oh, Dad! That's disgusting! I'm never using that thing again!"

Bill half-smiles and pats his daughter's knee.

"But now for the *good news*. Here is the exhaust vent of the StormBurst." I shine the light above the hole. "Watch as no dust escapes—are you ready?"

"Yes!"

Growl—grind—whoosh.

Their eyebrows rise simultaneously.

"Oh, Dad! That's so *cool*, isn't it?"

He grins. "Yes, it sure is, honey."

Just as I start shrinking the sofa cushion, we hear the doorbell. Before I know it, two other teenage girls stand beside me, waiting in anticipation.

"Oh, Diana, would you mind doing it again—I just want my friends to see. It's *so* cool!"

"Well, of course! I'd be happy to."

Bill's eyes twinkle and the cushion shrinks flat inside the plastic bag.

"See! Isn't it *cool*?"

The girls take off for Harveston Mall, and we continue. Bill's enthusiasm never fades.

"Are you ready to go to Ireland, Bill?"

"Absolutely! Let's do it."

"Okay, close your eyes for a moment!"

"Well, holy moly! My goodness sakes!"

"That's what we call the Breath O'Ireland fragrance. Isn't it great?"

"It sure is! Boy, Maggie would sure like that, wouldn't she?"

"You bet she would, Bill!"

"Too bad she had to miss that part."

I reveal the murky Pot O'Water and gently guide him to the close. "Now wouldn't you rather have all of this *dirt* outside?"

"I should hope so!" He giggles.

"So if I could make it *possible* for you to own a StormBurst today, you'd be interested, wouldn't you!"

"Well, after seeing the look on Maggie's face, I'd say I'd better be!" He winks.

"Well alrighty then!"

"But how much do these cost?"

"Well, the StormBurst, with *all* the attachments you see here, is fourteen thirty-seven."

"Oh." His smile vanishes.

"But we have lots of payment plans available—"

"Well, yes, but I—I'm just not sure I could swing it, with a price tag like that, you know what I mean?"

"Oh, sure. I understand, Bill. But I'll tell ya, I've been able to work out some pretty good deals for a lot of customers who didn't think they could swing it either."

"Well, I still don't—"

"And you know what? I can give you credit for your old vacuum cleaner, too—a hundred dollars!"

"Well, that's real nice, but it's still—"

"Tell me Bill, how low would I have to get your monthly payment to comfortably fit this StormBurst into your budget? Name your price!"

He smiles at the carpet and rubs his hands together. "Well, gosh, I suppose around ten dollars or so?" He looks up at me hopefully.

"*Ten* dollars?"

He squints his eyes. "Yeah. Or maybe closer to five—any chance?"

"Oh, well, let me, uh, see what I can do. Can I use your phone?"

"It's in the kitchen."

"Great. Oh, and just out of curiosity, how much could you put toward a down payment today?"

"Down payment?" His eyes widen. "Oh, well, I suppose I could do…fifteen?"

"Okay, I'll just, uh, make that call now." I feel my stomach begin to percolate as I dial for Brenda Sue.

"*Five* dollars a month? *Five* dollars, Diana? Who *are* these people? Are they living on the *street*?"

I try to whisper as softly as I can into the phone. "No, he's in a singlewide in Live Oaks."

"Well, we've sold a million StormBursts to people in singlewides! Does he have a job? Disability? Hell, Diana, even our customers collecting unemployment can do better than five a month! Now here's what I want you to do…"

I go back to the living room and try to force a smile, a reassuring smile. I sit on the demo case and pick up my clipboard. "Okay, so I think we should be able to work something out for you, Bill—"

"Oh, that's terrific!"

"But first I'll just need to ask you some prequalification questions so we can set up that payment plan, all right?"

"Oh, sure."

My stomach gurgles loud enough for Bill to hear. "Great. Okay, so are you working Bill?"

"Yes, ma'am. I'm on graveyard over at the plant."

"I see. And what's your position over there?"

"Janitor."

"Great. And what's your current salary?"

"Salary? Oh, well I get paid by the hour—$7.25 an hour."

"All right. And are you married—or have you been?"

"Well, yes, I was married fourteen wonderful years." He smiles fondly. "But my wife died when Maggie was just ten."

"I'm so sorry."

"We are too." His eyes water, but he blinks it away.

"Okay, where was I?" I look down at the clipboard and feel the heat pressing down on me, squeezing the sweat out of my pours.

When I get up to make another call, my stomach muscles are clenched so tight I can hardly stand up straight. I force a smile as I leave the living room.

Brenda Sue says she hates to do it, but we'll have to work out a deal for a *used* StormBurst. When I ask about Marcie & Reggie's machine, she laughs. "No, honey. We're going to sell that one for a *lot* more than $500—in fact, we already have!"

Bill cheerfully signs the papers for his five-dollar-a-month payment plan. He withdraws the fifteen dollars' down payment from a Mason jar in the kitchen cupboard and shakes my hand. "I sure appreciate your understanding about this."

"My pleasure, Bill."

The next afternoon, I stop by to deliver his new, *used* machine. It's got orange buckles and an orange Storm Chaser—with a black scrape over the front corner.

I force a smile. "Well, it doesn't have the fancy exterior of the new model, but believe me: a StormBurst is a StormBurst!"

And according to the StormBurst annual sales incentive program: a sale is a sale.

❧   ❧   ❧

"Hello?"

"Hi, I'm a student at Harveston University and I'm trying to earn some money for my tuition and books—and I found this company that's paying just for demonstrating their new product to people. My name is Diana."

"Demonstrating?"

"Yeah, and you don't have to buy anything. I just come to your house when it's convenient for you and your family and all you have to do is watch and then tell me if you think it's a worthwhile product or not. Your friends, the Hiddle-sons, said you might be willing to help me out."

"Oh, they did? And you get paid just for that?"

"I sure do! So I'm trying to get as many demonstrations as I can before school starts—can I count on your help, Jerry?"

"Oh, well, I suppose—"

"Oh, thank you so much! I can come over any time of day or night—weekends too, whenever you and your *family* have got the time for me! So when would be best, Jerry?"

"Well, let me think here…I suppose Thursday evening we should all be around."

"Terrific! How about 7 o'clock?"

"All right, that'll work."

"Oh, thank you so much, Jerry! You have no idea what this means to me!"

"Heh-heh. Oh, it's no trouble at all."

"Then I'll see you folks Thursday night at seven!"

❀   ❀   ❀

It's so hot out that I wear a tank top, even though I know my bra straps show. But then: I'm not supposed to look professional. I'm just a kid, in college, trying to earn enough money for tuition next—well, this year.

I'm on my way out to Dairyway Lane off of Highway 24, just west of Cornston. Even along the coastal highway, the pastures are as brown and dry as the lawns of Harveston. The only green in sight is the little fir trees that dot the sides of the hills.

I turn up Dairyway Lane and drive along a whitewashed fence for miles, until I reach a yellow farmhouse with an old, red barn. It's got a little square-shaped turret on the top, just the kind of place you'd expect an owl to live. I don't see anyone outside, not even a cow. And all I can hear is the screech of a hawk somewhere in the distance. But the smell of manure—and decay is intense. My eyes water as I walk to the door.

"Hi, I'm Diana!"

"Art Grayson!"

"Vivien!"

"Nice to meet you!"

The gray-headed couple smiles and thanks me for the steak knives. Vivien offers me a glass of pink lemonade.

"Wow! Did you squeeze this yourself?"

She giggles, "Well, if I knew where they grow pink lemons, I might give it a try sometime." She adjusts the little pearl in her earlobe.

I comment on the handsome man in uniform, framed above the piano, and let them boast for a while about their son who served in the Gulf War.

"He'd only been out of high school two years!" Vivien shakes her head, "We were worried sick."

Art coughs a little. "He's in Texas now."

Vivien holds up a silver-plated frame and smiles. "This is his wife and our two granddaughters. They're on the base with him."

"That's nice. Have you ever been to Ireland?"

"Pardon?" Art looks at me kindly, as if he's sure he misunderstood me. "Did you say, *Ireland* dear?"

I grin, "As a matter of fact, I did!"

"Well, good heavens! I can't say as we have…" Vivien looks over at Art, curiously, then they both stare at me. "Why do you ask?"

I rub my hands together, "*Well*…if you'll wait while I get my things together, I'd like to take you there!" I flash my best smile.

Art adjusts his belt and grins at me.

Vivien smiles and throws her hands up in the air. "Well, I can't see why not!"

"Great! You guys can just get comfortable there in the living room, and I'll be all ready in no time!"

They sit on the sofa and giggle as I drag in my equipment. Art chuckles, "Goodness sakes, you must get a good work out hauling that all around!"

"I sure do!"

I finally take my seat on the green demo case and pick up the Ray O'Sun. "Okay, then. This…" I gesture to the Ray O'Sun as if it were a sparkling necklace on display, "this is what we call the *Ray O'Sun*. Now, you know how sometimes the sun shines in the window at a certain angle?" Click. "You can see all the dust and pollen that floats in the air, can't you?"

Vivien smiles as she holds up her hand to block the view and looks the other way, "Oh, Diana, can we just pretend it doesn't exist?" She chuckles.

Art laughs with her.

"Oh, Vivien, I wish it were that easy, don't you?" I smile.

"Oh, yes." She grins and folds her hands in her lap.

"Well, don't take it personally, Vivien. According to the EPA, 40 *pounds* of dust accumulate in the average home *every* year." I raise my eyebrows for impact.

"But, Vivien, I'll bet you know the best way to trap dust don't you—with a dry dust cloth or a damp one?"

"Oh!" She looks a little startled. "Well, I know I've always used a moist cloth for dusting."

I grin at Art, "See, you married a genius!"

We chuckle.

"That's because *water* is Mother Nature's little helper, isn't it?" I nod.

They nod back.

"Just like when it rains outside and helps keep the dust down, right?"

Art sits up, "That's right!"

I follow Vivien into the kitchen to fill the Pot O'Water.

"Diana, you're just like a ray of sun, yourself! You seem so at ease talking with folks and—you have such a delightful personality. Why, have you thought about—"

My stomach gurgles.

"Well, you could be like one of those spokes model girls on Star Search!"

"Oh, Vivien, aren't you sweet!" I press the Pot O'Water against my stomach as we return to the living room.

She calls out behind me, "You're certainly pretty enough, too!"

When I ask her to bring me her vacuum, Vivien pushes an old Bag-A-Breeze upright across the floor. "Well, I'm not sure if this is what you had in mind, Diana—this was actually my *mother's* originally! I always figured we'd replace it one day, but the darn thing just keeps going!" She and Art chuckle together.

I smile, "Well, you just never know, do you?"

As I shrink the sofa cushion, Vivien shouts, "Boy, that *is* a fancy machine!"

Art just nods and smiles.

I invite Vivien to take the StormBurst for a test drive.

"Oh, I'd love to! I don't think I've ever seen such a fancy rug cleaner in all my life—and I'm sure my mother never did either!"

We all laugh together.

"Now, I promised to take you to Ireland…are you folks ready for a vacation?"

Art grins, "Well, I should say we are!"

"All right then! Why don't you two just settle in and get real comfortable…and close your eyes…"

Growl—grind—whoosh—

"And here we go!"

Drip. Drip. Drip.

"Isn't that terrific?"

"My goodness, yes!"

They keep their eyes closed and I watch their chests rise as they take deep soothing breaths.

Drip. Drip.

"Now doesn't that smell just like a spring rain?"

Drip. Drip.

"It certainly does, Diana!"

They both smile, perfectly relaxed on the sofa.

Click.

"Well then, what do you say we take a look at how that Pot O'Water's doing?"

Vivien blinks her eyes open. "All right." She smiles.

I hold up the beige water and shine the Ray O'Sun up through it. "So, what do you think of that?"

Vivien shakes her head and smiles down at the floor.

Art grins, "Well, I'll be…isn't that something?"

"Now, you folks would have to agree this is a pretty amazing machine, isn't it?"

"Oh, yes indeed." Vivien smiles and folds her hands on her lap.

"Absolutely!" Art nods and smiles. "You've done a fine job showing it, too."

"Oh, well thank you." I smile. "And I can tell you folks would rather have all this dust and pollen on the outside of your home, now wouldn't you?"

"Well, of course!" Vivien giggles.

"Who wouldn't?"

"So then, if I could make it *possible* for you to own a StormBurst today, you'd be pretty interested, wouldn't you?"

Their smiles evaporate.

"I mean, if I could make it *possible*, of course," and I try to smile again.

They look at each other, and at the floor.

Finally Art clears his throat. "Oh, well, Diana, I'm sorry for the misunderstanding, but I thought my sister told you on the phone that we wouldn't be able to buy anything today?"

"Oh, you're right, she did tell me that. And that's just fine!"

Vivien smiles nervously, "She told us you'd get paid just for showing it to us—we just wanted to help you out, for your school money and whatnot."

My stomach gurgles.

"Oh, absolutely! And I definitely appreciate your help!"

Art smiles a little, relieved.

"I just thought that since you two seemed to like it so much, I might be able to find *some* way to make it possible for you folks to get one."

Art looks at Vivien who is still looking at the floor. He looks back at me, uneasily, "Well, we sure appreciate that honey, but I can assure you, it's just not going to work for us today."

"That's fine!" I smile and they smile back at me. "I just wanted to let you know that we have several kinds of payment options, including a wide variety of payment plans, so if you guys could just give me a ballpark figure of what your monthly payments would need to be, I'll be happy to see—"

Art clears his throat. "Well, that's real kind of you, Diana, but like I said, it's just not going to work for us today. But thanks for coming anyway." He stands and reaches out to shake my hand.

I pretend not to notice his hand and look him in the eye. "Okay, well I can understand that today may not be the right day. After all, just because today's the day I showed up in your lives and in your home, and introduced you to the amazing StormBurst, that doesn't mean you have to be ready to buy it right here and right now, now does it?"

Art drops his hand to his side. "Thanks for understanding."

I look over at Vivien. She looks up from the floor to her husband with her lips held tightly together.

"No problem. It just makes me proud to know how much you folks like this little machine—say, just out of curiosity, could you folks give me any idea of when—in the future—it might be a *better* time for you to get a StormBurst?"

Art takes a long, deep breath, and his hands find their way into his pockets. "Oh…well…I don't suppose that's going to be for some time…" He glances toward the window and looks out at the red barn.

"But seriously, I've worked some real miracles for folks. I even got someone a payment plan for just *five* dollars a month!"

Art continue to stare out the window at the bright red barn. White letters above the barn door read "Grayson Farms since 1893."

Vivien has turned her head to look out the window behind her.

I search my memory for the appropriate StormBurst Revelation.

Turn their reservation into a brand new conversation.

"That sure is a lovely barn—looks like a postcard or something!"

Vivien begins to sob against the back of the sofa.

Art shoves his hands into his pockets and continues to look out the window, his jaw locked in place.

Turn their fight into a double delight!

"Well, Mr. And Mrs. Grayson, I can tell how much you both like this amazing machine, but that it seems Mr. Grayson still has some—"

Art turns toward me, his eyes brimming with water.

Suddenly Vivien runs down the hallway.

SLAM.

Art's eyes flash and a tear spills over onto his cheek. He growls, "I think you've done enough here now…If you don't mind, we've got things to do," and he walks out through the back of the house.

I walk across the silent room to unplug the Ray O'Sun, and stare at the handsome soldier above the piano as I wind the cord.

Thunderheads roll in from the east as I load up the Rabbit. They're moving fast—faster than me. I feel a drop on my bare shoulder as I open the driver's side door, and more land on my windshield as I pull out of the driveway. The drops seem to build on each other, getting heavier, falling faster, and louder on the roof of the Rabbit. I turn my wipers to the highest setting, but it's not enough. They flap frantically back and forth like the broken wings of a bird. But I drive on, faster, putting distance between the Graysons and myself.

The lines on the road begin to blur: first the yellow, then the white line too, and I feel the Rabbit slide over the water, gliding straight toward the whitewashed fence. The tires grip and we lurch forward, this time toward the opposite side of the road. I lift my feet from the pedals and pull up hard on the emergency break.

Well, not everybody's cut out for this line of work, are they?

The wipers flap and flap in vain. I turn them off, then the engine, and I watch as the rain blurs across the windshield in ripples and in sheets. Specks of white begin washing down the glass. I take a deep breath and watch as the sheets of rain transform into shards of ice, dumping from the black sky above. Inside the Rabbit, it sounds like a thousand gunshots, firing round after round after round. I cover my ears and look out the side window to where I can see, between whitewashed boards, a thousand hailstones ricocheting off soggy mats of straw. And I feel a drop slip down my cheek, down my neck, and onto my chest.

"There you are! We've been worried *sick* about you, what with this storm coming on so suddenly and—when we called the Graysons to see if you'd left they just said to not ever call there again, and, well, what on earth happened, Diana? What went *wrong*?"

I look at Brenda Sue and take a deep breath. I can see the rim of her green contact lens edging onto the white of her eye. "Oh, it's a long story. I'll tell you later."

Berta munches a burger, wide-eyed, as she watches the downpour outside.

"I have to get some lunch—and a change of clothes." I feel the damp card between my fingers and remember why I'm standing there, dripping on the orange shag carpet.

"Are you all right? You're soaked to the bone! And you look a little pale, darlin'."

"Yeah, I'll be fine. I just need to get some food in me. But, um, can you maybe get someone to cover my three o'clock? Here's the referral card."

"Well you know, statistically speaking, you've been way ahead of the game for some time, Diana. Now don't let one silly little *non-sale* get you all down in the mouth. You've still got a *big* future with StormBurst—and don't you forget it!" She winks a green eye. "And besides! I was just checking in with regional headquarters—and you'll never guess who's in *sixth* place for the first week!" Her eyes flash. "Well, let me get you some paper towels so you can dry off a bit!"

I can see her reflection walking away in the glass door. Then I refocus my eyes and see the blue raindrops painted across the glass. Then all I can see is the rain on the other side.

"Diana?"

"What, Berta?"

"You can have th'rest of my fries if you want." She sets a half-filled carton of French fries on the counter in front of me.

I feel a paper towel press against my head. "Now you've got to take good care of yourself darlin' if you're going to win that Snow Tiger—you can't go getting sick now!"

"There's no chance of me getting that Snow Tiger now."

"Well, maybe not, but you could still win the trip to Hawaii!" She blinks her emerald eyes.

"Yeah." I reach out and pull a single French fry from the carton.

"Now, whatever went on with those mean-old farmers, you just don't let it discourage you too much. You're still one heck of a salesman, Diana!"

I watch her walk away in the reflection of the glass. On the other side, the water streams across the parking lot to the drain beside the Rabbit, still parked in the space closest to the door.

❧   ❧   ❧

The rain has stopped. But the gutters still flow like they did during the downpour. The thunderheads are rolling out as quickly as they'd rolled in. And the sun is shining so brightly that it glares off the puddles in the alleyway.

I hesitate before entering the cottage, and decide to sit down on the porch instead. I cross my legs in half-lotus position, feeling the stiffness in my knees and hips that haven't bent this way since spring term. My back aches as I try to sit upright and press the palms of my hands together.

Snots. My legs are shaking.

I try to breathe into the tight muscles to get rid of the tension, but they won't let go.

I look out on the yard, where everything drips. The browned camellia leaves, the rose brambles, the clothesline and T-shirts, the gutters around the porch, the ivy along the fence.

Drip. Drip. Drip. Drip.

Drop. Splash. Drop. Splash.

Splat. Splat. Splat.

I close my eyes and listen carefully to the overlapping music that surrounds me. I take a long, deep, soothing breath and exhale.

"SHOOO."

Holy snots. I'm lonely. I'm so completely and utterly lonely. No one would even know if I never came home today.

Gulp.

I uncross my legs and look around the yard again.

"Kerouac! Kitty-kitty-kitty!" Where would he be on a rainy day like this? "Kerouac! Kerouac!" My voice trembles, "kitty-kitty-kitty-kit—"

I can't help it. I start to cry.

"Come on, Kerouac! Come on, kitty!"

The camellia leaves part a moment and a rain-drenched cat appears before me. He sits there, about ten yards away, not-staring in my direction.

"There you are!" I wipe my nose with my shirttail. "Come here you silly cat."

He doesn't move.

"I'll get you some towels. Come on, Kerouac!"

He waits.

"Come on!"

Sneeze.

I clear my throat. "Blanco?"

He trots toward me and gives a wet rub against my shin.

"Vvvr."

I laugh as I wipe at the tears. "Yeah, I guess I should have known."

❧   ❧   ❧

"Hello?"

"Hi. I'm a vacuum cleaner salesman. Please feel free to hang up at any time."

"Is this a prank call?"

"Nope. Believe it or not, I really do sell vacuum cleaners."

"Well, young lady, I *definitely* don't want to buy a *vacuum cleaner*."

"I understand. I wouldn't want to either!"

"Say, what kind of a salesman are you?"

"Well, actually, I'm a college student. I'm just doing this to help pay for my tuition this year."

"That's kind of a funny job for a college student, isn't it?"

"Tell me about it. My parents think I've gone off the deep end. Sometimes I do, too!"

"Well, what do you *really* want to do?"

"To be honest, I'm not really sure! Part of me thinks I should be a teacher, but some people tell me I should get into computers instead."

"Yeah, computers is got a big future, that's for sure."

"I think so too. I just don't want to end up sitting in front of one for the rest of my life, you know?"

"I hear ya."

"Well, I'm sorry if I interrupted anything by calling this evening. I know how annoying telemarketers can be."

"Ain't that the truth! Well, if it makes you feel any better, you're about the nicest telemarketer that's ever called here—but if you don't mind my saying so, maybe you ought to try something other than sales. I think you're going to have to be a lot tougher in order to get somebody to buy a *vacuum cleaner!*"

"Oh-ho! You're right about that. Well, fortunately for *me*, I get paid just to show it to people."

"You do?"

"*Well*...I do when people decide to buy it!"

"Ha! Well have you managed to sell any of these *vacuum cleaners* yet?"

"Yeah, a couple. But the hardest part is actually finding people willing to listen to me in the first place. I don't suppose you'd know anybody who'd be willing to watch a short vacuum cleaner demonstration, do you? You get free steak knives just for watching it, too."

"Well, I can't promise that any of my friends would, but how long does it take?"

"Oh, half an hour to an hour."

"And I don't have to buy anything?"

"Nope—not unless you decide you *want* to. You just have to watch. Then if you have any suggestions or anything about it, you can tell me and I'll pass it along to the company."

"Really? Well that doesn't sound too painful—and you say we get steak knives just for watching it?"

"You sure do!"

"Huh. Do you ever do these demonstrations on weekends?"

"Do I? I demonstrate this thing whenever anybody'll let me! Would Saturday work for you—maybe at eleven?"

"Well, I guess so. Sure! Now what'd you say your name was?"

"Diana. Oh, but I have to make sure that if you're married your wife will be there too—otherwise I don't get credit."

"Oh, sure, Betty will be here too."

"Great! Gee, I sure appreciate it! It's so hard to get anybody to even *listen* to me, you know?"

"Yeah, I hear ya."

"Oh, let me get your address."

"Sure, it's 1436 Lincoln Street."

"Great, I think I know right where that is."

"Say, Diana, next time you might try starting with something about you being a demonstrator instead of a *salesman*—you know what I mean?"

"Yeah, I see what you mean. Hey, thanks a lot—Fred."

"Glad I could help."

❇️   ❇️   ❇️

He lives around the corner from gorilla boy and two blocks over from Marcie and Reggie. But Charlie Hunt's house is on the very edge of the development. Every house on his street faces a woodsy growth of scrub oaks and blackberry brambles, instead of other houses. It's kind of a pretty view, actually.

I get my demo case and slide between the juniper hedge and the Ford pickup parked in the driveway. When I get up to the open garage door, I see a rusty 60-something Mustang, and as I'd predicted, Charlie Hunt. He looks up from under the hood and gives me a grease-smeared grin.

"You must be Mr. Hunt."

"Call me Charlie!" Pale blue eyes light up as bright as the rust-colored fuzz on his head. He reaches out a blackened hand for a shake, then flinches. "Oh, sorry 'bout that!"

We both chuckle.

"No harm done. I'm Diana. Nice to meet you."

Charlie scrubs up in the kitchen sink while I set up in the living room. Rust- and brown- and gold-colored furnishings are complemented by sections of the Sunday newspaper. As I set the Ray O'Sun on the carpet, I notice little bits of sawdust between the fibers.

Charlie sits down in the brown easy chair and sets a wrench on the table beside him. "So what's this thing called again?" He scratches the red and silver stubble on his chin.

"Oh, it's a *StormBurst*." I plug in the cord behind his TV cart. "Have you ever seen one before?"

"StormBurst, huh? What does it do?"

"Well, actually, it does a lot of things…but instead of just *telling* you all about it, I think I'll just let you see it for yourself. Seeing is believing, right Charlie?"

"All righty." He smiles gently and waits.

"Great." I take a look around the room, at the Sunday comics on the coffee table, and bluest eyes of Mr. Charlie Hunt. "Have you ever been to Ireland?"

Charlie explodes with laughter.

So do I. I look out the window and wipe a tear from the corner of my eye. We finally settle down again. I sit on the end of the demo case. "Oh, lord. I don't know how many times I've had to ask that question this summer."

He's still shaking from laughter. "I'm sorry about that, honey. It's just that, well, I guess the question just really took me by surprise, out of the blue and all!"

"I know what you mean." I give him a wink.

Charlie scratches his stubble thoughtfully. "Ireland, huh?" He grins. "No, I never have been to Ireland. But if it helps, I've been to Korea, Japan, Hawaii, and I was stationed in Germany for six years." His blue eyes twinkle. They're big and round as moons, and just as bright.

"Well, I'm not sure about any of those other places, Charlie, but if you can just imagine the Irish countryside, after a good *Irish* rain—" he nods and smiles. "Well, even right here in Harveston, doesn't the air always smell so fresh and sweet after a good rain?"

"It certainly does, Diana."

The twinkle never leaves his eyes, throughout the entire, somewhat abbreviated and entirely ridiculous, demonstration.

"You know there's dust in the air, right Charlie?"

"Well, sure."

"Great. This funny-looking lamp is made to help show you that dust."

Click.

"Well, how about that?"

"Let's see…now, I'm also supposed to show you how *your* vacuum cleaner blows dust all over your house. Do you want to see?"

"Sure! Shall I go get it for you?"

"Okay."

I hold the Ray O'Sun over the exhaust vent of the Karmair.

Click.

Poof.

"Can you see it, Charlie?"

"I sure can! Well, how about that?"

I turn off the Karmair. "Yeah, all the vacuum cleaners I've seen do that. But you know, they still keep the big stuff in the vacuum bag—the lint and what-not."

"Good thing too, eh?"

Charlie and I laugh.

"Oh, I can also shrink a cushion in a plastic bag, if you'd like to see?"

"Well sure, why not?"

"You can also use this thing to blow up a raft, or things like that. I have some balloons so I can show you how fast it inflates things. Do you want to see?"

"What the heck!"

I flip open the demo case and grab the Breath O'Ireland bottle. "All right, now don't laugh *too* hard, but now's when I take you to Ireland—kind of."

"Well I can hardly wait!"

We laugh together.

"Okay, see what you think of this."

Drip. Drip.

"Well…" Charlie closes his eyes and takes a long, deep, soothing breath O'Ireland. "That *does* take me back."

"You like it?"

"Oh, absolutely."

I turn off the StormBurst and kneel down to remove the Pot O'Water.

"All right. This is the really disgusting part where I shine the light through the water, and tell you about all the disgusting stuff that's in there. Are you ready?"

"Bring it on!"

"Here you go!"

Click.

We laugh.

Charlie sits up in his chair. "Well, I never said I was the best housekeeper!"

I laugh even harder and hear myself snort. I can feel a tear welling up in my left eye.

I set the Ray O'Sun and Pot O'Water on the carpet. "So there you have it Charlie. That's what they call a *StormBurst*."

He smiles, looks down at the floor, and rubs his stubble thoughtfully. Then he looks back up at me.

I sit down on the demo case. "So now I'm supposed to ask you if you agree it's a pretty amazing machine?"

"Well, Diana, I surely would, except that I know if I do agree, you're gonna try and sell me one!"

We laugh.

"Well, I am a vacuum cleaner salesman, you know."

We both smile in the silence.

"Well, the truth is, Charlie, I'm done with the demonstration now. So if you absolutely *hate* the StormBurst and you *never* want to see it again, I'll be more than happy to pack it up and haul it away."

"Would you now?" He lifts his rusty eyebrows.

"Well, I might try to find out *why* you hate it first!"

We both chuckle.

"Well, tell me, Diana, how many amps does this machine here have?"

"Amps? Oh, right. Well…to be honest, I can't remember exactly. They did tell me once, back in training…But I do remember it's *supposed* to be more powerful than all the other vacuums on the market—except the Sputnik."

He chuckles, "The *Sputnik*, huh?"

"Yeah, it looks like a big silver bullet—I think they must have forgotten the antennas!"

Charlie laughs harder and wipes a tear from his eye.

"Who knows—maybe they'll have them on next year's model! Like a big old chrome porcupine…creeping down the hall behind you!"

We both laugh so hard, we can hardly speak.

He shouts "The next new feature from Sputnik—home security!"

I laugh harder and fall off the demo case shouting, "Heel, Sputnik! Sick'em!"

Charlie looks like he's having trouble breathing now. He wipes the tears from his eyes and wheezes as I try my best to hold my tongue.

We gradually quiet to just giggles, when Charlie adds: "You know, it won't do much good though, until they come out with the cordless model."

And we're in hysterics all over again.

At last, I see the StormBurst, sitting on the carpet, with the Storm Chaser hose inserted into its *anus leprechauns.* I take a long, deep breath, and I sigh. "So, I guess I should wrap this up now."

"Yeah, alrighty then." He winks.

"You asked about amps and I don't know. I suppose I could get back to you with the exact number, if that's going to make or break the deal?" I try to make eye contact—without laughing.

"So how much does one of these go for nowadays?"

I grin, "Oh, so you are interested?"

"Heh-heh, I didn't say that. I just asked the price."

"Right, well, the StormBurst…" I look around at the attachments, "It's *one thousand, four hundred and thirty-seven dollars!*" I laugh out loud.

"Whe-hoo!" He snorts and I try hard not to. "My-oh-my!" He slaps his thigh and twinkles his eyes at me. "That sure is a lot of money, isn't it?" He raises his eyebrows at me.

"Yeah, it sure is." I laugh a little more. "That doesn't even include the burglar alarm!"

We grin.

"Hmm." He rubs the rust and silver on his chin and smiles, "Well, Diana, I sure think you're a nice little salesman—and darned honest too."

"Well, I appreciate that, Charlie."

"So I'm going to have to come clean with you. You see, I wasn't totally honest with you…"

My stomach gurgles.

"You see, I *have* seen a StormBurst before." His eyebrows lift and his eyes twinkle. "In fact, I used to sit on a case just like that one you've got there." He grins. "Except it was orange—and as I recall, it didn't have gold buckles."

"You're kidding."

"Nope. But that was a long time ago—back in '52, by golly!" He slaps his knee and chuckles to himself.

"You're *kidding.*"

"No, well I wish I could say I was! I only lasted about three weeks I think, but you know? It looks like you've lasted a lot longer than that. How long've you been doing this, Diana?"

I look out the window at the scrub oaks and sigh. "Well, that's a good question. I guess it's been, oh, just over three months now."

"*Really*?" He shakes his head. "Well, at fourteen thirty-seven a piece, I'd say you must be one *hell* of a salesman, Diana!"

I grin. "Oh, I am. Believe me, Charlie, I *am.*"

He laughs at that, then laughs even harder. His eyes are tearing up as he says, "Have you ever been to Ireland? Oh! I just couldn't believe it when you said that!" He loses himself in a fit of cackling.

And I cackle too.

"Wee-hoo! But I suppose it's a lot better than the way we started out in '52!"

"Really?"

"Yeah, imagine this—" Charlie puts on a serious face. "Have you ever experienced a rainstorm in your *living room*?"

"You're kidding!"

"I tell you, boy, to think back when I did it, it was a different world then! That's for sure!" His ears and face turn scarlet.

"Tell me, Charlie. Did they hate vacuum cleaner salesmen as much back then as they do now?"

He nods, "Well, I can't say we were America's most-loved boys…" he shakes a callused finger at me, "but we did seem to have a certain credibility…somehow." He nods his head for a moment. "But then: maybe everybody seemed to have more credibility back then."

"Did you have to make cold calls?"

"Cold calls? Well, I can't say as *I* did—not in my short career! Back then we just went knocking on doors."

"Are you serious? That must have been awful—I mean, I can only take so much of people hanging up on me, but slamming the door in my face? Oh, I wouldn't last a day."

"Yeah, you had to have a thick skin—say can I offer you a soda pop, or maybe a beer? It's so hot out!"

I stare out at the brambles a moment.

"Oh, well, I know you've got your schedule and what not—I don't mean to keep you."

"You know, Charlie, it's a *perfect* day for a beer. I'd love one." I give him a wink. "And maybe you could tell me some more about your stint as a *vacuum cleaner salesman*—if it's not too painful for you?"

He grins, "Oh, sure! I'll be right back."

I stand up and take a look around the living room, at the attachments sprawled out across the coffee table, at the sawdust floating in the Pot O'Water, at the Ray O'Sun lying on its side with the jaundiced bulb staring up at me.

"You know, the porch gets a little breeze about this time of the afternoon." He hands me a Green Hornet.

"Sounds lovely."

We sit out on the front steps and he fills my head with stories of housewives, floor polishing attachments called "Lightening Wands," and the adventures of Charlie Hunt, dressed in his Navy uniform and standing on porches flashing his blue eyes at the ladies. He tells me about how they used to play up the responsibility of the housewife, and how the StormBurst could help give a housewife a sense of pride in the only job she had.

"Oh, man."

"Yep. Bet that wouldn't go over nowadays, eh?"

"Not on your life." I take a sip. "Plus, now you've got to be sure and show it to both the husband and the wife at the same time—or the *domestic partner, significant other, trans-gender friend* or whoever the heck they live with."

"Heh-heh! Yeah, things have changed all right. For one thing, we sure never had any salesmen on our staff that looked anything like you, that's for sure! No offense, of course."

"None taken, Charlie." Gulp. Ahh. "There really weren't *any* women though?"

"Only to answer the phone!"

"Yikes."

"Are there lots of you nowadays?"

"Oh, well, no...I guess not." I take a sip.

"Yeah, I don't suppose it's really all that *safe*, either. You should be careful, you know?"

"Yeah, I know." I sip the beer. "Actually, one of the owners is a woman."

"No kidding? I'll bet she's shrewd as the devil himself! You know, like I said, you've got to have a thick skin—and being a woman to boot!"

"Oh, she does." I picture Brenda Sue with her swath of blond hair and those gold chains diving into her cleavage. Then I see Harold, with his bulges hanging out as he writes on the whiteboard. Then there's Charlie, right here on the porch with me. "So why'd you give it up so soon—if you don't mind my asking? Was it the going door-to-door?"

He smiles and takes a sip. "Well, Diana, it's pretty simple."

"It is?"

"Yes, it is. You see, I'd reached my goal!"

"Your goal?"

"Yep. I already had a regular job, but my wife and I, we had our first baby on the way. I just joined StormBurst because I thought I could do it on the weekends and save up enough for this baby carriage Irene had seen down at Sears—fancy thing! She wouldn't say so, but I knew she wanted it. So I worked until I had enough to buy it, and then..." he holds his hand up in the air and takes a sip.

"And then what?"

"Well, then I got on with my life!"

"Oh."

"So what about you?"

"What do you mean?"

Charlie smiles, "What's your goal, Diana?"

"Oh, well, I'm not sure I really have a *goal* exactly. I mean, I took the job 'cause it sounded a heck of a lot better than making ice cream cones or flipping burgers all summer, you know?"

He grins and shakes his head. "I see. So when do you expect you'll be ready to get on with your *real* life? Didn't you say you're in college?"

"Yeah." I look out at the scrub oaks. "Fall term starts in a couple of weeks."

"Have you had a good summer?"

"Sure…Well, I've made way more money than I thought I could. Mom and Dad won't have to help me at all this year."

"That's not what I meant."

"Oh." I take a sip. "Well, I've kept busy."

Charlie shakes his head and takes a sip. "So tell me, do they still give that bonus for a cash sale?"

"Yeah, a $100 bill."

"Well that hasn't changed either! Too bad!" He snorts. "$100 sure bought a lot more in '52 than it will now!"

I take the last sip from my bottle. "Well, I suppose I should get packed up now. I have to make some phone calls this evening."

"Yeah, alrighty then."

He takes my empty bottle and disappears into the kitchen while I wind up the cord on the Ray O'Sun. I kneel down to start packing the attachments, when a calloused hand appears in front of me, holding a check for one thousand, four hundred and thirty-seven dollars. I turn around and face Charlie.

He grins, "Now I'll give this to you on two conditions: First, I want you to put your commission into your savings for tuition and school stuff—if not for this year, then whatever comes next. And second, I want you to take your cash bonus and do something *fun* you can tell somebody about fifty years from now." He winks a blue eye.

I pull myself up onto the demo case. "Oh, Charlie. Charlie—that's *terribly* nice of you, but I can't take your money like that. I—I know you don't really even want one of these—and that's a *lot* of money, Charlie!"

He's still smiling. He shakes his head and holds the check out to me again.

"Look, I appreciate the gesture—I *really* do. But Charlie, I can't take your—"

"Now listen to me, Diana. I'm an old man. And I've worked hard and saved up a lot of money over the years so my wife and I could enjoy a nice retirement. Only my wife passed on a bit earlier than we'd expected, and now it's just me. And I don't get the chance very often to do things that make me feel good—good about still kicking around this place." He looks around the living room. "But *this* makes me feel good. So take it, and have some fun, kid." He winks.

I can't help it. The tears roll down my cheeks and I can't get a single word out.

"And besides, I need *something* to pick up all this *dirt* and *dust* and *filth* I keep tracking into the house!" He chuckles as he retrieves the wrench from the side table, then walks out through the front door.

As I carry my demo case out, I stop to shake Charlie's hand. "Well, I sure never saw that one coming!"

He's grinning from ear-to-ear. "Like I told you, Diana, you're one hell of a salesman! But I'm sure that you're much more than that, too, kid. Good luck with it all." He gives another wink.

"Thanks, Charlie." I walk toward the Rabbit. "Thank you."

❁   ❁   ❁

Brenda Sue rushes out the front door with a demo case in her hand. I pull the emergency break and step out of the Rabbit, parked beside her.

"Where are you off to?"

She hoists the demo case up and into the trunk of her Cadillac. "Oh, I've got to go cover a demo for one of our *former* dealers." She races around to the driver's side.

"Who?"

She backs out, then peels out as she pulls onto Blume Boulevard.

I set my demo case down on the carpet against the front of the reception counter, where Berta can't quite see it. Inside it is my green cell phone and a note to Harold and Brenda Sue:

> ❧
>
> *Thanks for the opportunity.*
> *——Diana*

Berta slurps away at her soda, flipping through a magazine.

I walk back out to the Rabbit, then return with the shampoo wand. I set it up, across the reception counter. "Hey, Berta! I think there's something wrong with this one."

"Ah, just leave it there on the counter."

"Okay." I walk back to find Harold sitting behind Brenda Sue's desk, punching Sudafed tablets from a foil packet.

"Harold!"

He bolts upright in the chair, almost knocking the bottle of cough syrup off the desk.

"Good news!" I flash Charlie's check in front of him.

He gasps, trying to catch his breath, through his mouth. "Oh, good job, Diana. Uh, here," he opens his wallet and hands me a crisp $100 bill, then pulls a handkerchief from his pocket and gives a tremendous blow.

"Thanks, Harold!"

He pats his nose with the handkerchief.

"I'll leave the receipt with Berta."

"Yeah, okay." He washes down the Sudafed tablets with a swig from the cough syrup bottle.

"Are you okay, Harold?"

He groans and rubs his nose with the handkerchief again. "Yeah, it's just these damned allergies. That rain must have tricked all the plants into thinking it's spring—it's making everything bloom all over again! Can you believe it, in September?" He pinches the bridge of his nose between his thumb and forefinger.

I hand Berta the envelope with Charlie's check and sales receipt. "Hasta la vista!" I step outside to the Rabbit, parked right up front in the best parking space in the lot. I back out of my parking space carefully, and blow a kiss to the sign that reads "Dealer of the Month: Diana Jensen."

"WAHOOO!"

My final paycheck arrives in the mail a week later.

❊   ❊   ❊

I'm standing at gate twenty-two for twenty-five minutes until, at last, her plane arrives. The stream of people ebbs and flows until out walks Christina: tall, tan and beautiful. Her hair has been lightened by the sun.

"Diana!" She hugs me hard and plants a kiss right on my cheek. "Oh, my god! I missed you so much!" She turns to the dark man standing behind her and beams. "This is the guy I told you about: Enrique!"

"Enrique?"

Enrique smiles, sheepishly, and nods at me. He has dark brown eyes and hair and lips that look as soft as pillows.

"Oh, god. Didn't you get my letter?"

I smile and try my best not to look at his mustache.

"He got accepted to the student exchange program at *Harveston*—can you believe it?"

Gulp.

"No!" I force a smile.

Enrique flushes red.

"It's just for six months—you don't mind another roommate do you, Diana?"

"Roommate?"

Christina turns and kisses Enrique on the cheek.

"Well, the more them merrier, right?"

"That's right!" She mumbles something to Enrique in Spanish and they giggle.

"So, did you bring a friend for me?" I wink at Enrique.

Enrique looks at Christina.

"Oh, he doesn't speak a *word* of English, but don't worry, I can translate for you!" She jabbers something at him in Spanish and he laughs and nods at me.

As we begin walking to baggage claim, Christina takes my arm and whispers in her most concerned voice: "Did you lose weight, Diana?"

I whisper back. "No, I'm just not wearing a bra."

"Oh!" She looks at me again and giggles.

On the way home I break the news to her about our *other* roommate. She translates to Enrique who laughs heartily from the back seat. "Blanco!"

"Si, Blanco! Señor Blanco!" Christina chuckles.

I turn up the alleyway and see Kenny dragging a stick along the fence. He turns and waves his little fingers in the air as we pass.

I run inside the cottage to open all the windows and let the heat out before we carry in the suitcases. Christina squeals as soon as she sees the entertainment center with the TV and DVD player.

"Did you rob a bank?" She traces a finger around the 27-inch TV screen.

"In a manner of speaking—I'll tell you later.

Her eyes bulge. "Okay…"

"So, do you guys want to watch a movie tonight? I've got some there in the cabinet—although tonight's the season premier for all the best sit-coms. I was thinking we could get take-out and—"

"Bullshit! We're going out tonight and painting the town *red*!" Christina carries her bags into her room and shouts, "OH MY GOD! I forgot!" Her bags thud to the floor. "I still don't have a frickin' bed!"

She takes the first shower while Enrique disappears into what is now "their" bedroom.

The cottage has changed already. It feels like somebody else's home. Their home. For a moment it's almost as if the summer and the drought and the demonstrations and the eyeless cat never happened. I push open the door to my room to make sure the ridiculous trophy and plaques are still there on the windowsill.

After while, Christina comes out of the bathroom, towel-drying her hair. She asks, "So, Diana, what did you do all summer?"

I laugh and take sip of Green Hornet as I settle into the beanbag chair. "Well, I'll be honest with you Christina…"

She stops drying her hair.

"I was a vacuum cleaner salesman." I wiggle my eyebrows and grin.

The towel drops to the carpet. "All right. Cut the bullshit, D. What did you *really* do this summer?"

I hang a wet pillowcase over the clothesline as I consider my new major: Dramatic Arts. I figure it's as practical as anything else I've studied and, so far, it's a lot more fun.

"YEE-OWL."

He rubs his cheek against the fence by the entrance to the alleyway.

"Blanco! How's it going?"

"YEE-OWL." He shifts his eyeless head toward the alley.

"Where've you been lately, handsome? Haven't seen you around."

He paces back and forth at the edge of the path, waiting for me.

"All right, buddy. You lead the way."

He turns left onto the alley and I follow, carefully negotiating the gravel beneath my bare feet. Smoke from a barbecue drifts through the alley, and I can hear soft music as we stroll through the center of the block. "It's a perfect day for a beer."

Blanco turns into the yard of a small cottage. It looks a lot like mine.

Gulp.

He sits there on the porch steps, singing softly as he strums a guitar. His eyes are closed in concentration. Or maybe it's bliss.

Blanco wastes no time crossing the patch of grass toward the source of the music and rubs up against his shin.

"Hey, guy. How's it—oh! I see you brought a friend with you." He grins at me and lifts a blond eyebrow. "Is this your cat?"

Blanco flops onto his side on the lowest step and turns his head toward me.

"Oh—no, he's not *my* cat." I tuck a strand of hair behind my ear and try to think of what to say next. "He's just a friend."

"Oh, good." He sets the guitar aside. "I'm Chris." He reaches out his hand and shakes mine, with a wink.

"Hi." I feel my cheeks heating up. "I'm Diana," I smile. "Diana Jensen…I go to Harveston."

A hearty thanks and round of Green Hornets to the following:

Tim Rivoli, who could never be thanked enough for his contributions as a sounding board and second set of eyes for this project. YEE-OWL.

Melissa White, Anne Tillinghast and Jason Cortlund, who test-drove the prototype some four years ago—growl—grind—whoosh—and offered helpful feedback, suggestions and encouragement.

Elizabeth Davis and Petra Ulrych, who provided expert last-minute advice and unbridled enthusiasm: "Yes!"

Stephanie Harralson and Hana Packard-Haas, who generously let me read from over their shoulders and gave uncensored commentary. Gulp.

Lillian Brand, matriarch of The von Trapp Family Storytellers, who Scrabbled me as a wee wily wordsmith and fortified my funny bone. "Wouldn't you agree?"

Jan Bateman and Ruth Good, two of the unsung heroes of public education, who let me have my way with words early in my career. *Thanks for the opportunity.*

Karen Ford, who taught me to read like a writer; and Paul Dresman, who inspired me to (get off my duff and) work like one. "Do you want to see the proof?"

Robert Grudin, who helped me to recognize and maximize those fleeting moments of grace. SLICE—

And Chang-rae Lee, who taught me that good stories (like good sales pitches) are shown, not told.

"And that's the demonstration!"

0-595-27950-3